T0283710

STAR TREK™
STRANGE NEW WORLDS

ASYLUM

STAR TREK™
STRANGE NEW WORLDS
ASYLUM

Una McCormack

Based upon *Star Trek*
created by Gene Roddenberry
and
Star Trek: Strange New Worlds
created by
Akiva Goldsman & Alex Kurtzman and Jenny Lumet

GALLERY BOOKS
New York   London   Toronto   Sydney   New Delhi

G⫿

Gallery Books
An Imprint of Simon & Schuster, LLC
1230 Avenue of the Americas
New York, NY 10020

This book is published by Gallery Books, a division of Simon & Schuster, LLC, under exclusive license from CBS Studios Inc.

First Gallery Books hardcover edition November 2024

GALLERY BOOKS and colophon are registered trademarks of Simon & Schuster, LLC

Simon & Schuster: Celebrating 100 Years of Publishing in 2024

For information about special discounts for bulk purchases, please contact Simon & Schuster Special Sales at 1-866-506-1949 or business@simonandschuster.com.

The Simon & Schuster Speakers Bureau can bring authors to your live event. For more information or to book an event, contact the Simon & Schuster Speakers Bureau at 1-866-248-3049 or visit our website at www.simonspeakers.com.

Interior design by Kathryn A. Kenney-Peterson

Manufactured in the United States of America

10 9 8 7 6 5 4 3 2 1

Library of Congress Cataloging-in-Publication Data has been applied for.

ISBN 978-1-6680-5136-8
ISBN 978-1-6680-5138-2 (ebook)

For Verity,
who knows why

STAR TREK™
STRANGE NEW WORLDS

ASYLUM

2233

STARFLEET ACADEMY
INDUCTION DAY

Ensign Christopher Pike, Personal Log

Nobody wants to take a sabbatical this early in their career, but needs must when the orders come from on high, by which I mean my CMO. Also Robert April. Not that he's my CO, but he's my mentor, and when your mentor and one of Starfleet's finest says, "Son, you're taking a sabbatical," first you look the word up in a dictionary, just to be sure of the meaning, and then you take the sabbatical.

"You need some time," said April. "Clear your head before the hearing. Think things over." Which sounds to me like a fast route to sitting around feeling sorry for myself about everything that happened, and, frankly, I don't need any encouragement to do that. I said that (okay, not exactly that, but the gist of that) to April.

"Go camping," said April. "Go riding."

I could, I guess, but my leg still hurts.

"For pity's sake, Chris" (I sure hit the limits of April's patience pretty quick), "if you can't just sit on your ass for a few weeks without making a damn drama out of the whole business, I'll find you something to keep you busy."

Anyway, that's why I find myself back in San Francisco, in an apartment right next to the Academy campus, special instructor of a bunch of classes. Apparently I have a reputation back here. Good or bad? I didn't ask. But the commandant seems to think that I have something to say, and that the cadets will listen. I'm close enough to them in age, but far enough along in my career that I've learned something.

I wonder if I should tell them about what I've learned? Not about the circumstances leading up to my sabbatical, that's for sure. I don't want to send them running for the hills.

Pretty strange being back on campus. They say you can't go back, and then you do. You find yourself right back where you were only a handful of years ago. The place is deserted. Fun, huh? The semester doesn't start for a couple of weeks, so the cadets aren't back. The campus is bereft of life, and, with fall on the horizon, it feels kind of melancholy, but I'm trying to put a stop to that feeling; I suspect that it would fall into the category of making a drama about the whole business. So let's look for signs of life. I guess . . . there's a growing sense of anticipation around the place. Because you know that the paths, lawns, and buildings will soon be full of life. Filled with cadets, who are in turn brimming with optimism, enthusiasm, and ambition, whose eyes are fixed on the stars.

And all I have to do is make sure I don't sour them on all that. Tell them what I learned in my first few years in Starfleet. Keep myself distracted till I get the date for the hearing. And try not to think too much about what happened while at the same time get everything straight in my head about what happened.

I need a pal. I need a drinking buddy. And I really do need to get started planning these damn lectures. They don't prepare themselves. Who knew that being an instructor at the Academy wasn't a walk in the park? Thought so when I was a cadet. It's going to be interesting to see what life is like on the other side. See the cadets: who are they, and what they're shaping up to be. That'll keep me busy. That'll keep me from thinking about what happened.

[Note to future readers: I did not have to look the word "sabbatical" up in the dictionary. But if you check further, you'll see that "gullible" is missing. They took it out.]

There was no doubt that Earth was beautiful, Anxha thought, looking through the port. It was like mist on the mountains; like a painting she had done to remember being in the peaks in summer. Pale blue and white; wisps of cloud and filled with promise. Like, but not enough. Anxha looked away. There was nothing to be done about that, so she tried to put such thoughts out of her head. The *Helena Molony* would commence docking within the next couple of hours, and their new life would begin.

Anxha looked around for her cubs. The two youngest, the twins, Tilxho and Mexhano, were easiest to spot, weaving around between the seats in a fruitless attempt to burn up some of their apparently limitless energy. Always in motion, those two; always busy, and so close to each other that sometimes Anxha herself could not separate them. Paws and tails, forever entwined. She signaled to them that they should not start the game, which they were clearly contemplating, of seeing who could jump farther from one of the chairs. They went back to a less hazardous game of tag. Once she was sure they were in no imminent danger of damaging themselves or their surroundings, Anxha checked on Halexho. The loner of the family, thoughtful and curious, he was reading from a padd, one of several stacked up beside him. His tail shifted leisurely from side to side. He would start telling them something soon.

Last of all, sitting opposite Halexho, was Naxhana. The eldest, her beautiful daughter, poised on the brink of adulthood, but still so achingly young. Naxhana was sitting a few seats away, right by another port, but she was not looking out at their destination, and what the future might hold. Her head was turned away. She was staring down at the carpet, the toe of her shoe marking out the pattern over and over again. She was unhappy, Anxha knew, deeply unhappy—but there was nothing Anxha could do about the cause of that unhappiness. Naxhana wanted to go home. But there was no going home.

Anxha padded over to her daughter and sat beside her, resting her paw upon Naxhana's. *I know why you're sad*, she thought. *I feel the same way. We can do nothing—only make the best of our situation. Find new people and places to love.*

Halexho, looking up from his padd, cleared his throat. "Fact," he said. Anxha suppressed a smile. She caught Naxhana's eye and winked. Naxhana's whiskers twitched, ever so slightly. That was a start.

"Go on, Hax," said Anxha. "What have you got for us this time?"

Hax facts, they called them; the pieces of information that, from the thousands he must learn each day, he considered particularly worthy of offering up for their consideration. Like a hunter, bringing back prey. It was a mixed pleasure, sometimes, listening to Hax. He was exactly like Anxha's father, now long gone, who had never learned to read, but somehow knew everything about everything, and whose curiosity remained undimmed, right up until the end, and despite everything that had happened to him.

"The largest animal ever to have existed on Earth is *Balaenoptera musculus*"—he said that slowly and carefully—"the blue whale . . . Oh!" he said, and stopped.

"Go on," said Anxha.

"It says here they were nearly hunted to extinction." He frowned. "I don't like that . . ."

"Excuse me . . ." A quiet voice, but not shy; gently but insistently intruding. Anxha looked up and came face-to-face with her first Bolian. A dapper little woman, wearing a richly patterned dress whose intricate design almost confounded the eyes, and who was as blue as the sky above in the mountains north of Rechzan, back home.

"May I help you?" said Anxha.

"Rather the reverse," said the woman, who had a kindly look in her eye. "The two little ones—"

"Oh no," groaned Anxha. "What are they doing now?"

"Nothing *yet*," said the woman. "But if I know children—and I'm the mother of three—I *think* they may soon be climbing up the walls. I was rather wondering whether you would allow me to take them in search of a treat." Her eyes twinkled. "I promise I'll steer away from Bolian cuisine. My human friends tell me that it's an acquired taste."

"Those two will eat anything," said Naxhana.

Anxha hesitated. There was so much she didn't know about this new world in which she had found herself. The Federation was supposed to be a safe place; yes, of course, that was why they had come here. But the particular stresses of the last few years meant that her immediate instinct was to keep her cubs close, where she could see them. She saw realization dawn in the other woman's eyes; she saw compassion. Anxha was long past resenting such things. She was grateful for the understanding.

"They'll be safe with me," said the Bolian gently.

Anxha took a deep breath. Letting the boys out of her sight was a risk.

"Mamma," said Naxhana. "They'll be fine."

"Yes, of course." She smiled up at the Bolian woman. "That would be very kind, thank you."

"Are you Bolian?" said Halexho, who was staring at the woman.

"Hax!" chided Naxhana. "Don't be rude!"

He blinked up at his older sister. "I'm not being rude. I'm being interested."

The woman laughed. "It's a fair question. And you're quite right. I *am* Bolian. My name is Waneha." She listened attentively as Anxha introduced herself and her litter, then said, "May I ask in turn—are you Chionian?"

"No," said Naxhana, fiercely, exactly as her mother said, "Yes." Naxhana glared at her. Anxha went on, "I mean—yes, in terms of our official designation."

"Otherwise, no," said Naxhana. "We're Euxhana."

The other woman, looking carefully between them, said, "Of course. Of course . . . I understand. Well, shall I take those two youngsters and put something sweet and sugary inside them and then hand them back?" She looked at Halexho. "Would you like to come too? See what treats they might have hidden away round here?"

Halexho looked at his padds, and then at Waneha. The struggle, thought Anxha, was very real. Hax was still wavering on that line between cubhood and adulthood.

"Oh, go *on*, Hax," said his older sister. "The facts aren't going anywhere."

Hax nodded seriously, taking her point. He sprang to his feet. He wrapped his paw around Waneha's blue hand. Waneha gave Anxha a kind smile.

"I'll have them back within the hour," she said. "Please don't worry."

She went off with Hax, who called out to the twins to join them. "Tixh! Mexh! We're going hunting. For *cake*."

Anxha, watching them go, could feel the force of her daughter's resentment.

"I don't like it when you call us that," said Naxhana.

"I know, *xhixhi*. But it makes things much easier—"

"That's what they say back home, isn't it? If we'd only call ourselves Chionian, everything would be so much easier."

That hurt. "That's not fair, *xhixhi*—"

"None of this is fair, *Maxhi*. In case you hadn't noticed."

Tears sprang to Anxha's eyes. She turned away so that her daughter would not see. *I am trying my very best*, she thought. *But this is impossible.*

"I wish we were back home." Naxhana's voice was low, but sharp, tight, and angry. Anxha hated hearing her sound like this. "I wish *Edxhi* was here."

But Tarxho, Naxhana's father, the father of all four of Anxha's children, was not here, and could never be. Anxha burrowed her face into her daughter's soft fur. "I know," she murmured, nuzzling her, comforting her. "I know . . ."

"I wish we hadn't come here," said Naxhana wretchedly. "But I don't know where else we could go."

"We'll make something here," said Anxha. "We'll make a home."

"It won't be home. It *can't* be home."

Naxhana stood up and walked a few seats away, sitting down again, alone, and staring through the port. Anxha, who knew her daughter would not welcome any approach when she was in this mood, sat quietly, taking the opportunity to look once again through all their documents. Could anything go wrong at this late stage? Surely not. That would be too cruel. The thought of being sent *back*.

The boys returned an hour later. (Waneha looked perfectly cheerful, as if their excursion had troubled her not one jot.) There

9

had indeed been cake, and Waneha had also prevailed upon her connections to the crew to get access to the gym. The twins—and Hax too—had worn themselves out on the trampoline. The ship docked not long after. When they were given the all clear to disembark, Anxha gathered up her cubs and their bags, and made her way to the main concourse. Everyone she spoke to was friendly and helpful, and there was even someone to meet them: a human woman, holding up a sign that spelled out Anxha's name in Euxhana letters. She had to turn away, briefly, at the sight of that—here, in public—to cover the tears that had sprung into her eyes.

The woman came forward. "Aynur Lavin," she said. "I'm with World of Sanctuary."

Their sponsors. The people who had made the journey here possible. Anxha remembered this woman's name now; the lawyer who had completed all the paperwork that Anxha had been holding on to like a lifeline.

"Oh," she said, reaching out her paw, "thank you. *Thank you.*"

"Welcome to Earth," said Lavin. She looked around at the cubs, and her face crinkled into a delighted smile. "I'm so very glad you're here. I'm so very glad to meet you all at last."

Lavin picked up a couple of their bags and led them through the concourse to the public transporter, listening to Hax ask for facts, and supplying them as best she could. So this was Earth, and Anxha could not fault the people or the welcome. But what Naxhana had said had stuck, circling round and round her brain.

It wasn't home, and it couldn't ever be home.

"Cadet Chin-Riley! You stop right there and go *no* further—I want a word with you!"

Una Chin-Riley (rising star of the Academy and brightest light of her senior year) had been walking through campus with her roommate, Theresa Mullins, in search of coffee. Now she turned to see one of their instructors heading toward them at pace.

"Oh god," muttered Mullins. "We can't be in trouble already. The semester's only fifteen minutes old."

Lieutenant Commander Pelia, whose idiosyncratic engineering courses were the bane of cadets from wide-eyed plebs to world-weary seniors, was certainly on the warpath, covering the ground toward them faster than one would have thought possible from one so petite.

"Shush," said Chin-Riley.

"She's daft as a brush," muttered Mullins.

Chin-Riley broadly shared that opinion, which was in fact the consensus across the cadet body. Pelia was . . . eccentric? That surely was not a controversial thing to say. It was one reason that she'd avoided taking any of Pelia's courses. Until now. This semester, Chin-Riley had taken the plunge and signed up for Pelia's elective on Starship Maintenance. Rumor (which meant the previous year) had it that the formal aspects of the course were a breeze (Pelia sometimes being vague when it came to details such as exams and so on), but that the experience was second to none. Pelia wasted no time throwing them into real-life situations, to see how far their technical expertise would take them. Chin-Riley was curious to see how well she would be able to adapt. Better now than later.

Pelia, reaching them, ground to a halt. She bent over, placing her hands on her knees and gasping for air. "Give me a moment . . ." she said. "Oh, I am much too old for this kind of nonsense. Why do you cadets have to move so *quickly*?"

See? Mullins mouthed over her head. *Daft as a brush.*

Ssh! said Chin-Riley. "Anything we can do for you, Commander?" she said, politely, as the instructor gathered her wits and her breath.

Pelia, recovering herself, stood up straight and, nodding at the padd that Chin-Riley was holding, said, "Is your schedule on that?"

"Yes, Commander," said Chin-Riley.

"Lemme see that," said Pelia, grabbing the padd from Chin-Riley's hands. "I want to see what you're doing."

"You'll need my access codes, Commander—"

Pelia snorted. She had already bypassed the security on the padd and was scrolling through Chin-Riley's schedule for the coming semester.

"Do you still have space left anywhere?" Pelia said. "No, of course you don't, you're Cadet Chin-Riley. You're auditing at least three extra courses and will still have time to star in this year's Gilbert and Sullivan production."

"It's *The Mikado* this semester," said Chin-Riley, trying to keep the excitement out of her voice. Last semester she had rocked Mad Margaret from *Ruddigore*. The parts for *The Mikado* weren't cast yet, but Katisha was surely hers. She'd already memorized the part. In fact, she'd already memorized the whole libretto. "I don't want to miss *The Mikado*, sir."

"I'm not saying you should," said Pelia. "But whatever else you are doing, I want you to make room for one more course."

Chin-Riley, retrieving the padd from the instructor's grasp, started thumbing through her schedule. "Commander, I honestly don't see much room here—"

"You must. You've heard of Christopher Pike, haven't you?"

"Of course, Commander!" They had not overlapped in their time here, but every single instructor at the Academy reminisced fondly about Cadet—now Ensign—Pike. His skill, his charm, his cool under fire. Some of the cadets cursed his name; others, Chin-Riley included, found the myth intriguing, wondering how all these stories could possibly come close to reality. She knew her own reputation among her peers and instructors, and how that might be recounted once she had graduated. She also knew—unlike anyone else—how different that reputation was from the much more complicated truth.

"He's at the Academy this semester," said Pelia. "He's giving a series of lectures in the run-up to Thanksgiving."

"Oh," said Chin-Riley. That did sound interesting. She started searching through her schedule again. Was there space? If she stared hard enough, perhaps she could see some cracks.

"Remember *The Mikado*," murmured Mullins. "The world can't miss out on your Katisha."

"That would surely be a loss to civilization," said Pelia. "Not to mention the general gaiety of life. I'm not saying drop it, Una. Heaven forbid." She leaned over Chin-Riley's shoulder. "What is this? Astrotheory 101? Bit late for that, isn't it? You can drop that. Command Psychology?" She snorted. "Absolute waffle. Sipek doesn't know what he's talking about, and you'll get everything you need from my Starship Maintenance course. Look, I don't care what you do, what you drop, but do *not* miss a single one of Pike's lectures! *Capiche?*"

"Understood, Commander," said Chin-Riley. "But, um, what are they *about* exactly?"

"You'll see!" Pelia said. As she left, she called back over her shoulder. "The same goes for you too, Mullins. And I would also like to remind you that a *truly* good brush is a superior—no, a *triumphant*—piece of industrial design."

"Yes, Commander," said Mullins, flushing scarlet. "Sorry, Commander."

"Warned you," whispered Chin-Riley.

Mullins tapped the padd. "What *are* these unmissable lectures?"

"Um, there's a few of them," said Chin-Riley, scanning through the titles. "'What to Expect from Your First Two Years Aboard Ship.' That seems reasonable. 'What Ensigns Do Badly and What They Do Well.' I guess he'd know. 'How to Ace Your First Test Flight.'"

Mullins laughed. "He fancies himself, doesn't he?"

"Maybe he has cause," said Chin-Riley.

"Maybe," said Mullins. "One thing this place does is give some people a *real* sense of their own worth."

"As long it's an *accurate* sense, I don't see what's wrong with that," said Chin-Riley. She read through the rest of the lecture titles. All were oriented toward Pike's practical experience. Pelia's course seemed to have the same emphasis. "They're really trying to make us think beyond the Academy, aren't they?"

"I guess it's not long till we get our first postings," said Mullins. She sounded less enthusiastic about that prospect than one might expect from a senior. "You're not going, are you?"

"Hmm?" said Chin-Riley.

"These lectures."

"I think I will," said Chin-Riley.

"What are you going to drop? Not Command Psychology?"

Chin-Riley found the add form for Pike's lecture series and began to fill it in. "Can you imagine Sipek's face if I did?"

"It would certainly merit an eyebrow. So what's going? What are you dropping?"

"Nothing," said Chin-Riley. "I'll make it work. I always do. But you know what? I think Pelia's right. I think you should come too."

Mullins shook her head. "Nuh-uh. I've got plenty to do."

"You're always complaining that you don't get to see enough real examples," said Chin-Riley. "That some of the instructors are teaching the last generation of cadets, not the next generation. You can't say that about Pike. He was here a couple of years ago. And he was on board ship a couple of months ago. He'll know the score."

"I know, Una, but—"

"It's a short lecture series. It's not like it's a complete course. There's not even an assessment listed. We can try out the first one, and if he's hopeless we don't bother with the rest. Look, this first one is about this test mission. Let's see what he's made of. Let's see if we should believe the hype."

"Oh, all right," Mullins said grudgingly. Quickly she sent off her own add form. "But if he turns out to be some self-satisfied flyboy, I'm holding you personally responsible. Okay?"

"Okay," said Chin-Riley. "Shall we get that coffee now?"

"Yes. Though I'm gasping for a cup of tea."

They strode off across campus, talking and laughing. It was a glorious day, the best that September could offer, filled with the thrill and the promise of a new term, a new year. This, Chin-Riley thought, was everything she had wanted from the Academy; everything she had wanted from being part of Starfleet. Good and challenging work, fun extracurricular, and some really great friends who liked her. Her last year at the Academy. She had great plans for it, and for everything that would come after. The risk was paying off. She'd always known she could make a success of Starfleet. She was doing fine. More than fine: she was doing brilliantly. If you didn't know better, you'd think she deserved to be here.

Ensign Christopher Pike had learned from an early age that you had to roll with the punches. Recent events had brought a number of punches that meant he was still limping on damp mornings. The medicos promised this was a temporary thing, and, when it came to it, wasn't everything temporary? Take this sabbatical, for example, which would last only as long as that damned limp hung around, and until the hearing date was set. Pike wasn't punishing himself, he was young, but he wasn't stupid, there were plenty of daily therapeutic exercises to be done. And he'd taken the plunge and gone out riding. April had been right. He should have done it weeks ago. It had been good to get back on a horse. There'd been no physical side effects, and he felt a thousand times more cheerful afterward.

April had also been right about not sitting around waiting to be called to testify. Thinking about his lectures had kept him oc-cupied. ("Scare the bejesus out of them," said April, darkly, when they were discussing the possible topics of the lectures. "Or at least get a few of them to stop doing damn fool things. *You* might be the luckiest devil to serve on board a starship, but the vast majority of them are not.")

Seeing what life was like not as cadet, but as instructor had been a revelation. Take Sipek, for example. He had been the terror of the cadets, with a turn of phrase that could freeze your heart. Turned out he was mostly bark (with a little bite), and that nobody knew the cadets whose development was in his care as individually, thoughtfully, and intelligently as did Sipek. His class, Command

Psychology, cut in many directions. A practical application of a highly theoretical subject. On reflection, Pike shouldn't have been surprised. You knew how good the instructors were. But it was only really now, on the other side of the fence, watching the meticulous thought and care that went into these courses, the constant fine-tuning and refining of the material, that Pike realized how good.

Pelia was another example. Everyone in Pike's Academy class had a theory about her. She'd been part of the board that founded the Academy. She had six old masters stashed away in a lockup in east London, kept as a nest egg in case money ever made a return and she needed to make a fast buck. She'd met Jesus. One time, Pike sat mesmerized through a long diversion in one of her lectures where she talked about Johannes Gutenberg as if they'd been best friends. They'd come away convinced that she must have had a hand in inventing the printing press. His theory was that whether or not Pelia had steered the course of human technological history, she certainly didn't mind leaving you with that impression. As a cadet, listening to her, he'd found her rambling, diffuse, with the slightest air of a charlatan. The past couple of weeks talking to her as a colleague set him straight. Pelia was sharp as tacks, knew her stuff, and you were mistaken if you thought she rambled. She was surveying a few thousand years of experience, and picking out the exact detail she wanted you to know.

Best of all, she was a great drinking buddy. Every Wednesday and Friday evening since his arrival in San Francisco, they'd met to debrief and trade stories. They took turns to try to find a bar that the other had not discovered. Pike, to the surprise of both, was way ahead on this score. Tonight they were in a "real English pub" run by a guy from Oxfordshire who had somehow wound up in San

Francisco. So crusty was the place that you would not be surprised if a troop of Morris dancers suddenly jingled through.

"How do you find a dive like *this* in San Francisco?" muttered Pelia, glaring toward the far side of the bar, where a couple of fiddle players were about to commit folk music.

"How do you *not* find them?" said Pike.

"I've had a gutful of fiddles over the centuries," groused Pelia. "You cannot imagine my relief when finally jazz arrived. It was like being released from jail! Not that I have firsthand experience of being released from jail, you understand, let me make that clear."

"Sure," said Pike. "Anyway, I like this place. It's warm. It's friendly. The beer's good. And at least the music's live."

"The music is on its deathbed. And the beer is not good. The beer is full of twigs. Twigs have their place, yes. And that is on trees. Not"—she waved her forefinger at him—"in beer."

"Whisky for you, then, Pelia?"

"Hell yes. And make it a double."

Pike went up to the bar, brought back the drinks, and settled into his chair. There was a real fire crackling away in the hearth. A couple of patrons were playing a game that seemed to involve rolling dice in the shape of skulls and knocking back shots. Pike had tried a few of these pub games when he was a plebe. There was a whole weekend of his life he couldn't quite account for. Carefully, he stretched out his left leg and gently kneaded the area above the knee, which had been twinging all afternoon. Was this what it would be like to be old? Constant twinges? He was too young to be thinking about getting old.

"Everything okay with that?" said Pelia, nodding at his leg.

"Stiff," he said. "No hiking for me this weekend."

"I should hope not." She took a slug of her whisky. "First lecture tomorrow."

"Yep," he said. He sipped his beer. She didn't know what she was talking about. This stuff was great. Fed the soul. He'd got into a dumb debate once, at the Academy: "What was humanity's greatest achievement?" Beer had narrowly lost out to the bag, which, another cadet had argued, was the basis of human civilization, allowing people to collect what they needed while keeping their hands free. Beer, they'd argued, had occurred only because people could collect and carry things.

"Prepared?" said Pelia.

"I guess. I imagine you don't know until you're in the room."

"If you know *that*, then you're prepared," she said. "Want some tips?"

"Sure," he said.

"Watch out for any seniors present."

"Oh yeah? Any particular reason why?"

"Seniors are always know-it-alls. And this year they're . . ." She gave a wry smile. "Some cadets, you know? They're practically perfect in every way."

"Is that a problem, Pelia?"

"Well, it can be. If they never learn to roll with the punches. You must have seen this, Chris. Sometimes it's the less stellar colleagues that turn out to be the most consistent. They've made mistakes. They've learned. Nobody can keep up perfection indefinitely." She winked. "Not even you."

He wasn't particularly feeling this alleged perfection at the moment, but he took her general point. "Huh."

"You got a date for that hearing yet?"

"Nope," he said.

"You want me to leave this subject alone for now?"

"Yep." Absently, he rubbed at his leg. "So you've got some *too*-perfect cadets at the moment, huh? Think they know everything? Think they've seen everything?"

"More that they don't always get what it is we're offering them. You'll see." She gave a smug smile. "I've sent a couple of them your way."

"Thanks, Pelia. Remind me to return the favor."

"They'll keep you on your toes. Stop you from getting lazy."

"That's my problem," he sighed. "Not enough action. Too much sitting down."

"Too much beer with twigs," she agreed. "Nobody needs that many calories."

Over on the other side of the pub, the fiddlers started up. A jig.

"*Jeez*," muttered Pelia, slinging back the rest of her whisky. Pike hid his smile behind his pint glass. "I'm gonna need at least another one of these." She made a run to the bar. When she got back, she lined up her two new shots of whisky. "There's one I'd like you to keep an eye on."

"One of those too-perfect cadets?"

"Sort of," said Pelia. "One of the smartest in her year. Best debater. Mind like a steel trap. But I get the feeling her heart isn't really in Starfleet."

"No?"

"No. In fact, I think she might be better suited to something else."

"Diplomatic corps?"

"Maybe . . ." Pelia didn't look sure. "She's got a lot of extracurricular activity going on."

"Fun stuff?" said Pike. Everyone did that. It wasn't insurmountable, even in your third year, though at some point you did have to knuckle down and do the work.

"Quite the contrary. Activist. Politics." Pelia shrugged. "Maybe I'm wrong. Her name is Theresa Mullins. Look out for her. She consistently gets some of the best grades across the board, along with Una, of course."

"Una?"

"Cadet Una Chin-Riley." Pelia smiled, rather wolfishly. "Oh, you'll see. I imagine that Una will make herself known to you very quickly."

"Why do I get the feeling you're setting me up?"

"A man takes me to a bar with fiddle music," said Pelia darkly, "he's gonna pay a price."

The lecture hall was one of the biggest on campus, and with twenty minutes to go it was almost full. Una Chin-Riley and Theresa Mullins found a couple of leftover single seats near the front, right at the end of the rows, one behind the other. They grabbed these, Chin-Riley in the foremost seat. She turned to talk to her friend. Anyone looking at them would think that they were the epitome of a couple of seniors, sitting relaxed and confident, coffee cups in hand, padds laid out in front of them. As they talked about their schedules and gossiped about their peers, someone stopped in the aisle beside them.

"Excuse me," said a soft voice. "Are you Cadet Chin-Riley?"

Chin-Riley turned to see a very young-looking plebe (When did they start looking like *babies*?) who was tugging in embarrassment at her uniform collar.

21

"Una," said Theresa, "you're famous."

"Yes, sir, she is," said the plebe. "Sorry to interrupt you while you're talking to your friend. I heard about your performance as Mad Margaret last year. Everyone has been raving about it."

Chin-Riley offered her hand. "Yes, I'm Una. And you're . . . ?"

"Fatima Nahas. Hi." She shook Chin-Riley's hand. "I love Gilbert and Sullivan, and I'd really like to join the society." She took a deep breath and launched into the patter song from *Ruddigore*.

"If I had been so lucky as to have a steady brother

"Who could talk to me as we are talking now to one another—"

Wow, thought Chin-Riley. That particular song was a real tongue twister. Nahas had set off at a real pace, and wasn't showing any sign of tripping over the words. She let Nahas do the bulk of the verse and joined in for her favorite bit at the end:

"This particularly rapid, unintelligible patter

"Isn't generally heard, and if it is it doesn't matter!

"This particularly rapid, unintelligible patter

"Isn't generally heard, and if it is it doesn't matter!"

There was a smattering of applause from the cadets around them. Nahas gave a tiny mock bow to their appreciators. "Honestly," said Mullins, rolling her eyes.

Chin-Riley and Nahas looked at each other and burst out laughing.

"You're *great*," said Chin-Riley, with real enthusiasm, and sent contact details and rehearsal information over to Nahas's padd. "First rehearsal's this evening. Whatever your plans—cancel them. We definitely need you!"

"Oh, I shall!" said Nahas, eyes shining.

"This *Mikado* is going to be *fantastic*," said Chin-Riley. The pair then launched into a dissection of the best parts (Katisha, they both agreed), but their mutual enthusiasm was halted when Pike appeared, ambling onto the dais and over to the lectern.

"Nineteen hundred!" said Chin-Riley. "The Mohammidi Auditorium! It's over on the east side of campus," she added, considering that the plebe might not yet have found where everything was.

"Got it!" said Nahas. "See you later!" she promised, and dashed off to find a seat.

Ensign Christopher Pike was tall, dark-haired, and seemed to be favoring his left leg. *What happened there?* wondered Chin-Riley.

Mullins, leaning forward, whispered, "Una, he's gorgeous."

Chin-Riley studied the ensign. He was handsome, she supposed. His haircut—which was slightly too long and floppy—made him look like he'd stopped listening to new music three years ago. Chin-Riley supposed she could see what other people might see, but truth be told, she was far more interested in what Pike had to say. "I guess."

"Una," hissed Theresa, "sometimes I'm not sure you have a pulse!"

Pike smiled out at the class benignly. "Hey," he said, "more of you than I was expecting, particularly at this time of the morning."

Some general laughter around the room.

"I'm Chris Pike. Ensign. Five years ago I was sitting right where you're sitting now, wondering when my damn lecturer was going to get started so that I could get back to the pool table."

More laughter.

"First of all, let me say that I appreciate your appreciation for my jokes."

Mullins tapped her on the shoulder. *Dad jokes,* she mouthed. *He tells Dad jokes.*

Shush, mouthed Chin-Riley, getting ready to take notes. *He's nice.*

"Coming back here to the Academy so soon after graduating is interesting, to say the least. Being on this side of the lectern is even more so, and"—he gave a laugh—"more than a little intimidating. But I've picked up some experience in the past couple of years, and the commandant thinks that this could be useful for you, as I am slightly closer to your age than that bunch of ancient—sorry, those venerable luminaries."

More laughter. Chin-Riley rolled her eyes. *Get on with it, Pike. Cut to the good stuff.*

"Right. This first lecture, I'm going to talk about a test mission I flew straight out of the Academy. It's so textbook that they're putting it in the textbook. I chose this for my first lecture so that you'd go away absolutely sure that I am competent. I'm saving the cock-ups for later in the semester, and I promise you that you don't want to miss those lectures. I look like a real fool in most of those. But today I want to impress you. So let's get on with it."

He cut to the good stuff.

Almost an hour later, Pike stopped to take a drink of water. Chin-Riley, sitting up and flexing her hand, realized she hadn't stopped taking notes the whole time. Pike could certainly spin a tale—and his stuff was gold. Frank, honest, and straight from the source. More of their courses needed to be like this—although some of the cadets in the hall looked like they'd just been dropped down a turbolift shaft.

"Okay," he said. "Let's get this ship landed. Here's how we handled reentry."

Two minutes later, Chin-Riley sat up, stared at Pike, and then reached for her padd and began searching for the piece of information she knew was in there somewhere. Five minutes later, the lecture ended to rapturous applause. Pike, to his credit, looked rather endearingly relieved. Chin-Riley turned around to speak to Mullins.

"He made a mistake," she said.

"What?"

"In reentry. There's a whole series of protocols he didn't go through." She held up the padd. "Look," she said. "It's in the regs."

"Is that what you were doing the last five minutes? Checking the regs? I thought you looked happier than usual—"

Chin-Riley grabbed her padd and her bag and stood up. "I'm going to tell him."

Mullins, following suit, said, "You're what?"

"I'm going to tell him. He made a mistake."

"Let me get this straight," said Mullins. "You're going to go up to Christopher Pike, guest lecturer and darling of the Academy, and tell him he didn't follow regs?"

"Yes," said Chin-Riley.

"Can I come?"

"Sure," said Chin-Riley.

"You never know," said Mullins, "you might need a witness."

They inched their way through the crush of cadets heading off in the opposite direction toward the exit. They all looked enthused about everything they'd heard. At the front, Pike was packing up. He had bitten into an apple. He took it out as they approached.

"Cadets," he said, "is there something you needed?"

"I had a question, sir," said Chin-Riley.

"A quick question?" said Pike. "I have a meeting across campus in five—"

"You made a mistake, sir."

Pike, who had been scooping up his bag, stopped. "I did what?"

"You made a mistake, sir. In reentry, there's a series of protocols surrounding checking fuel reserves that you didn't observe. If you forgot—it was a mistake. If you didn't forget—it was still a mistake." She held out the padd. "It's right there in the regs."

Pike took another bite of his apple and chewed slowly. "What's your name, Cadet?"

"Una Chin-Riley."

Something flickered behind Pike's eyes. Had he heard of her? What had he heard? And how? Chin-Riley didn't like thinking that people were having conversations about her behind her back. It made her feel suspect, and she had very good reasons to not like feeling suspect. She put the feeling aside, squared her shoulders, and looked him straight in the eye.

"And I'm Theresa Mullins, for the record."

"Cadet Mullins," said Pike. "I've heard about you too."

"About me?" Mullins laughed. "Sorry, sir, but that *never* happens."

"Theresa," murmured Chin-Riley, "you're famous."

"Do *you* think I made a mistake?" said Pike.

"I don't know, sir," said Mullins. "This is the regs we're talking about. I'm not the one that's into the regs. I'm the one that's into the law. You want to know something about the perils of working within multiple and sometimes competing legal systems, then I'm your cadet. But when it comes to the regs, nobody can beat Una."

Pike smiled and reached for his bag. "You know, I do have to run," he said. "But we should meet later and talk this through."

"Should we make an appointment, sir?" said Chin-Riley. "My schedule's pretty full until next week—"

"Well, I want to hear what you have to say sooner than that," he said. "I'm not really here as an instructor. I'm just doing the odd lecture here and there. Why don't we meet for a drink later?"

"A drink?" said Chin-Riley, wrinkling her nose.

Mullins stifled a laugh.

"Yes, you know, a drink," said Pike, shouldering his bag and taking another bite of his apple. "In a bar. You do know what a bar is?"

"I'm not sure she does, sir," said Mullins. "Now, if you offered to meet her in one of the study zones, she'd be absolutely clear—"

Chin-Riley gathered up her dignity. "I know what a *bar* is. I just . . . have a lot to do."

"Nineteen hundred?"

"Oh, it's first rehearsal on *The Mikado* tonight—"

"Gilbert and Sullivan, huh?" Pike's eyes were twinkling. "Very model of a major general."

"Yes, sir, although there's more to Gilbert and Sullivan than that—"

"Is there? Let's say twenty-one hundred. Tyulia's? You can tell me more about Gilbert and Sullivan. As well as the regs."

"Tyulia's?" said Chin-Riley. She'd never heard of the place.

"It's on Archer Street," said Mullins. "Specializes in Efrosian cocktails."

"That's the one," said Pike. "Look, I'm sorry, I really have to go." He gave them both an outsized grin. "Cadet Chin-Riley. Cadet Mullins. Pleasure to meet you both." He turned, threw the apple core straight into the recycler—hole in one—said, with some satisfaction, "*Boom!*" and went on his way.

"You know," said Mullins, watching him go, "I think this might be the start of something special."

"What?"

"You. Him. A bar on Archer—"

"No," said Chin-Riley firmly. "Absolutely not."

"You sure about that?"

"Really, Theresa? It would be like dating your older brother."

"Not my older brother." Mullins sighed. "Shame. You two would look amazing side by side. The kind of thing you engrave on a plaque and send out to the stars to show aliens the high point of our species. Did they include any Gilbert and Sullivan when they sent out those probes?"

"I hope he didn't think I was interested," said Chin-Riley. She was getting worried now, and the direction Mullins was taking was making her uneasy. Not to mention there was no time in her schedule for a relationship and, besides, relationships meant opening up, intimacy, telling . . . Well, telling secrets, and Chin-Riley wasn't up for telling anybody any secrets. She wasn't up for that at all. *Was* he interested? She needed to make clear, absolutely clear, that it wasn't in the cards.

"Okay," she said, making a decision. "You're coming with me."

"Wait," said Mullins. "What?"

"To this bar. You can come too. I mean, he didn't say that he only meant me, did he?"

"Una," said her friend, "I have a life of my own, you know."

"Yes, but—"

"I already signed up for this talk against my will. I'm not playing chaperone while you decide whether or not to date the handsome ensign."

"It's *not* a date," said Chin-Riley, "and that decision is made."

"I believe you," said Mullins. "Thousands wouldn't."

"Well, it definitely can't be a date if you're there."

This was delivered with such an air of finality that Mullins sighed and said, "All right! All right! But you *owe* me, Una. Big-time."

She was fine with owing Theresa a favor. Because she'd be safe with Theresa there. She'd have sent the right message. No chance of misunderstandings; no chance of any messy mistakes that might leave her open to scrutiny.

They headed out of the hall and into the bright midday sun. "You're a good friend, Theresa," said Chin-Riley, meaning it in more ways than Mullins could possibly know.

"You know what?" said Mullins. "I really am. See you at Tyulia's. Twenty-one hundred. Try not to dazzle him."

2260

STARSHIP ENTERPRISE
DIPLOMATIC INCIDENTS

First Officer's Personal Log

The *Enterprise* will shortly arrive at Starbase 1, where our esteemed passenger and guest—Ambassador T'Maal of Vulcan—is scheduled to open trade negotiations with representatives of the planet Xhio. This world is home to a species known as the Chionians, whose territories lie close to a number of outlying Federation colony worlds. It's hoped that these negotiations will enable the Federation to formalize trade and shipping routes through Chionian space, enabling Starfleet to reduce significantly the time taken to bring necessary supplies and resources to many planets. Life on these more remote colonies is undoubtedly hard at times, and many of these worlds will benefit from more regular and reliable shipments of medical, farming, and infrastructural supplies.

While the negotiations are primarily to discuss access to Chionian space, the captain has suggested that the choice of Ambassador T'Maal as the lead might also signal that an application to join the United Federation of Planets might be under consideration by the Chionians. This seems logical to me: Ambassador T'Maal has successfully negotiated the admission of six worlds, and is presumably keen to learn more about the Chionians. While it's early days in our relationship with the Chionians, we cannot help but be conscious of the wider implications. Missions such as these are about presenting the Federation in the best light possible: showing that we are partners to be trusted and demonstrating the principles that hold the Federation together.

Information on the Chionians is comparatively limited. Physically, they are humanoid, bipedal (and digitigrade); in many respects, they are similar to such feline species as the Caitians. They are long-eared, appear slender, and their fur—which, so far as we can make out, ranges in hue from pale yellow through various shades of gold to russet—is marked with dark spots and stripes. The captain has said that they remind him of an Earth mammal known as the serval. It's helpful to have a visual cue in advance of meeting face-to-face. They are a warp civilization. In terms of their culture and society, we know very little beyond what we can infer from their communications with us. While they have made files on their language available to us, our universal translator is having problems parsing it. Ensign Uhura has been immersed in studying it (hoping to add another language in which she is conversant), and her analysis is that the language is structured to show a courtesy of tone, and a degree of attention to formality and regulations. I find that reassuring (as does Lieutenant Noonien-Singh). The decision to send a Vulcan ambassador, given the formality with which they also approach significant occasions, should also help achieve the best outcome. (As a side note, Spock has informed me that T'Maal is from an old, highly respected Vulcan family. He believes the ambassador has worked alongside his father on several occasions. Spock indicated that, given the current status of his relationship with his father, it might be logical for him to limit his contact with T'Maal. The captain has suggested we play it by ear.)

There has been only one disruption to our preparations, which was a request from the Chionians, two weeks ago, that we move the location of the talks from Starbase 1 to the *Enterprise*. The request was formal and highly courteous but offered no specific reason beyond a general statement that having reviewed the information the Federation made available, they believed a starship location would be preferable and more suited to them. Perhaps they did not like the décor on

Starbase 1 but were unwilling to say anything impolite. Since *Enterprise* is well equipped to handle negotiations such as these, the request was granted, and I believe Lieutenant Noonien-Singh is happier now that security is directly within her purview, rather than the responsibility of her opposite on Starbase 1. This is not intended as a slight toward the security team on Starbase 1, which is first-rate, and under the watchful and entirely competent eye of Lieutenant Zhovell, a respected and decorated officer. Lieutenant La'An Noonien-Singh simply prefers to be in charge. (I wholeheartedly agree that if you want a job done properly, you do it yourself.) But perhaps I should note here, in passing, that I have sensed a restlessness in my friend and colleague in recent days that I am struggling to explain. I'm hoping that immersing herself in the minutiae of the mission will go some way to helping her deal with whatever is currently preying on her mind.

I should, I suppose, finish this entry with some reflection on my own position. It's now several weeks since my court-martial. I thought that I was facing expulsion from Starfleet and, potentially, a lengthy jail sentence. Several weeks! It seems like it happened years ago. Looking back over incarceration, the investigation, and then court-martial, the whole experience seems like a bad dream. I wake each morning feeling . . . *light*, there is no other word for it. A huge burden has been lifted, but, more than that, I have never felt so whole. I have never felt so accepted. I continue to be grateful for the support extended to me by my crew, my friends. I don't know what I would have done without them. I feel more at home on *Enterprise* than ever before; I have found the sanctuary that I always knew Starfleet could provide. I trusted that people would be good; and they are.

One unanticipated aspect of the whole business has been to hear from people with whom, simply as a result of the passage of time, I had fallen out of contact. Old friends from the Academy. People with whom

I served on my first ship. Someone with whom I briefly corresponded about the history of performances of *The Pirates of Penzance*. I guess it's been good—it's been extraordinary—to find out that I was held in esteem, despite the secrets that I was forced to keep. Throughout my life, I have had to keep my own counsel, keep people that I love at arm's length. Habits of a lifetime are hard to unlearn, and I doubt I will ever break completely through this reserve of mine that, if it was not innate, has become so by force of habit. At the same time, each day I feel the benefits of being able to live authentically, without the knowledge of the big lie that existed between me and the rest of the universe. That lie did far too much damage over the years—to me, and to those around me. I am glad to be free of it, at last. Nobody should have to lie in order to be able simply to live.

Echet Linchar A'Chevar, empowered by the Chionian government to speak on behalf of both branches of the Family of Xhio, said, "I am particularly eager to meet the Vulcan T'Maal."

Her aides, Marachat and Texho, were both present. They were, Linchar thought, polar opposites, as different as the valleys and the mountains. Not simply in their physical characteristics—the differences there were, obviously, marked—but in age, manner, and background. The specific tasks she had set them in advance of these negotiations were inflected rather differently too. Marachat she had asked to survey Federation culture, to find points of sympathy and similarity. This was not an assignment she would have considered giving to Texho, even though he was her senior aide. Texho had taken the lead on communicating with Starfleet and finalizing the details of their time on Starbase 1.

Texho—broad, often gruff, round faced and blue eyed, with

silver-gray fur and a distinctive rosette on his brow—said, "Why the Vulcan in particular, *Echet*?"

"Our civilizations seem to have followed similar paths," said Linchar. "They set a high premium on reflection, prudence, moderation. They value harmony, not only in their arts and architecture, but in their social arrangements. I believe, too, that T'Maal comes from a highly respected kinship group. She will understand the burdens of authority." Linchar was proud of her lineage, the web of relationships that stretched back several centuries prior to unification. "I believe that we have much in common. I hope this turns out to be true."

"My sense, *Echet*," said Texho, "is that you've had the most success when you've found a personal connection to your opposite number. Remember the Stavilite ambassador?"

"How could I forget!"

They shared a smile.

"I must hear *this* story," said Marachat, smiling in turn.

"Texho tells it best," said Linchar, and her aide nodded his gratitude at this compliment. It had undoubtedly been a risk, all those years ago, taking Texho onto her staff, and many of her colleagues had warned her privately that it was only a matter of time before his true nature was revealed. *Euxhana don't change their spots*, more than one said. But Texho had more than rewarded her faith in him. She could not imagine going on any of these missions without him. Always he had the right piece of information to hand. Always he anticipated what might be needed. True, his manner could be—What would be the best word? Blunt, perhaps? Yes, blunt—and there was still, after all these years and despite the boarding school, the faintest hint of the mountains in his speech, but the dewclaw in him was long since pared away, as the saying went. He was exceptional, in many ways, and particularly so for a Euxhana.

Marachat was the absolute opposite. Young, and with an impeccable pedigree, easily as good as her own. Linchar had studied with Marachat's mother at one of the elite schools in Ghezha—oh, too many years ago, now! In turn, Marachat had attended the same establishment. Linchar did not, as a matter of principle, give posts to the children of her friends and colleagues, believing that merit had to be demonstrated. But Marachat's achievements and reputation were so outstanding that many people were pursuing him. Linchar had persuaded him that, for the moment at least, his future lay in the diplomatic corps, and that she had a great deal to teach him. He was graceful and elegant, his pelt a particularly handsome gold, his stripes regular, and he was surely destined for great things. She hoped that she could keep him a while yet. He was a jewel in her crown.

She liked, too, how he interacted with Texho. There was no awkwardness or overfamiliarity. He treated Texho with respect. He treated Texho like his superior.

"I'm curious, *Echet*," said Marachat. "What *exactly* is your hope for these discussions?"

"Trade routes, for one," said Texho.

"Yes, trade, of course—but I sense there's something more."

"Your ears have been twitching again, Marachat," said Linchar.

"Oh, I'm always alert to what is happening around me. 'The gates of the compound are well protected.'"

That, as Linchar knew full well, was a quotation from Charavar's fifth ode. Marachat always had the right phrase: the benefits of a classical education. They smiled at each other in mutual recognition; Texho looked on.

Linchar stretched out on her couch. "It must be clear by now that the United Federation of Planets has emerged as one of the major powers in this part of the quadrant," she said. "But we have been caught rather unprepared for this outcome. Wisdom for many years was that the *Klingons* . . ." She tried to suppress her distaste, but with limited success; they were so *uncouth*. ". . . would emerge as the superior power. Had that been the case, we would most certainly have kept our distance. But the Federation is . . ."

"More nuanced?" said Marachat.

"Precisely," said Linchar. "Many of their worlds—and not only Vulcan—bear the hallmarks of civilization. So"—she nodded at Texho—"an agreement on trade routes is one goal. But there might be others. We want a better understanding of the Federation. Its internal workings. How it is governed . . ."

Texho rumbled his approval, a deep and instinctive sound that came from the barrel of his chest. She had never quite broken him of that habit. Marachat, meanwhile . . . She could see his clever mind at work, thinking through the implications of everything she had disclosed.

"*Echet*," he said, "are we considering applying for membership?"

Clever cub. "No," she replied; and then, since obliqueness was more the Chionian way, added, "At least, not right now."

That stopped Texho's rumbling. "Membership in the United Federation of Planets?" he said bluntly. "Are we ready?"

Statements like that were what, ultimately, reminded one that Texho was not quite the same as everyone else. Linchar raised her fine brows. Marachat cleared his throat.

"The question, surely," murmured Linchar, "is whether or not they are ready for us."

"Of course," said Texho, "that was what I meant."

Marachat smiled politely.

The Chionian civilization was rich and varied, and its achievements significant. They would bring great things to this federation of worlds and species. But if Linchar was being scrupulously honest with herself (and one did not succeed without being scrupulously honest with oneself), she could not help feeling a strange desire for approval from the Federation. They represented progress in her mind—forward-looking, expansive, energetic. Xhio sometimes seemed oddly *timid*. No, that was not fair. Circumspect. Careful. Meticulous. All of which were fine qualities, ones that arose from cultivation. The Federation's energy might also be seen as impulsivity. Brashness. Clumsiness. But still, there was that *vivacity* to them.

"Surely we can learn from them," she said. "'An open mind is the height of cultivation.'" She saw Marachat smile at that nod to the sixth ode. "And I am sure that the three of us can show the Family of Xhio at its very best. Show everything that *we* have to offer."

Agreement from all around. She liked it when they were all in concord. A light flashed on the comm bracelet around Texho's wrist, and he checked the message.

"We're approaching Starbase 1," he said. "I'll see to the formalities, if I may, *Echet*?"

"Please do, Texho," she murmured. Both her aides rose from their couches, and Texho left. But Marachat held back, indicating with a discreetly raised paw to Linchar that he wished to speak to her further. When the door had closed, leaving them alone, Linchar said, "Was there something else?"

"Yes," said Marachat, in his soft and cultured voice. "You'll quickly understand that this is not the kind of matter best raised in front of Texho . . ."

Linchar, who thought she might be able to guess what was coming next, shut her eyes briefly. "Oh no," she said, with a sigh. "Where now?"

"Achionis. The gilt quarter."

Linchar shuddered. Her fur stood on end. Achionis was the second-biggest city on Xhio's second-largest continent. The gilt quarter was in the very heart of the old town, a deeply treasured place, layered with history. Some of the buildings there dated back several thousand years before unification. There would have been many tourists. Educational groups. *Cubs . . . ?*

"A much more significant target than ever before," noted Marachat.

"A calculated assault on our shared heritage," said Linchar. "Has anybody been hurt?"

"One of the instigators seems to have been killed."

"I meant, anyone who matters."

The merest pause, and then Marachat said, "Of course. I understand that a teacher was injured protecting her charges."

"So brave . . ." said Linchar. "Sometimes I wonder how this will ever end," she went on. "We open schools, we build homes, we create systems that allow people to rise up the ranks, and in return our cubs are threatened and our history attacked."

"I do understand the frustration," said Marachat.

"Frustration!" Linchar almost hissed—but her cultivation was sufficient to hold this in check. "This goes beyond frustration!"

"It is slow work," said Marachat. "Each individual setback is not necessarily a backward step. We have to keep moving forward. Otherwise, I ask, what is the alternative? You can't force cultivation on people. You have to teach it by example. 'The strongest of all warriors are time and patience.'"

41

Linchar, puzzled, inclined her head. "I don't recognize that quotation, Marachat."

"It's from a human writer, *Echet*," he said. "I know you asked me to explore primarily Vulcan art and literature, but I have been drawn toward the human texts."

"Your conclusions?"

"They are certainly cultivated in their own way. There is something quicksilver about them. I find their dynamism and adaptability quite fascinating."

"I have chiefly concerned myself with the Vulcan," admitted Linchar. "The *Enterprise* is crewed substantially by humans. Perhaps I should have explored more widely."

"We ought to advise the Federation about this attack in Achionis," said Marachat. "I'm happy to do that, *Echet*—"

"Why would we do that?" she said. "This is a Family matter. Besides, my understanding is that Starfleet and the Federation have strong prohibitions against interference in the internal affairs of other civilizations. We don't want to inadvertently offend—"

"*My* understanding of that particular general order," said Marachat, "is that it applies chiefly to pre-warp civilizations. What we might call less cultivated societies—"

"What else are the Euxhana?" said Linchar.

Marachat tilted his head elegantly, a sign that—with her permission—he intended to disagree. There was such ease to everything he did. Texho, for all his hard work, would never achieve this innate degree of polish.

"Go on," said Linchar. "You believe we should inform them? For what purpose?"

"There could well be security implications, for one thing," he said.

"There's no sign that Euxhana terrorists have ever operated beyond Xhio," said Linchar. "I'm not convinced they would have the wherewithal to do so, never mind the expertise. I am not sure that complicating our visit with extraneous details would be useful, Marachat. The Federation has extensive intelligence networks. If this information is relevant to their interests, they will surely have learned about it through their own sources. But it is, ultimately, our business. Not theirs. A Family matter."

"Very well, let us by all means mind our own business." But he was not yet quite finished. "Do you truly believe that these extremists have limited resources?"

"I believe that an attack on a place as high-profile as the gilt quarter of Achionis speaks more of desperation than confidence," said Linchar.

"So you think these outrages may finally be drawing to an end?" She heard the note of eagerness in his voice. She sympathized with him. Who could not? More than half a century of conflict, of trouble. Surely the Euxhana must see that they would never win. That would not—that could not—be permitted. *That* was a step backward; a step away from civilization.

"Time will tell," she said.

"I suppose so," said Marachat.

Linchar understood. She too longed for peace at home, for harmony between both branches of the Family of Xhio. Surely the Euxhana did too? They were at heart the same people. But the Euxhana had (now what was their expression?) strayed from the pathway. They should be guided back.

"Keep me informed on the situation as it unfolds, Marachat. And . . ." She sighed. "You might find a way to broach the subject with Texho."

"I usually pass on the reports," said Marachat. "We tend not to discuss the contents."

"No," said Linchar. "No need to complicate his life further, I suppose."

"Your second deserves all the support we can offer him, *Echet*," said Marachat.

"A cultivated viewpoint, Marachat," said Linchar. This was the highest compliment one Chionian could pay another, and he inclined his head graciously. As he started for the door, she said, "What else have you learned from your explorations of Vulcan and human culture?"

"An interesting question, *Echet*, and I'm not yet qualified to do it justice."

"You're too modest."

"Then . . . I would say that it seems to me that the difference between the Vulcans and the humans is very like the difference between the two branches of the Family of Xhio."

"The humans being the Euxhana in this comparison, I assume?" said Linchar.

"Yes—younger, less cultivated—"

"Of course," she interjected, "the Euxhana have not produced any high art."

"Ah . . . Indeed not," he agreed. "How could they? And that is an important difference."

"Still," she said, "it bodes well that there are two cultivated species to whom we can speak. The Federation is broad enough that there will be more."

"I agree, *Echet*," he said, and went on his way.

Alone in her exquisite cabin once again, Linchar pondered her mission and what it might mean. She knew—all Chionians knew—of the hard work that had been done to bring the Family of Xhio—the *whole* family of Xhio—to this point in their history, when they could step forward proudly and show other worlds their grace and dignity, their cultivation. She understood from her meticulous and careful preparation that part of the Federation's philosophy was that their diverse worlds could learn from each other. In her heart, she believed she had more to teach than to learn. She was eager to meet the representative from Vulcan, another cultivated species. She was sure that T'Maal would understand.

The commander of Starbase 1, Ylezia Wass, was Bolian. Linchar did not know the extent to which Bolians were cultivated, but there was no doubt that Commander Wass gave them a nuanced welcome to the base, speaking warmly and enthusiastically about the forthcoming negotiations, and managing a fine and formal welcome in their language.

"The *Enterprise* should be docking later this afternoon," said Wass, leading Linchar through the corridors of the base. "There's a reception this evening with the two delegations and the senior staff of both Starbase 1 and the *Enterprise*. Afterward, at your request, I have arranged for an informal face-to-face supper between you and Ambassador T'Maal. I have also organized a short tour of the base for your security staff. But I imagine that before anything else you're keen to see your quarters, *Echet*, and make yourselves comfortable."

Linchar concurred with all these arrangements. The base, as they walked through, struck her as rather more serviceable than she had expected, the design leaning more toward functionality than subtlety, but she could not complain about her quarters. Clearly some effort had been made to discover what she might find aesthetically pleasing, and the room was warmed by gentle amber lamps. The overall effect reminded Linchar of her clan's country cabin in the lush green valleys of Praichinais, where she had spent many happy childhood holidays. Linchar's overall favorable impressions continued when, after Wass left, she found on the comm unit a short message from Ambassador T'Maal. She was hoping that Linchar was pleased with her accommodations on Starbase 1, adding that she was anticipating their first face-to-face meeting later that day. What a cultivated touch on the part of the Vulcan ambassador; what a thoughtful and nuanced welcome. This all boded well for the future, and the nascent friendship between their two civilizations.

After refreshing herself (and being fortified by a short nap, which she took stretched out along the couch), Linchar decided that she was sufficiently at ease in these quarters to take out her *chera'char* from her luggage. This, although her hosts could not know it, was one of the highest compliments Linchar could pay them. The *chera'char* was one of Linchar's most prized possessions, inherited from a grandmother, the individual carved blocks and the patterns inked onto them building up to provide a visual representation of her whole clan stretching back generations. The practice of laying down one's *chera'char*—cherishing each part, studying the whole— was both meditative and spiritual, and Linchar tried to carry out the exercise daily. Today, she got no further than placing the first few blocks before she was interrupted by the chime on the door. At her instruction, the door opened, and both her aides entered.

"There's been an attack," said Texho.

"In Achionis?" said Linchar. "I know."

"A second attack," he said—almost interrupting her, but she let that moment of bluntness pass, as she often did with Texho.

"Where?" asked Linchar.

"Chianaise," said Marachat.

"That's near the border," she said. It was also not far from a Federation colony world . . .

"*Echet*," said Marachat, "I strongly recommend that we inform the Federation of this—"

"No!" she said quickly. "This is a Family matter!"

"It might be prudent," said Texho.

"No," she said, again.

There was a brief and embarrassed pause. Linchar stretched and attempted to regain her self-control. "Is there anything else?"

"I believe so," said Texho. "Whether or not we inform the Federation, there are security concerns. You are a high-profile individual, and this is a significant meeting. We must make sure that we keep you safe."

"Very well," she said. "But what can we do? We can hardly ask for discussions to be moved to our ship—"

"That could certainly be construed as an insult," said Marachat. "But is there anything we can do to disrupt Euxhana expectations? Confound any preplanned attack?"

"Is such an attack *likely*?" said Linchar. "How would they reach us here?"

Another pointed pause. "There are Euxhana in Federation space," said Texho quietly, not inviting further interrogation.

"Of course," said Linchar delicately. People who had not been willing to do the work needed to bring about harmony in the Family of Xhio. Not to mention people who had broken the law and elected not to face the consequences.

"I suppose a further change of location . . ." said Texho, and shook his head. "No, no . . . Too difficult at this stage, surely."

"I'd like to hear your thinking at least," said Marachat.

"Starbase 1 was preparing to receive us," said Texho. "The *Enterprise* offered more security in the wake of the demonstrations in Iomionia."

Demonstrations that had turned deadly.

"You believe we might be able to move the talks back here?" said Marachat. "To Starbase 1?"

"The security arrangements here were well advanced," said Texho doubtfully. "I reviewed them myself. We could ask?"

Linchar pondered this. They had already asked for one change of location, which had been met with courtesy. Would a second be too much of an imposition? Would questions come in the wake of such a request?

"It's your decision, *Echet*," said Marachat.

Was there genuinely a threat to her life? What did she know about those Euxhana who had left Xhio? What *could* she know about them? Their lives, their intentions, were completely opaque to her.

"I believe that we can *ask*," she said. "Texho, perhaps could you approach the base commander—discreetly, please!—and ask whether we might remove the talks back to Starbase 1. Ensure that everyone concerned is clear that this is not meant as a slight to the arrangements made by Captain Pike and his crew." She clawed at her head, thinking of what would need to be said to make this request without giving offense. "Oh, Marachat! I think perhaps you may be better suited for this task!"

She regretted these words as soon as they came out, implying, as they did, that Texho lacked sufficient nuance and cultivation for the errand. But there was no way to withdraw the remarks without further damage—and, besides, Marachat *was* better suited.

"Of course, *Echet*," he said quietly.

And Texho—dear Texho, saving her from the humiliation of her own clumsy mistake—said, "I shall be glad to liaise with the security officers on both *Enterprise* and here on Starbase 1, and ensure that all concerned understand that no insult is intended."

She grasped immediately the deeper nuances of this statement—and she was grateful to him once again. Sometimes Texho surprised her—but why should she be surprised, after all this time, and everything he had done? Everything that he had, against all expectations, proven himself repeatedly to be.

Glasses chinked, plates clinked, voices murmured, soft music played, and the *Enterprise* security chief was supremely confident in her preparations for the forthcoming negotiations. La'An Noonien-Singh tugged her dress uniform straight, grabbed a plate, and began piling up delicacies.

"You're starting early," said a voice behind her. "The speeches haven't happened yet."

Noonien-Singh didn't look around. "I always find speeches more digestible when accompanied by a generous portion of finger food." Turning to the speaker, she saw her superior officer's own more-than-respectable plateful, and gave a wry smile. Lieutenant Commander Una Chin-Riley wasn't holding back either. "Did you miss lunch?" ·

"Never," said Number One briskly. "Only fools skip meals." She speared a Grasanian salad pinwheel. "And you should always sample what other places have on offer." She chewed and swallowed. "These are *nice*."

"Do I see a comprehensive review of the menus offered on board *Enterprise* for diplomatic receptions looming on the horizon?" said Noonien-Singh.

Number One nudged her arm. "Wanna help out?"

"I would say there are *definitely* security implications surrounding the food that we serve to visiting diplomats," said Noonien-Singh. "I think I should be *very* closely involved."

Number One munched on a sweetened Naxian olive. "You're cheerful today," she said. "Almost chipper."

"Is that a problem?"

"No," said her friend. "Quite the contrary. You've seemed . . . down, the past couple of weeks."

"Mm?" said Noonien-Singh noncommittally, and through food.

"Don't worry," said Chin-Riley. "I won't press you for details. I doubt you'd tell me anyway. But whatever it is, or was, it's nice to see you more like yourself. Not least because that means I can assume that you're happy with the security arrangements at last."

"Well," said Noonien-Singh, "it was rather sprung on me at the last minute. So, yes, I think I can take a moment to be satisfied with a job *exceptionally* well done."

They stood side by side, friends and colleagues, and surveyed the room. There was a lull in the music, and Ambassador T'Maal moved to the front of the room. The Chionian ambassador—*Echet* Linchar—with whom T'Maal had been deep in discussion, came to stand beside her. They were both striking figures, dressed to the nines. Dressed to impress.

"Oh well," said Noonien-Singh with a sigh, reaching out to restock her plate, "here come the speeches."

The security chief listened stoically to the usual welcomes and platitudes and expressions of goodwill and wishes for future friendship, and made short work of some Atuanati lemon wild-wings. As she was nibbling around the bones of one of these, she saw one of the Chionians slip into the room late. A broad, silver-furred individual whom Noonien-Singh knew by sight from the discussions about the security arrangements. Chin-Riley nodded over the room to the new arrival.

"Which one of their team is that?" murmured Chin-Riley. "The one who just came in?"

"That's Texho," Noonien-Singh whispered back. "Linchar's second. Why?"

"*Ssh!*" someone hissed. They went quiet until the speeches were done, applauding politely with the rest. People began to mingle. Texho went directly over to speak to Captain Pike and Commander Wass. Meanwhile, *Echet* Linchar was moving gracefully around the room, led by T'Maal, nodding as she was introduced to various people.

"They are the most spectacular species," said Noonien-Singh. Grand and grave, and extremely poised; they really were very beautiful. "I wouldn't like to get on the wrong side of one of them. Look at the size of those paws . . . I bet a swipe from one of those could do some serious damage."

"Trust me," said Chin-Riley softly. "They can."

Noonien-Singh eyed her superior officer with interest. "How do you know that?"

"I've been at the wrong end of one of those paws," said Chin-Riley.

"What? *Recently?*" How had this not come up before?

"No," said Number One. "It was a long time ago."

"I didn't think we'd had encounters with this species before."

"I'll be honest, La'An, I didn't realize we were dealing with the same species until he walked through the door. Texho, I mean. He's exactly like the ones I met."

"When was that?"

"On Earth. When I was at the Academy."

"Oh, you *did* mean ages ago."

"Hush," said Chin-Riley. "I'm briefing you."

"Oh, sorry, I thought you were coming up with your explanation for why you hadn't mentioned meeting them before. Surely this should have come up sooner?"

"I'm explaining that, too, if you'll stop interrupting. The people I met were from a distinct cultural minority. See how Texho's fur is more silver than gold?"

"I thought that was probably because he was older," admitted Noonien-Singh. But now that she looked more closely, she could see that there were many differences between Texho and the other two members of the delegation. He was broader, his face was much rounder where Linchar's and Marachat's were narrow, and his eyes were ice blue rather than jewel green. Yes, really quite different, when you thought about it.

"A minority?" Noonien-Singh said thoughtfully. "Tell me more."

"The people I met back then"—the commander lowered her voice—"were refugees. Asylum seekers. They spoke a language completely different from the one in the files that the Chionians sent over. And I don't think I ever even heard them use the word 'Xhio' to talk about their home planet. They certainly didn't refer to themselves as Chionian. Euxhana. That's what they called themselves. It means 'the people of the mountains.'"

"Refugees?" Noonien-Singh raised her eyebrows. Refugees implied some kind of unrest. Which implied, in turn, a certain amount of internal instability on Xhio. And while Chionian domestic affairs were—quite specifically—not her affair (or, indeed, the Federation's affair), in Noonien-Singh's experience internal instability could, on occasion, disrupt external relations. And anything that might disrupt this meeting between the Federation and the Chionian representatives was, without a shadow of a doubt, Noonien-Singh's affair. "None of that has come up in any of our briefings."

"Maybe the situation has resolved itself," said Chin-Riley.

"I suppose it was a very long time ago," said Noonien-Singh. But she was already making a mental list of questions she wanted answered.

"Thank you for the reminder," said Chin-Riley.

"You're absolutely sure you haven't made a mistake? You're quite sure that this is the same species?"

"One big cat looking much like another, you mean?"

"I . . . do not mean that," said Noonien-Singh. "Because that would be rude. I was merely asking whether your memory of the distant past was completely reliable."

"Because that *isn't* rude?" said Chin-Riley.

"Not in quite the same way," said Noonien-Singh. "Not in such a way that could cause a diplomatic incident, for example."

"Heaven forbid either of us causes a diplomatic incident," said Chin-Riley. "I suppose there's one way to find out. We go over to Texho, you introduce us, and I say hello in Euxhana."

"That should do the trick," said Noonien-Singh. They wove their way through the little groups of people chattering and gossiping, over to where Texho stood, peering around the crowd. "Ah," he said when he saw Noonien-Singh. "Lieutenant. I'm glad I've found you." His voice was low, and came from deep within his chest. "We have a few things that we need to discuss . . ."

"Of course," said Noonien-Singh. "First, allow me to introduce Lieutenant Commander Una Chin-Riley. First officer of the *Enterprise*."

"A pleasure to meet you," he said.

"And you," said the commander warmly. "And I wanted to say . . ." She took a deep breath. "*Xhe'ana euxh on'axhi. Axhena mezh, alxho alxhena.*"

Chin-Riley had about half a second of looking pretty pleased with herself, and then saw Texho's reaction to her words. His face froze. His bright blue eyes went icy, and a quiet rumble sounded deep within his chest. Noonien-Singh got the distinct impression that he was ready to pounce on her superior officer, and her hand strayed—almost imperceptibly, but steadily—toward her phaser. Her eye fell on those massive, powerful paws. After a moment, however, Texho took a deep breath and gave Chin-Riley a curt nod. "Excuse me," he said. "I must speak to . . . to Ambassador T'Maal."

He turned his back on them and walked away. Noonien-Singh observed that he did not go over to the ambassador, but instead left the room.

"What the hell happened there?" said Noonien-Singh.

"I have absolutely no idea," said Chin-Riley. She looked stunned.

"What did you *say* to him?"

"It was a greeting," said Chin-Riley.

"He took it like it was an *insult*."

"Honestly, La'An—I'm as baffled as you are," said Chin-Riley. "The people I met all those years ago—they taught me the expression. It means 'From my high peak to yours, I salute you. May you breathe the clear air of the mountains all the days of your life.'"

"Well, it *sounds* very nice," said Noonien-Singh. "It's very pretty—"

"It's meant to be the most courteous greeting you can give!"

"Fashions in courteous greetings appear to have changed since then. Mind you, it must be . . . What? Half a century ago, now?"

"A *quarter* of a century . . . You know, precisely *none* of this is making me feel better."

Behind them, someone cleared his throat. Noonien-Singh turned to see another member of the Chionian delegation. Marachat, the junior member of the team. He was giving them both an apologetic smile. "Do excuse my colleague's somewhat abrupt behavior," he said. "I'm afraid you rather touched a nerve."

"I should be the one apologizing," said Chin-Riley frankly. "It's a while since I've met any Euxhana, but I certainly knew enough to be able to guess that this might be a touchy subject. Would you pass on my apologies and my deepest respects?"

"Of course." Marachat looked at her with keen interest. "You say that you've met Euxhana before?"

"A long time ago," said Chin-Riley. "Before I was a serving officer. I knew a family who had come to live on Earth. Only briefly, but enough to pick up a few words here and there. Greetings, and so on." She looked ruefully across the room to the door through which Texho had left. "Perhaps it might have been better if I hadn't."

"I am certain that Texho was more startled than offended," said Marachat. "There are some . . ." He took a moment to find the right word. "Some *sensitivities* surrounding the use of the Euxhana dialect in public, but surely one could not be other than delighted to hear one's mother tongue spoken?" His green eyes sparkled. "Even with your accent, which, Commander Chin-Riley, I regretfully have to say is execrable."

Noonien-Singh laughed; Chin-Riley looked piqued. "I didn't really get much of a chance to practice. But I certainly didn't mean to offend. Quite the opposite."

"Speaking for myself"—Marachat looked around and lowered his voice—"I am of the opinion that Texho should be proud of his origins. And not only because he has come so far despite all that they entail."

"That seems very . . . very forward-thinking," said Chin-Riley.

Noonien-Singh wasn't so sure. It sounded a little too close to the kind of prejudice she faced when she said her name.

"I'll take that as a compliment, Commander." Marachat tilted his head, then crossed the room and introduced himself to Spock, who was deep in conversation with *Echet* Linchar.

"Damn," said Chin-Riley under her breath.

Noonien-Singh felt her pain. Marachat had been more than gracious, but this was a misstep. The commander prided herself on her professionalism and discretion, so this would be particularly galling. "Do you want to fill me in on what just happened?" Noonien-Singh said. "Because I feel like I'm missing a few steps, and I also feel like this has the potential to become a thing."

"Texho is from a cultural minority," explained Chin-Riley. "They're called the Euxhana. I thought he'd welcome hearing a few words in his language."

"And instead he didn't like being reminded of where he came from," said Noonien-Singh. That, at least, was understandable; something to which she could relate.

"I should have known better," said Chin-Riley.

"On the plus side," said Noonien-Singh, "and knowing how you like to be best at everything, only fifteen minutes into a diplomatic mission before the first walkout might be a Federation record."

Chin-Riley glared at her.

"Don't look at *me* like that," said Noonien-Singh. "You're the one that's screwed up."

"Thanks for your support." Chin-Riley sighed. "I'd better find the captain. Let him and T'Maal know about this."

"Here's your chance," said Noonien-Singh, and nodded to a figure heading their way. "Better get it over with."

Pike came to a halt in front of them. He looked fraught. Very slick, and smart, in his dress uniform—but definitely fraught.

"Captain," said Chin-Riley, "I need to loop you in on something that just happened—"

"Is it serious?" he said.

"A . . . minor diplomatic misstep," she said. "Possibly major? Is that serious enough?"

"It'll have to wait, Number One," he said. "We have a more pressing matter on our hands. Our esteemed guests are asking to move the negotiations back to Starbase 1."

Noonien-Singh nearly spat out her Intissian *vol-au-vent*. "They want to do *what*?"

Pike put his hand on her arm and began to maneuver his chief of security toward the exit. "Bring that plate with you, La'An," advised her captain. "I think it's gonna be one of those days. In fact, I think it's gonna be one of those missions."

2233

STARFLEET ACADEMY
SETTLING IN

Ensign Christopher Pike, Personal Log

The regs? You spin a yarn of excitement, adventure, derring-do, set on that cutting edge where the genius of experimental hull design meets the nerve of the test pilot, and some cadet comes up to you and starts quoting regs. Pelia said to look out for Cadet Mullins, but it's Cadet Chin-Riley that I want to know more about. Regs!

Other than that, the lecture went well. I'd already realized there was nothing to be gained trying to position myself as just another cadet like them but older; there is nothing more pathetic than an old man like me trying to pretend I'm still one of them. I bet even my haircut makes me look ancient. So I went for the corny jokes and hoped that the detail of the flight would win them over. Which, on the whole, it did.

With one exception.

One other good thing is that I've spent so much of today thinking about Cadet Chin-Riley and the goddamn regs that I didn't think about the hearing. I might not have thought about it at all if I hadn't got a message from Robert April, asking how the first lecture went, and telling me—yet again—that it wasn't my fault and that I need to remember that. That set off a downward spiral, wondering whether he'd heard something that I hadn't . . . I'm okay now. The thing is . . .

Damn right it wasn't my fault.

Am I moving from denial to anger? Could that be a *positive* thing?

The regs. The ever-lovin' regs . . .

The first few days on Earth were, naturally, more than a little disorienting. Living in a city the size of San Francisco was enough to get used to. Anxha's experience of big towns was limited to Iomionia—Rechzan, as she knew it—a settlement of about eight thousand people, with perhaps another three hundred administrators and their families. These people lived in their own compound, and with their arrival, Rechzan had changed completely. Anxha's grandfather still remembered a time when the population would drop almost to nothing during the summer months, as Euxhana went out into the mountains to walk the pathways. Once upon a time, he said, Rechzan (he always refused to call it by its new name) had been a city of tents: warm and snug for the winter months, but quickly packed away during the summer. By the time Anxha was born, tents were limited to the far edge of the town, and it was not easy to get permission to raise them. The old sites were more or less gone; new buildings were there now, apartment blocks and light industrial units. Homes and jobs for the Euxhana. Her grandfather had hated his apartment from the moment he'd been relocated there. He called it the "box," or when he was particularly morose, the "cell." He'd died in that box; he never walked the pathways again.

This Earth city—San Francisco—with its huge shining towers and bright lights, was like nothing Anxha had ever seen. Even the biggest cities back home could not compare, although Anxha suspected that this was exactly how the government wished their cities would look. They talked so much—the administrators, those in power—about progress, cultivation, growth, and moving forward. You could not help but think that they were inadvertently revealing their sense of inferiority.

Anxha's sponsors—the people who had helped them leave Xhio and bring the family here—had found her a small house. Anxha liked it very much. The area was quiet, the house had plenty of space around it, and you could see hills. If you closed your eyes and listened to the breeze and imagined very hard, you might even think you were back in the mountains, with the day's walk ahead, and the children running around, spying out the land, looking for the next set of old, old markers that had been left by those who had walked here before to guide you along the pathway. The little ones, whose patience had been severely tried on the long journey, loved the place. The big garden seemed boundless when compared to the little ships they had been inhabiting for weeks. Anxha was grateful for their resilience, even as she wondered what memories they would retain of their homeland. Hax had been restless, anxious about missing out on learning, until their sponsors arranged courses of study for him to do at home. He and Anxha were still making a decision about a school. Schools were a fraught question for Euxhana. Hax would choose in time.

Naxhana, her daughter, was Anxha's main worry. Naxhana, who remembered home distinctly; remembered her father, and the wider family; even remembered walking summer pathways with her mother before Hax came. Naxhana, who had not wanted to leave for Earth, and who, when they arrived, had refused to leave the house for many days, staying in her room, almost as if she was in mourning. Three weeks passed, then one morning, Naxhana emerged and joined them for breakfast, as if nothing had happened. She announced that today she was going to go into the city. Anxha had been so startled that Naxhana was gone before she could say anything. After that, she went out almost every day, coming home with the sunset. Her style began to change. Little glimpses of her

Euxhana heritage appeared. She painted her dewclaws crimson, a color far, far brighter than would ever be dared at home. She wore beads made from bluey-white stones. Perhaps it helped. What Naxhana had not done was mention friends. Not yet.

Her daughter came down this morning at the usual time, standing by the table rather than sitting with the rest of them, clearly eager to be on her way.

"Where are you going today, Naxha?" said her mother.

"Not sure yet. Maybe the waterfront."

"Can we come?" said the twins. Something about the ocean thrilled them, although the thought of open water made the fur on Anxha's neck stand up.

Naxhana lidded her eyes. "Absolutely *not*."

"Awww . . . *Maxhi*, make her! *Maxhi*, she's always going off on her own! *Maxhi*, it's not fair! Why can't we go along with her?"

"Not today, *xhixhi*," said Anxha, quickly, to the pair of them. "We'll go later in the week," she promised—adding bravely, "I'll take you on a boat."

"You on a boat?" murmured Naxhana. "I might come along. I'd like to see that . . ." She grabbed a selection of dried meats (Anxha had been experimenting with the matter synthesizer to see what she could emulate of their familiar diet) and headed for the door.

"What time will you be back?" said Anxha. "Aynur's coming later. She was going to bring information about schools—"

"*Maxhi*," said Naxhana, "I told you I'm not interested in going to school. It's not the Euxhana way."

"Yes, but—" But now they lived on Earth.

"I'm off!"

"Yes, but what time will you be back—?"

"For supper," said Naxhana. "Don't worry!" And with that she left, closing the front door behind her. *Don't worry.* That was all Anxha had done, for years now. But they were safe here, on Earth, weren't they? And Naxhana was showing signs of life again; showing interest in her surroundings, showing independence—that was such an improvement over the last few weeks that surely Anxha could take heart.

The two little boys, rushing and tumbling, went out into the garden. Hax curled up in the living room, a stack of padds beside him. The house was suddenly very quiet. Anxha wondered what to do with the morning until Aynur arrived. Back home, the children were in school all day, as central law demanded. Anxha, as a mother, was exempted from a full work levy, but she was obliged to provide a number of hours a week to ensure that she kept their apartment.

Here on Earth . . .

Nobody worked at anything they didn't want to do. Nobody would track her working hours, to ensure she wasn't shirking (everyone knew that Euxhana were shirkers). Nobody would issue a fine if they heard her forget herself and call out to the children in their mother tongue. She could speak the way she liked. She could get out the paint box again, if she wanted, and if she could remember what to do after so long. And once their papers went through, she could—if she really wanted—pack up and leave this nice little house and take the children high into the mountains, to wander whatever pathways this world might have to offer. As Anxha thought about this, the freedom that this new world might give her and the children suddenly felt overwhelming. They could be happy here, couldn't they? They could make a place for themselves here on this kindly and bountiful planet, couldn't they?

Only it wasn't home.

"*Maxhi*," said Hax. "Did you know that the highest mountains on Earth are found in a range called the Huh-marlias?"

Grateful for her son's interruption, Anxha went to sit with him. "I think that's said 'Himalayas,'" she told him.

"Oh," he said, and practiced the word until he was content that he had it. Interesting that he was finding out about mountains. "Do you like it here, *xhixhi*?" she said to him.

"What?" Hax blinked at her. "Oh yes! I can study at my own pace. And choose whatever topics I like. School back home was so *boring*." There were reasons for that, of course, and Anxha assumed that Hax knew them as well as she did. The lessons were limiting; they were taught only what was felt they needed to know. They were not expected to excel. "I miss the rest of the family," Hax said, "but I'm glad we're here. Maybe they'll come and join us."

Maybe they would. Mother and son spent a happy hour or so going through some of the course, finding out more about their new home. These mountains looked like a place they should visit. The comm chimed and Anxha looked up in surprise. She wasn't expecting a call. (Who, really, did they know here yet?) Perhaps Aynur was delayed? She went and read the message, and then had to stand for a while with her back to her son, taking deep breaths, and wiping her eyes.

"What was that, *Maxhi*?" said Hax. "Was it anything from home?"

"Nothing," she replied, keeping her voice steady—cheerful, even. The bell on the door rang. She took a moment to compose herself, then went to answer. Aynur was on the step, all smiles—until she saw Anxha's stricken face. Gently, she took hold of Anxha's arm and guided her back inside. Anxha showed her the message.

"Hax," said Anxha brightly, calling back over her shoulder, "you've been inside all morning! Why don't you take that out into the sunshine?"

"Okay," he said—sweet cub, darling cub—and padded out to

join his brothers. Anxha reached out for Aynur, who drew her into a hug. "I'm so sorry," she murmured into Anxha's ear. "I'll try to find out whatever I can."

But what was there to find out? The whole family was missing; and when people went missing these days, they didn't, on the whole, come back.

Tyulia's was awful. There really was no nice way of saying it. Like a dank cave, the sort of place where you feared you might die on an away mission.

"Have you been here before?" Chin-Riley asked Mullins, who was wiping down her seat with a bar mat. Something blue and sticky came away.

"Once or twice," said Mullins.

"You mean you came *back*?"

"Only to use the bathroom." Mullins shuddered. "Now, that was a *bad* mistake."

"Do you think he knows?" said Chin-Riley. "That it's . . ." She waved a hand around helplessly. "I mean—why here of all places? Do you think he *knows*?"

"You'd hope not," said Mullins. "Otherwise—kind of an insult, isn't it?"

"Why didn't you *say* when he suggested the place?"

Mullins shrugged. "I thought it would be funny to get a look at his face when he walks in and sees the state of the place."

"You're trouble, Mullins," said Chin-Riley, laughing. They sat down, blue and sticky drinks in hand, watching the door.

"This is nice," said Mullins, taking a swig at her appalling cocktail. "We should double-date more often."

"It's *not* a—"

"Hey," Chris Pike said from behind them. "I was sitting over there. Guess you didn't see me in the murk."

Mullins covered her laugh, and they both moved around the table to let him pull up a chair. He didn't have a blue and sticky drink. He seemed to be drinking whisky. Good choice. Music started. Talarian head beats on Efrosian drums. Chin-Riley's eyes began to water.

They exchanged a few pleasantries. How was he settling in? Did he like being back on campus? Pike turned to Chin-Riley, a distinctly challenging gleam to his eye.

"So," said Pike, "Cadet, these regs of yours."

"They're not my regs, sir. They're Starfleet's."

"Right. I am not denying the importance of regulations. They're great and all that—"

"I think I know what you're going to say, sir," said Chin-Riley. "That they're great in theory. But once I'm out there—"

"Space is unforgiving," said Pike. He was looking down into his glass, and his mood had altered, suddenly, subtly. He was no longer joking; Chin-Riley could see there was something more serious going on. Mullins had seen the shift, too, and mouthed to her: *What's going on?*

Chin-Riley had no idea. "I don't want you to think I'm inflexible, sir," she said, hoping that going over their point of contention would bring him back to the present moment. "I do know that the regs aren't there to forbid action. But they represent a body of experience, don't they? They're there to help. To protect everyone. That's my understanding."

She was saved from embarrassing herself when Mullins's comm chirped. "Excuse me," said Mullins. She jumped up from her chair and headed toward the door.

Chin-Riley drank a little more of her sweet, lurid cocktail. She resented the implication that she knew nothing about the real world. Every day, she negotiated what the real world demanded of her. She kept a whole part of herself hidden, because of the "real world." Suddenly, Pike relaxed; leaned back in his chair; was himself again.

"You're right," he said. "What I'm saying is, you don't want to find yourself locked into a particular course of action because of rules. Sometimes, you have to follow your instinct. You work the situation that's unfolding before you, not look for an example in the book."

"I get that, sir," she said. "I really do."

"Here's what happened. We were testing a new alloy on the hull. I knew *exactly* how much fuel I had in reserve. What I didn't know was how the asymmetries I'd detected in the reentry plasma would affect the whole flight. Fuel was what I was focused on. Think of it this way," he said. "We weren't testing the regs. We were finding out what new regs needed to be written. Do you see?"

"I see why *you* did what you did, sir," she said. "I think . . . Can I speak freely?"

"What? Sheesh, of course!"

"Thank you. I think I would have done things differently. But then, I'm not a test pilot."

"No?" He was looking at her very keenly now. "What are you, Cadet Chin-Riley?"

I'm Illyrian. "I'm . . ." She smiled. "I'm the person who knows the regs, sir."

"Never fancied being the one who writes them?"

Mullins came back in. She looked flustered. "Una," she said, "I'm really sorry but I to have to go."

Don't! Don't leave me alone with him! Chin-Riley was about to mouth, but Mullins was obviously worried about something, so Chin-Riley didn't plead her case. "Everything okay?"

"Yes . . . just . . . something has come up with the group I volunteer with." She glanced at Pike. "Sorry, sir."

"That's fine. I hope everything works out."

"I'll see you later, Una," said Mullins. "Ensign Pike, sir," she said, a twinkle in her eye, "would you make sure Chin-Riley gets home safe? Usually, she's tucked up in her rack by twenty-one hundred, with only the regs for company."

"I'm sure she can take care of herself," said Pike. "I'm the ancient one. Good night, Cadet Mullins."

They watched her go. "She okay?" said Pike.

"I think so . . . She works with this organization. They help refugees and asylum seekers. It takes up a lot of her time. Probably more than it should, but it matters to her."

"Uh-huh." He nodded and looked around. "You know what?"

"What?" said Chin-Riley.

"This bar is *terrible*."

"Yes," said Chin-Riley. "I know. Sir."

"Why didn't you say?"

She thought, *Because you're an ensign and I'm a cadet and I don't want to offend you?* He must have seen something in her eyes, because he went on, "You know, my first captain, she used to say to all the ensigns, 'You must never hold fire. If you think I'm about to make a mistake, tell me. At the very least I can explain my reasoning.' "

Chin-Riley laughed.

"If you can't tell an ensign that you think his choice of bar is lousy, Cadet, then you're not going to make a good first officer."

Whoa, where did that come from? "Me? A first *officer*?"

"That's the plan, isn't it?" he said. "At the very least."

"I've not graduated yet!"

"Don't tell me you haven't thought about it."

"Have you thought about being a captain, sir?"

He grinned. "Ever since I was a tiny wee boy."

"You're an *ensign*—"

"And I'm not messing about. I mean to go places. And I'm pretty sure that you're the same. So—don't hold your fire." He sat up straight; cleared his throat. "What do you think of my choice of bar, Cadet Chin-Riley?"

"I think your choice of bar is lousy, Ensign Pike."

"You're right."

"Are you going to explain your reasoning?"

"There wasn't really any reasoning," he said. "I wanted to try somewhere new. I was walking around the city, I saw this place. It wasn't here when I was at the Academy, so . . ." He shrugged. "You live and learn. Did you think of telling me what you thought?"

"I guess I thought that . . . this must be your kind of thing."

"What? Holy fresh guacamole, no! Talarian head beats? I'd need something stronger than this." He held up his glass and finished his drink. "Shall we hit the road?"

"Please," said Chin-Riley fervently.

"You hungry?"

"Hungry?"

"I'm starving." He slapped his left leg. "And I need to stretch my legs. There's a place nearby—"

"Is it going to be as bad as this?"

"I doubt it. How bad can somewhere be?"

She gestured theatrically. "Look around, Ensign."

He laughed out loud, stood up, and grabbed his jacket. "Come on. Things will only get better."

They fled Tyulia's.

"Didn't you read any reviews?" she said as they walked briskly down Archer. His limp didn't seem to be holding him up right now.

"I did," he said. "Half were good, half were bad. But I'd rather form my own opinion." He glanced at her. "Did *you* read the reviews? No, don't answer that. You read the reviews, interviewed a few patrons as they came out, devised a series of metrics against which you measured the place—"

"I did not do *any* of those things—"

"Lighting, atmosphere—"

"Very funny—"

"State of the bathrooms—"

"Stop it!"

"Whether each individual pour is exactly the same as the previous one—"

"Chris!"

"Oh good, we're on first-name terms at last." He grinned. "Una."

Was it weird to like hearing him say her name? No, that wasn't weird. That wasn't anything at all. "So . . . you said you know a place nearby?"

"Yep. You willing to take another chance?"

"Sure. Impress me."

Naxhana spent her days wandering around the city. In this, she was truly Euxhana. She was solitary: she had made no friends and she saw no need for them. The pathways she wandered were alien, and the friends she might have made were not her own people.

Earth tried its best to beguile her. The weather was good. Whoever she spoke to was friendly and welcoming. There were no long and boring school days, stuck inside for hours with no time or space to wander, knowing that every day would be the same, until she left school and went to work. Now she was free to do what she chose. And yet Naxhana was angry, and because the people who were making her angry were out of reach, she reserved most of her fury for her mother. Why had *Maxhi* brought them here? What was Naxhana supposed to do here? No wider family, no paths—just a mother and three little brothers, each annoying in their own particular way. Her wider family was not overbearing—they were too dispersed, too nomadic for that—but you could always find them when you needed them. Not here. There was nobody here. However much they smiled, however much they extended the hand of friendship—these people were not her people.

Sometimes, the days seemed very long. She looked at alien buildings, studied alien art, listened to alien music, and tried alien food, but she did not have the context to appreciate any of it. She resisted the opportunities that she knew were there to learn. One day she found herself near a big open area—green grass, with huge buildings beyond—but when she tried to enter, she found the way barred. A security officer came up to her and explained, very nicely, that this was the part of the Starfleet Academy campus where the cadets lived, and you had to have permission to enter, or a friend to bring you through. Naxhana went away. The cafés nearby were full of young people—cadets, she guessed. They became a favorite haunt. She would sit and listen to their conversations, wondering what their lives and homes were like. They were all so confident. They all seemed to know what they wanted. Sometimes she longed to be like them. Sometimes she was angry at how easy and pleasant life was for them.

Naxhana knew that her mother wanted her to choose a course

of study, but she swore she would never go back inside a school again. Too many unpleasant memories. The teachers at the central schools—who were not Euxhana—thought they all needed discipline. There were hundreds of stupid and meaningless rules about how you were supposed to dress and where you had to be by certain times and how you should never be alone at any time. Naxhana was done with all of that, but that meant her days were unstructured and meandering. She longed for something to do, but she did not know what. So she roamed this strange city, watching the lives of others, and aching for home.

After another day spent watching the cadets, eavesdropping on them, Naxhana came back to the house and knew immediately that something was wrong. Her mother was sitting on the couch. Aynur was sitting beside her, arm around her mother's shoulder. At the sound of the door opening, her mother sprang to her feet. "Naxhana!" she said, far too brightly. "There you are! Have you had a good day?"

Naxhana looked at both of them in turn. Her mother looked tired, more tired than usual. Had she been crying? No, *Maxhi* didn't cry. Something wasn't right. "What's going on?"

"Nothing—"

"Have you been crying?"

Her mother gave a forced smile. "I . . . got a little overwhelmed by everything," she said. "But you mustn't worry. There's absolutely nothing to worry about."

Naxhana didn't believe her. She glanced at Aynur, but the human woman was staring at the floor. "All right," Naxhana said slowly. "Nothing to worry about."

"Aynur brought the information about the school—"

"*Maxhi*, I've told you already that I'm not going back to school—"

"It won't do any harm to look," said her mother. "Everything is different here, Naxha. You can study whatever you like, at your own pace. The way they think about education is different. You might enjoy it—"

"I won't. And I don't *want* things to be different—"

"There's no hurry," said Aynur quietly. "And there's no compulsion."

"I just want you to be happy here, Naxha," said her mother. "I want us all to be happy here." But she looked the very opposite of happy. She looked very, very sad.

Aynur left shortly afterward. Naxhana tried again to find out from her mother what was going on, but when *Maxhi* called the boys back inside, she knew she wouldn't be able to get an answer. Not in front of those three. She tried a couple more times over the next few days, but her mother always evaded the question. By the end of the week, Naxhana was none the wiser, and her mother was no happier. Perhaps it *was* time for her to make some friends. But not those cadets. She had nothing in common with those carefree cadets. She wanted to talk to people who would understand her. People who were like her, who knew where she was coming from.

She went out one afternoon and walked down to the waterfront, looking for Dock Street. Just before they'd left home, her uncle Falxho—her father's brother—had given Naxhana an address in San Francisco and some names. "These are friends of mine," he said. "Well, friends of friends. They've been on Earth awhile. They'll help, if you need it." He whispered, "Don't tell your mother."

With help from some passersby, Naxhana eventually found the address she was looking for. It turned out to be a small café on the corner of a quiet block. When she opened the door, she nearly burst into tears. The place smelled exactly like home; of cured meats, mouth-wateringly spicy; of freshly squeezed *xhive* juice; she even fancied that, behind it all, she could smell the clear mountain air. She stood on the doorstep, uncertain, and looked around. A big black flag hung on the wall behind the bar, showing the silver triple-peaked mountain. The flag of the Free Euxhana movement.

"Are you coming in, sister?" someone called out. "Or will you stay standing on the step all day?"

Naxhana went in. A group of four or five of her people were sitting around one of the tables, and they moved to let her sit with them. They were playing a board game that her father and Uncle Falxho had loved: *trizhe*. Her father had promised to teach her one day, but never got the chance. Mesmerized, Naxhana watched their paws move the pieces around the board. Each of them still had their dewclaws intact. She breathed in deeply. She felt at home.

"You're Naxhana, aren't you?" said one of the women. "Tarxho's daughter?"

"Yes," she whispered.

"He was a hero," she said. "A real hero."

The whole group agreed. They told her about her father, remembering the man they had known. She had not had the chance to know him. "Have you heard from your uncle?" one of the men said.

"Uncle Falxho?" said Naxhana. "No. Why? Should I?"

There was some muttering around the table.

"Have you not heard the news, girl?" said one of the older men, who had been standing by, watching the game but not joining in. Naxhana wasn't sure about him. He had been staring at her the whole time, and he didn't blink much.

"No."

"There's been another crackdown in Rechzan. Do you know what that means?"

Of course she knew. People would be disappearing. It would be awful. Was that why her mother was upset?

"And nobody's heard a word from your uncle Falxho in days now. You didn't know, did you?"

"Leave her alone, Mexho," said the woman who had recognized her, whose name was Xenanxha.

"Cubs," he said. He moved closer to Naxhana. "Your father, now. He knew what we needed. Do you know, little cub? Do you know what your people need?"

"I have to go," Naxhana said, and stood up. "My mother is expecting me home."

"Don't listen to him, little sister," said Xenanxha. "He's bitter, and he's angry with himself because he ran away."

Mexho swiped at Xenanxha with his big paw. Xenanxha dodged him, easily, and laughed. "Missed me," she said. "Again."

Naxhana, suddenly afraid, ran for the door.

"Wait!" called Xenanxha after her. "Don't go off like that!"

Naxhana didn't wait. She dashed off down the road. She was some distance away from the café when she realized she had no idea where she was. The sun was setting. She thought about going back to the café, asking for directions, but she didn't like the anger she'd felt, and she definitely didn't want to see Mexho again. She wandered for a while, hoping she would see a landmark that she recognized, but it was getting darker, and in the end, she had to admit that she was completely lost. There was only one way to turn. She found a public comm unit and contacted the only person she could think of. Not her mother.

"Aynur," she whispered. "It's Naxhana. I went out and now I'm lost. I don't know where I am. I don't know where I am."

The human woman's voice was confident, reassuring, and very

kind. They were all so very, very kind, and that made it difficult to hate them.

"*Don't worry,*" she said. "*Nobody on Earth will hurt you. Let's work out where you are, and I'll send someone to help you.*"

Impress me. Was that how this was going to work? Pike was up for that. He wasn't a vain man, far from it, but he knew he could be impressive. He led Chin-Riley along Archer and turned left onto Chisholm. At the corner of Chisholm and Ferraro, there was a vendor making gyros from a food cart. A tall and vertical rotisserie was spinning slowly in the corner, and there were trays of salad and various vegetables in front of the counter. There was a line stretching down the street.

"Here we are," said Pike, joining the back of the line.

She looked along the line. "You're kidding me."

"No."

"I thought we were going to . . . like, a restaurant? A diner?"

What did she think this was? A date? Was that positive forward momentum? He didn't know. "It's a nice evening," he said. "Let's sit on a wall and watch people go by."

"Okay," she said, and laughed. "I've never had a gyro. What do you recommend?"

"I don't know," he said. "Never been here before." He peered over the shoulder of the people in front of them in the line, who were now placing their order. "That looks pretty good. I think I'll try that."

"Is that usually how you choose what you're having for dinner?"

"No," he said. "Sometimes I pull all the stops out. What do you think you'd like?"

"I'll have what you're having," she said.

"Okay," he said. "Go grab a spot on the wall. We don't want anyone taking the best seats."

Pike joined her a few minutes later, each hand clutching a pita bread stuffed to overflowing. He explained there were slices of lamb from the rotisserie, tomatoes and onions, tzatziki, garlic, and—he was pretty sure—there was cumin in there somewhere, and perhaps the tiniest bit of rosemary? Yeah, he was sure of that. He handed Chin-Riley hers, and they began to eat. He watched the street traffic—the flashing lights, the people—as he ate. It had been ages since he'd done something like this; not since he was a cadet. You couldn't turn the clock back, but you could savor these moments when life delivered them. He glanced at the woman sitting next to him. He wondered if she knew how impressive she was.

"Oh my," she mumbled, mouth full. "This is incredible . . ."

"It is, isn't it?"

"You said you'd never been here?"

"Nope. I walked past a few days ago, saw the length of the line, figured it would be good. My mistake with that bar was reading the reviews. I should have picked the one down the street." He glanced at her. "Do you ever follow your instincts?"

"It's not about following instincts, is it? It's about knowing what's possible. What's permissible."

"Those regs, huh?"

"You do understand what regulations are?"

"More or less. You do know that they're not holy writ?"

"I know they're not there to be followed blindly. That they're not a substitute for thinking—"

"Still, I wonder whether you're too fixed on knowing them."

"I figured someone aboard ship would need to—"

"I wonder what would happen if you followed your gut once in a while."

She didn't reply. Her face had gone very still. What was that about?

"You know," Chin-Riley said, at last. "Not everyone has the luxury of following their gut. For some, there's too much at stake."

"There's always something at stake, Una," he said. His leg was aching. He stretched it out and rubbed at it.

She said, "You haven't said how that happened."

"Nope."

"You gonna tell me?"

He could give her the basics. "It was a mess," he said. "A mess that shouldn't have happened. Someone died."

"Oh, Chris."

"Mm," he said. "There's going to be a hearing. I'm waiting to find out when."

"I had no idea," she said.

"Yeah," he said. "It stinks. I'm trying not to overthink it."

"I'm so sorry."

"Real life, huh?"

"Reckon the regs might have helped?"

"The damn *regs*," he said, with a laugh. "It's like a *religion* to you, isn't it?"

"Nobody goes wrong," she said, "memorizing the regs."

He laughed out loud, properly, for perhaps the first time in ages. He looked around the street again. Felt alive. Felt glad to be alive. Beside him, Chin-Riley sighed.

"You okay?" he said.

"Yeah. I've got to prep for tomorrow."

"Big day?"

"Class with Pelia."

"Big day," he agreed.

She finished up the last of the pita, rich with sauce and the juice from the meat. "This was great," she said, wiping her mouth. "Thank you."

"You're welcome."

"How long are you around, Chris?"

He wasn't going anywhere until the hearing. "A few weeks, I guess. I've got a half a dozen more lectures before Thanksgiving."

"I won't miss them."

"I hope you'll give me notes after."

"I hope I won't need to."

Pike laughed again. "Can I walk you back to campus, Cadet?"

"That would be very kind, sir."

When Chin-Riley got to the rooms she shared with Mullins, the lights were off in the sitting room. Chin-Riley tapped on the door of her friend's bedroom. No answer. She must still be out. Chin-Riley kicked off her shoes, made a cup of chamomile tea, and went through to her own room, a combination bedroom and study. A space of her own. She sat at her desk, turned on the lamp, and pulled out her notes for her class with Pelia.

Starship Maintenance was a deceptively simplistic name for a fiendishly complicated elective. It was hard to think of another course like it. What else could you expect from Pelia? The students studied in detail two historical examples from early manned space missions that had gone wrong, where engineering solutions came to the fore. The idea was to see how rapidly they could think, under pressure, and with only limited materials to hand. Chin-Riley had been assigned to the group studying the *Ares IV* mission to Mars of 2032; the other group was studying the Apollo 13 mission from 1970. Chin-Riley had been pleased to get the *Ares IV* mission. There were still many unanswered questions about what had happened to one of the crew members, therefore it seemed to offer more chances to get those elusive high marks that Pelia awarded for initiative. Chin-Riley sat and read through the case study yet again, annotating it, taking in the story of the mission: the two mission scientists—Rose Kumagawa and Andrei Novakovich—down on the surface, seeing sunsets that hardly anyone had ever seen. She wondered how they must have felt when they realized that they'd lost contact with the orbital craft, and that their commander, John Kelly, was dead. She thought about what those weeks must have been like, trying to survive while a craft was sent from Earth to rescue them. She wondered what they must have thought of the regs, how they would have rewritten them.

Chin-Riley shook her head. Nobody took up space there rent free, not even Chris Pike. She stretched and checked the time. Past midnight. She got ready for bed and lay down. Her mind strayed back over the evening's conversations with Pike. Follow your instincts. Easy for him to say, but the stakes were too high for her. She needed every possible protection; she needed to be better than everyone around her, know everything that they didn't know; and there was no room for mistakes. Take this hearing that Pike was waiting for. She didn't know in detail (he hadn't told her) what had happened, and she doubted that he was responsible (he wasn't a senior officer). Could she afford scrutiny like that? She couldn't. She would know the regs backward, and she would never be caught out.

The door to the set of rooms opened. Chin-Riley sat listening to her friend move through the shared living space, trying to be as quiet as possible, but then she bumped into a chair and swore loudly. Chin-Riley got out of bed and opened the door to the living room.

"Lights," she said.

"Oh, Una, I'm sorry," said Mullins. "I was trying not to wake you up."

"I wasn't asleep."

"No?"

"Lots to think about."

"I bet. Hey, I'm going to make some tea. How about you? Cup of tea?"

"Go on," said Chin-Riley. Tea was a serious business to Mullins, as close to ritual as Chin-Riley had ever seen. What the regs were to Chin-Riley, tea was to Mullins. Task complete, they sat down, cups in hand. Mullins pulled out a paper bag and passed it over.

"We should try these," said Mullins.

Chin-Riley peered inside; the bag seemed to contain boiled sweets, covered in what looked like fine sugar. "What are they?"

"They're a Euxhana delicacy," said Mullins.

"A who what?"

"They're a present," Mullins explained. "From the people I met with. Go on, try one."

"You know, I've had enough sensory experiences this evening," said Chin-Riley. "Between the Efrosian cocktail and the gyros—"

"Try one."

Chin-Riley took a piece out of the bag and popped it into her mouth. She had been expecting something sweet; instead she got *sour*. "Wow," she said. "That's strong!"

"*Rezhara*," said Mullins. "They're called *rezhara*. They're pretty addictive." She curled up in her chair, mug in hand. "How *did* the date turn out with the handsome ensign?"

"It wasn't a date. He's an instructor. Let it go."

Mullins eyed her carefully. "Okay."

"Thank you."

"What was it?"

"I'm not quite sure. A . . . teachable moment?"

"Really?" said Mullins.

"I think he thought he was teaching me," said Chin-Riley. What she didn't add was that the whole evening had felt strangely like an interview. Pike was going to be captain of a ship one day. He'd need an XO. She didn't say any of this to her friend. She knew that the other cadets talked about her ambition. She didn't need to add fuel to the fire. "I'd like to think I gave him a couple of things to think about."

"What was his advice?"

"I should follow my instincts more often. Worry less about the regs."

"I guess it wouldn't do you any harm," said Mullins.

"I'm not rule bound, you know," said Chin-Riley. "I'm just . . . *thorough*."

She caught Mullins's eye. They both burst out laughing.

"How did you end up spending your evening?" asked Chin-Riley. She jabbed her friend's leg with her toes. "After you shamelessly ran out on me."

Mullins took a deep swig of her tea. "Bit of a sad story," she said. "The legal advocacy group I volunteer with is working with Euxhana refugees. A mother with four kids—four cubs, I should say—and the oldest isn't settling. She ran off this evening."

"Theresa, is she okay?"

"She's fine. She was near where we were. I found her and took her home. She got lost and was bewildered by this big city."

"We all feel that way, sometimes."

"Yeah, and worse when you're exiled from your own home-world. They live up in the mountains. Una, it's so beautiful! Anxha—that's the mother—has shown me images. Imagine the Himalayas, but vaster. That's where they lived. They're nomadic, given the choice."

Chin-Riley's interest was piqued. "But they're not being given the choice?"

"No," said Mullins. "They're a minority—ethnic, cultural. The majority group controls the government, the institutions. They've been forcing the Euxhana into towns, into state-run schools. They're taught not to use their language. The Euxhana are watching their whole way of life disappear. If you protest, you're in trouble. Anxha had to come here, to Earth, to keep her cubs safe. To let them experience something like their way of life. But it's not the same, is it? Earth isn't their home. They're not in the mountains. I can't tell you how awful it is, Una," she said, shaking her head. "To be forbidden from living your life as who you really are . . ."

Something deep inside Chin-Riley went *twang*. It was not that some part of her broke, rather that a string of her soul had been plucked that she had thought had been stilled. Now it was echoing her friend's words. *To be barred from living your life as who you really are . . .* Mullins did not need to say more. Chin-Riley knew. She looked at her friend, sitting deep in thought, cup of tea in hand. Mullins was such good fun; they made each other laugh—but there was this other side to her. The work she did, it was so deeply felt that she gave hours of her life to help. What was Gilbert and Sullivan compared to that? What was memorizing the regs?

Am I playing at being Starfleet?

Now, that was a troubling thought. Chin-Riley could not afford to play. Starfleet was a serious business—and for Chin-Riley, more serious than most.

They went off to their bedrooms. Chin-Riley sat down at her desk and began a new entry in her personal log. Not a place for secrets, but it helped her think through priorities.

I can't seem to put the Euxhana out of my head. Theresa's commitment to them. A commitment to something bigger than herself. Talking to Chris Pike . . . It makes me think about how my time here at the Academy is coming to an end, and then there are going to be choices. Choices about what kind of officer I want to be. Pike says "follow your instincts," but that comes with risk. I can't afford to make any mistakes.

She stopped, dangerously close to saying something that she didn't want on the record. She looked back over her log and decided *enough*. She lay awake for some time, not thinking about her conversation with Chris Pike, or even about tomorrow's class. She was thinking about all that Mullins had said.

When she slept, she dreamed of mountains.

2260

ENTERPRISE
EVERYONE MAKES MISTAKES

First Officer's Personal Log

Best-laid plans? I guess even a perfectionist can make mistakes, but that doesn't mean I have to like it when it happens, and particularly when it might have an impact on a new diplomatic relationship.

On reflection, I should have known better than to speak Euxhana to Texho. I knew Anxha's family only very briefly, over twenty-five years ago, and from what I did know, I should have guessed it would be a sensitive subject. I knew that the Euxhana were discouraged from speaking their language in public, and I stepped in it and did exactly that. When in doubt, tread carefully—a basic rule of diplomacy. I should have brought myself up-to-date on what has been happening with the Euxhana in the intervening years. What can I say? It was so wonderful, so unexpected, to see someone Euxhana. I had absolutely no idea that they were in any way connected to the Chionians. Related, perhaps? Would that be a more accurate word? Related to the Chionians in some way. To see someone Euxhana again—I was reminded of Anxha, and her cubs. I was reminded of how I was welcomed into their little family, of the way that they opened up their home to me. How I met their friends, sat at their table, ate their food. I remembered all the good things about that time I spent with them.

I should have informed myself. Now that we know that the Chionians and the Euxhana are connected, this opens up all manner of questions about the Chionians, and exposes the limitations of Federation knowledge of Xhio. Anxha and her family were seeking asylum on the grounds of cultural persecution. The Euxhana were being oppressed; their way of life was being systematically suppressed, and was increasingly under threat. Schools forbidden to teach their language. Access to the mountains and their pathways limited. A whole host of measures designed to make it impossible to be Euxhana, in the way they had always traditionally been.

Now, I find myself asking: Is the situation for the Euxhana still the same? Has it improved at all? Has it gotten worse? What do we know exactly about what's going on back on Xhio? And—a pressing question this—does that make any difference to these negotiations and, most importantly, *should* it make any difference? Or is the whole question of the Euxhana firmly off the table? It is a domestic matter; the internal business of a world outside of the Federation. One thing I will say— I may be mistaken (and it must be clear to everyone by now that I am *not* an expert on Euxhana affairs; otherwise the situation with Texho would not have occurred), but I don't think that anyone could have risen to such a prominent position in the diplomatic service back then. One reason Anxha left her home was that the education her cubs could expect would have limited them in so many ways. (And I wonder where they are now, those four cubs, and what difference it made to them, growing up on Earth . . .) But like I say, that was twenty-five years ago, give or take . . . Perhaps the situation has changed. Perhaps the Euxhana have more freedom these days to express their culture. In which case, why was Texho so upset to hear me speak to him in his language? Why the shock? Marachat seemed to imply that Texho had overreacted. That he should be proud of his mother tongue. Does that signal that times have changed? The simple fact is that I need more information, but given what I know about the Chionians, they're unlikely to give us straight answers. They'll speak in allusions and evade.

I do have an idea of whom I can approach to ask. Someone I knew very well, whom I trust, and who was very good to me. We've not spoken in a while, but I'm sure she'll help.

It is so very strange to have this whole business come back around again. Strange, and, I have to admit, not entirely pleasant. Even after all this time—even after how everything worked out—I am still not sure about the choices that I made back then. I am trying not to be too hard on myself. I was young, a cadet, very sure of myself while still desperately insecure. No, not insecure. More than that. I was *scared*. I was terrified of what would happen if the truth about me was found out. As I went about my life, I tried not to think about any of that. I tried to blot out those feelings and not let them rise to the surface and steer everything I did. Of course I was scared, with good reason. But the truth is that frightened people act defensively, and that's what I did. Anxha's family could have suffered because of my choices. The fact that they didn't wasn't down to me. Nothing I did ensured their safety. That was down to the sacrifices of others.

This has brought all these memories to the fore—and I can't, in good conscience, say that I'm proud of the person that I was then. The choices that I made . . . A wise friend once told me to "be gentle" with myself. That cadet was doing her best under difficult circumstances. Perhaps I can allow myself to be gentle with her.

I'm due to brief the captain and the ambassador in thirty minutes. The captain and Commander Wass have been caught up in the ramifications of trying to relocate the negotiations on short notice. There are many questions surrounding that request; the Chionians continue to avoid answering questions directly, citing a desire for the most comfortable surroundings. Ambassador T'Maal has been with *Echet* Linchar since the reception, so maybe she has new information. I'm pretty sure that if there *were* any significant diplomatic consequences arising from my misstep with Texho, then I would have heard. But the broader questions remain. What do we know about the current status of the Euxhana back on Xhio, and will it have an impact on the talks? Given how elusive they've been over the requests to relocate the talks, I doubt very much that they'll give us the full story. I guess we'll be piecing it together from what we have, and what I can find out.

———

The remains of Ambassador T'Maal's private, one-to-one supper with *Echet* Linchar were still in evidence on the dining table: plates, an open bottle of sparkling Mantisian wine, and two wide bowls of uncertain use and origin.

"Please," said T'Maal, nodding toward the bottle. "Do help yourselves. It is displeasing to let good wine go to waste."

The commander looked at the captain, who nodded. *Yes, please.* The first officer located two clean glasses and poured the wine. Pike took the offered glass gratefully. He was still in his dress uniform, though it was looking somewhat disheveled by now. Chin-Riley sipped the wine. It was good. Well done, Starbase 1.

Meanwhile, the ambassador was shucking off her formal gear. There was something quite heartening about this. It implied that the ambassador felt no need to stand on ceremony with them. Off came the long, formal, stiff silken tunic—which T'Maal laid carefully across a nearby chair—followed by a fine pair of long and sparkling earrings set with green and red jewels. Last of all, and very carefully, T'Maal removed a brooch from her tunic: a *Kol-Ut-Shan*, symbol of Vulcan's most enlightened beliefs. She stowed this away in a small wooden box.

"How was La'An when you last spoke to her?" Pike asked quietly.

"Infuriated."

"Still?"

"I sympathize," said Chin-Riley.

"Mm. Me too," said the captain. "If we only had some sense of why they wanted the move. It's got to be something more than them taking a dislike to the décor on the *Enterprise*."

"La'An's not taking it personally," said Chin-Riley. "Not now. I think her main frustration—apart from the last-minute nature of the whole thing—is that security is in the hands of the team on Starbase 1. They're qualified, but . . ." She shrugged. "You know La'An. She'd rather have things under her direct control."

"We'll have to make it up to her somehow."

T'Maal came to join them. Her long dark hair, which had hitherto been arranged in an intricate and formal fashion, was now hanging loose around her shoulders, but she sat straight-backed in her seat. The ambassador looked about as relaxed as possible for a Vulcan. *Vulcan home life*, thought Chin-Riley, *what must that be like?* She could hardly imagine them kicking back, feet on the furniture. She must remember never to bring the subject up with Spock.

"Was your supper with Linchar a success, Ambassador?" said Chris.

"I believe so," said T'Maal. "We spoke in depth about the principles that lie behind *Kol-Ut-Shan*. The *echet* was intrigued to hear about the diversity of cultures within the Federation, and she asked how it worked in practice. I am not sure she fully understood. I believe she still thinks that there must be some kind of hierarchy at work. She reveals more about her own culture than she realizes."

Chin-Riley and Pike shared a look. It could not be denied that some Federation members were reputed to see their own culture as superior. Some Vulcans certainly thought so, although Chin-Riley was certain the ambassador was not one of them.

"*Echet* Linchar sets a great deal of store by what she calls 'cultivation,'" offered T'Maal thoughtfully. "Another word I heard her use repeatedly was 'nuance.' An ambassador learns to listen for these repetitions. They show habits of mind. I have not yet fully understood"—the ghost of a smile flitted across her face—"the *nuances* inherent in those words. I shall be paying attention. There is considerably more to the Chionians than the Federation has yet seen."

"I think I can shed a little light," said Chin-Riley. "I made a *faux pas* at the reception."

"Not like you, Number One," said Pike quietly. As ever, she appreciated his support, and his loyalty.

"Thanks, Chris. I was caught off guard."

"What happened?" asked T'Maal.

Quickly, Chin-Riley described her encounter with Texho. Her surprise at realizing that he was from a species already known to her, her greeting in his Euxhana, his anger, and Marachat's smooth and gracious intervention. "I'm not certain if I've done damage to our relationship with the Chionians," she said. "Although I presume, if I had, you would have said so, Ambassador."

T'Maal had listened to her account with interest and equanimity. "I agree with your assessment that no serious harm seems to have been done. *Echet* Linchar and I found each other's company both congenial and sensible, and that will surely provide a strong foundation on which to open discussion. Nevertheless." She drummed her fingers once against the arm of her chair. "I am unclear as to whether or not I should broach this with Linchar directly . . ."

"I'd say not," said Chin-Riley promptly. "We can't know if Texho reported my gaffe to her, and we might cause him further embarrassment if he's chosen to say nothing." She leaned forward in her seat.

"What really concerns me about this is that the Federation seems to have known far less about them than we thought. Have the Euxhana come up in *any* exchange we've had with them, Ambassador?"

"No," she said, "not by that name."

"Number One, you've met these people, the Euxhana, before?" said Pike. "When was this?"

She flushed slightly, and saw his eyebrows go up. "When I was a cadet," Chin-Riley said. "Senior year. Round about the time we met, Chris. Do you remember? I was involved with a volunteer group. They were providing support for asylum seekers and refugees. I got to know a family pretty well. They were Euxhana."

"This is ringing a few faint bells." Pike was no fool. "Didn't you step back from that work, Number One? You'd taken on too much? Senior year, and the rest of it. Wasn't there a production of *The Mikado*?"

Taken on too much. That was putting it mildly. Chin-Riley wasn't sure how much Pike had picked up on at the time. "Yes." Her eyes flicked in T'Maal's direction, and Pike took the hint. She'd tell him more later. Not now. Not in front of the ambassador.

"Euxhana," said T'Maal thoughtfully. "Interesting. My understanding from Starfleet Intelligence was that the Chionians have had trouble with a separatist group. The briefings we received indicated that these were fundamentalists, trying to return to a prewarp way of life, and not averse to using violence to ensure their goals."

"The information in briefings was supplied by the Chionian government," Pike pointed out. "We might be getting only one side of the story."

"I see your point, Captain," said the ambassador. "Nevertheless, I could understand the Chionians trying to stop violence from flourishing within their society. The viciousness of Vulcan's past was not easily put aside. It requires constant effort and attention. I confess it makes me unsympathetic to anyone that uses violence to advance their aims."

"The Euxhana I met were not like that," Chin-Riley said firmly. "A mother, four children—cubs. Their language was banned, and their way of life. Traditionally, they were nomadic. At the time I met them, there'd been decades of what amounted to forced resettlement in towns that were built for them."

"When you were a cadet," T'Maal pointed out. "Some time has passed since then."

Chin-Riley smiled wryly down into her glass. "As people keep *reminding* me . . ."

"Might the situation have changed in the intervening period?" said T'Maal. "Might the Euxhana that you knew not be representative of those who are now using violence?"

"I guess things might have changed," Chin-Riley said. The idea didn't sit well. "I knew other émigrés at the time. They were mostly artists, writers . . ." She thought of those evenings, spent in the company of these people, the aching sadness of their exile. "They'd been involved with protests, yes, but nothing serious . . ." Her voice trailed off. "It was a complicated situation."

The captain said, "We definitely know less about the Chionians than we should."

"But we can take heart," said T'Maal, "from the fact that a senior member of this delegation is Euxhana." The Vulcan stood up. "I have a meeting, tomorrow evening, with the representative of a group of Chionians who have relocated to the Federation. I'll try to gather more information then."

"I have a friend I'm trying to reach," said Chin-Riley. "We were at the Academy together. She was working with the Euxhana at the time. She might know more about what's going on now."

"The more up-to-date information we can gather, the better," said Pike. "I don't think it's going to come from Linchar and her team." He rose from his seat. "Good night, Ambassador. A rockier start than we might have wanted. Let's hope tomorrow is more productive."

T'Maal said, "We can only hope that that will be the case."

Leaving the ambassador's quarters, the *Enterprise* officers made their way to Starbase 1's transporter room. They were both unusually quiet. After a while, Pike spoke. "Number One."

"Yes, Captain."

"Something about this is hitting you hard?"

She took a deep breath. "I went through a bad patch back then, Chris."

"I remember," he said quietly. Of course he did. He was her best friend. "You'd tell me, wouldn't you," he asked, after a moment, "if there was something going on?"

"What? Of course!"

"No more secrets."

"I have no more secrets, Chris. You've got everything I have." She smiled at him. "You knew about the Gilbert and Sullivan. Not everybody knows about that."

They walked on a while longer, and then she said, "What would the Federation do if we learned that the Euxhana are still being oppressed?"

"What could we do? Offer asylum where appropriate. Monitor the situation. But beyond that?" He shrugged. "What else can we do?"

"Would the Federation carry on doing business with the Chionian government?"

Pike looked past her. "General Order 1 prevents us from interfering."

"You mean we *would* carry on doing business with them. That's disappointing, Chris, to say the least."

"There are two sides to every story," said Pike, but he didn't look pleased with the thought.

"But what if there *aren't* two sides to this story? What if this story is exactly as it appears? A government oppressing a cultural minority. Do we sigh, and shake our heads, and carry on 'doing business'?"

"You know we can't intervene. There's no way we can intervene."

"I know," she said. "Sometimes, though, standing by and watching doesn't feel right, does it?"

"Perhaps if they apply for Federation membership, then we might be able to exert some influence on them. Or . . . perhaps things really are much better now," he said. "Look at this Texho."

"Perhaps," she said.

"If you need to step back," he said.

She didn't give it a moment's thought. "I stepped back last time," she said. "And I wasn't proud of myself for that."

"If you're going to find it hard to stay impartial—"

"Impartial?" She smiled. "You know me, Chris. By the book. Always was, and always will be."

They reached the transporter room, where the officer on duty sent them back to *Enterprise*.

In her quarters on Starbase 1, *Echet* Linchar lit the round amber lamps and settled down on the couch. The few blocks from her *chera'char* that she had laid out earlier were still there. Normally, she would never leave them lying around in such a disorderly way, which pointed to her state of mind after her aides brought the news of the attack on Chianaise. She shivered. That was very close to the border. Could trouble like that be heading their way? Surely the Euxhana were not capable of such an operation? Yes, there had been attacks at home, and now this one, close to the border, but to infiltrate facilities run by the Federation? Surely that was unlikely? Surely that was not within their capabilities?

Texho and Marachat would keep her informed if any new information came in from Xhio's security services. Since Linchar could do nothing more, and Starfleet security was securing the room for the negotiations, she tried to put her worries about home out of her mind. Picking up the blocks that she had laid out earlier, Linchar set them down in front of her, in a line. Four of her grandsires. The foundation of her life. The layer through which she must pass to contemplate those who had gone before. Carefully, almost reverently, Linchar drew out the rest of the blocks that comprised her personal *chera'char*. She decided on the *echenesh* arrangement this evening, which always soothed her thoughts, and she began to lay them out, mandala-style. A human watching might think of Tarot cards, but while this was not a spiritual exercise to Linchar, it was a deeply felt cultural practice nonetheless. Primarily, use of the *chera'char* was contemplative: a consideration of her own personal past as it related to her family history, stretching back generations; a consideration of what had gone before her, what circumstances had led to her existence, what she owed to the past, and what she wished to carry forward.

She laid down a block that represented her great-great-grandmother, who had founded a college in the capital, Ghezha.

Linchar had met her once, as a very small cub, on a memorable and frankly terrifying occasion. Thinking of her great-great-grandmother put Linchar in mind of T'Maal. In truth, Linchar had found the Vulcan woman rather daunting—as, no doubt, was intended. Any serious diplomatic corps would surely choose its most impressive candidates for the post of ambassador. Linchar was considered such a figure back home: a senior member of an old family, whose territory stretched out through some of the most beautiful parts of the main continent, and whose Ghezha compound covered lands across three of its valleys. Still, Linchar had not been able to shake the feeling that T'Maal had looked on her rather like a grandmother might look on one of the family's youngest cubs. Some promise, but not yet seeing the route to its fulfilment. Linchar was not used to such feelings. They were disconcerting.

Perhaps there were other aspects to Vulcan society that she had not properly understood. This notion of *Kol-Ut-Shan*, for example, which seemed to be so significant. Linchar had admired T'Maal's brooch, and the Vulcan had been pleased that she recognized the symbol. T'Maal had given a short summary of the principles behind the device. *Infinite diversity in infinite combinations.* Linchar had imagined Vulcan society was like a mosaic, showing the ranks and files of Vulcan society, the lines of descent of the older echelons, the buds and shoots of the younger scions. The richness of an ancient culture whose members were bound together by hundreds and thousands of overlapping ties. Something very close to what she knew, in fact. After hearing T'Maal speak on the subject, and having seen a little more of the Federation up close, Linchar was starting to think that it might be something else. Something less formally structured. Something more . . . dynamic? No, that was not the word. Chaotic? Surely not. *Fluid* was the most generous interpretation, but certainly something less stable than she had originally believed.

Perhaps that was the influence of the humans. There was indeed a chaotic element to them that left Linchar feeling uneasy. They reminded her . . . Yes, she thought with a smile, Marachat had it right, didn't he? They reminded her of the Euxhana. The younger children of the Family of Xhio. The ones that needed guidance, direction—and, yes, sometimes chastisement and disapprobation— if ever they were to exhibit proper cultivation. Left to their own devices, the Euxhana would wander aimlessly around their bare mountains, doing nothing, achieving nothing. They would live in their odd, one-sided families, mothers only and no fathers in sight, spending half the year outside, putting their cubs' lives at risk, neglecting their education. Not living in the comfort and safety of a clan compound in a city, with access to art and music and books and culture. Their old way was no way to live. It was hopeless. It went nowhere. It lacked anything approaching cultivation. It amounted to nothing and was best forgotten.

Was this how the Vulcans perceived their human friends? Was this how their Federation worked? How else could it possibly work? Without one party to lead, while the others took direction. But there were so *many* of them—over a hundred member worlds, if she understood correctly. How did this function? Who led? Who followed? Who was the oldest child? Who were the younger? T'Maal, as far as Linchar could see, had spoken to Captain Pike and Commander Wass as equals. Was this courtesy to junior staff in front of strangers? Or was this how things were? Linchar could not be sure, and that was very unsettling.

She sighed and took out another block. Her sister's youngest cub, who now had a small cub of her own. Linchar looked down at the block lovingly. As she was considering where to set it, this newest and perhaps most treasured addition to her *chera'char*, the chime on the door sounded.

Texho was standing outside, looking worried. "*Echet*," he asked, "may I have a word?"

"Is something the matter?" Linchar felt a sharp stab of fear. "Has there been another incident?"

"What?"

"Chianaise," she said. "Has something else happened?"

"Oh! Oh no, nothing like that. I . . . May I come in and explain?"

"Of course, Texho," she said, and gestured to him that he should enter.

He padded in, light pawed for someone so big, and she gestured to the seat across from her own. As he sat down, he knocked the table slightly, disrupting the order of her *chera'char*. She only just caught the block that represented her brother's older cub before it clattered to the floor. It was an accident, yes, but it was ill-mannered nonetheless, compounded by the fact that he did not seem to even notice, never mind apologize. Discreetly, Linchar set the cherished blocks straight. Did he know the significance of this display? Surely he must. Did Euxhana have any similar traditions? She did not think they crafted to this level of sophistication, but she did not know for sure, and there was no possible way to ask.

She picked up her bowl of *chaola* and leaned back in her chair. "You look troubled, Texho."

"I am, a little. Something happened at the reception."

"Something serious?"

"I'm sure not, but I thought you were better informed than left ignorant."

"Go on," she said.

"One of the Starfleet officers spoke to me."

"There is surely no harm in that," said Linchar. "Quite the contrary. The whole event was for us to talk to each other—" She was smiling, but she stopped when she saw the seriousness of his expression. "Go on."

"She spoke to me in Euxhana."

Linchar folded her paws around her bowl of *chaola*. Texho had never mentioned his mother tongue before. She did not even know if he spoke it. Many of his age and background did not these days. The schools taught exclusively in Chion and had done so for more than half a century. Linchar would not even have thought to ask whether Texho had any knowledge of the language. For one thing, it would be thunderingly impolite, tantamount to implying that he had radical leanings. For another, it was not her business how he spoke to his family. They could communicate exclusively in grunts, as far as she was concerned. She and Texho spoke Chion to each other, as they should, and that was all that mattered. For a Starfleet officer to speak to him in Euxhana, and in a formal and public situation . . . How distasteful. Gauche on the part of the officer concerned, and wholly humiliating for poor Texho. No wonder he was looking so unhappy. To have his background brought up so publicly, and in such a crass manner.

"I'm very sorry to hear that," said Linchar gently.

"I'm afraid I was rather abrupt in my response to her, honored *Echet*," he said. "And I'm concerned that I may have offended the officer concerned."

"The offense was surely hers."

"I don't think that it was intentional."

"Nevertheless."

Linchar pondered the situation, watching him over the rim of her bowl. Usually he was a model of composure, particularly for someone so big, which was what made him so impressive. One saw first his physical strength, and then one saw how disciplined he was in the way he carried himself, the way he moved around in the world. Now he was sitting opposite her, paws drumming the arms of his seat. A further sign, like knocking over her *chera'char* and failing even to notice, that he was agitated. She had never seen him this way before. It brought his Euxhana heritage uncomfortably to the fore.

"Who was the officer, Texho?"

"Lieutenant Commander Chin-Riley."

The first officer on the *Enterprise*. A senior officer, not a youthful crew member wet behind the ears. "Would you like me to bring this up with her captain?"

"Do you think that's necessary, honored *Echet*?"

She would prefer not to, not least because hitherto she had thought the evening had gone so well, particularly in the connections she had made during her supper with T'Maal. But he was hurt, she could see that, and he was a valued colleague who had given flawless service over many years. She would certainly do this for Marachat, or any other pure Chionian on her staff, if they had been offended and if they asked. Why not for Texho? As Linchar thought of what she was prepared to do for him, she felt proud of herself.

"I would do it," she said, "if it would put you at ease."

Texho sat back in his chair. He looked at her with thankfulness, and more than a little admiration. "I think, *Echet*," he said quietly, "that was all I needed to hear. There's no need to take this further. I am sure the commander is as embarrassed as I am. Better to move on."

"I'm glad to hear that, Texho—and I'm grateful!"

"Grateful, *Echet*? I'm the one who is grateful—"

"No, no! My first conversations with T'Maal went so well. I'm thankful not to have raise something so disagreeable with her."

"Indeed, *Echet*," he said. Composed again, he sprang lightly to his feet. "I'll say good night. And . . ." He gestured down. "I knocked the table. Your *chera'char*. Forgive me. I was not myself."

"Oh, Texho!" she said fondly. "I do not know what I would do without you!"

After he left, she settled down again with the blocks and the *chaola*. Sitting with the display felt even better now; their conversation had heartened her, reminding her of the harmony that could exist between both branches of the Family of Xhio. Texho, she thought, filled her with hope for the future . . .

The door chimed again. Linchar gave an impatient hiss. It was Marachat this time, paw placed apologetically over his heart. She invited him inside and offered him a drink. It struck her that she hadn't offered one to Texho, and she wondered, briefly, why she never did that.

"Do try some of this *chaola*," said Linchar. "It really is superb. They've gone to some trouble to program these replicators with facsimiles of our food and drink. They seem to have drawn on the menus of some of the better restaurants in Ghezha." In fact, she was fairly sure she knew the restaurant from which they had devised their replicator menu. Not a fashionable one; an older establishment that had served the most beautifully prepared food for several generations.

"I do like to eat well," she said, "but after a few days of this kind of indulgence we will surely be longing to eat plainer food!"

Marachat took the bowl of *chaola* and lapped carefully. "I'm not sure I've tried better," he said. "But yes—too much of this and we'll be wanting to laze in the sunshine like cubs rather than work. Is there a polite way of asking for supplies to be sent over from our ship? Or are we making too many such demands?"

Linchar smiled at him. "Perhaps you could come up with a form of words."

They drank companionably for a little while, and then Marachat sighed. "I wasn't sure whether or not I should bring this to your attention," he said. "There was a minor incident earlier, with Texho."

"He's already spoken to me about that," Linchar replied. "I'm satisfied that he has nothing to answer for. A rather gauche mistake on the part of the Starfleet officer concerned, I think. No need for it to go any further."

"I agree," he said. "But I find myself wondering—if one of the Starfleet officers has had previous dealings with Euxhana refugees, might she have gained the wrong impression of us? If her impressions of our history have come from . . . nonpartial sources, shall we say?"

"What do you mean?"

"I would hate to think that, through no fault of their own, the Federation might already be prejudiced against us. Having heard only from extremists."

"That's certainly possible," said Linchar. "Although I had no sense of this from T'Maal. What do you suggest we could do?"

"We might provide them with a fuller briefing. Explain the situation with the Euxhana properly. How the story they have received is not the whole truth of the matter. I'd be happy to do this, *Echet*, if you like . . ."

He had been keen to brief them on incidents at home. Now this. She had seen this with many young people at the start of their service; eager to put themselves forward and give advice that was heard. Linchar considered his proposal. In truth, she could see no reason why they should discuss the Euxhana with their hosts. What was there to say? A group of troublemakers, unable to come to terms with the realities of modern life, desperate to turn back the clock and inhabit a world that Linchar doubted had ever really existed. Similar groups existed on Vulcan, or so she understood. Extremists, fanatics who would attack schools and learning centers in their misguided attempt to force Vulcan to withdraw from the Federation. Would T'Maal consider briefing them on these groups? Or would she, quite rightly, see them as an aberration, as unrepresentative of wider Vulcan society, as barely worth mentioning?

"I don't think that will be necessary, Marachat," she said. "We have no reason to hang our heads in shame, none of us. Quite the contrary. The shame is on those who try to split the Family of Xhio apart through acts intended to cause fear and mutual suspicions. Who try to terrorize us into giving them what they want. They are like children, willful and demanding, but—unlike children—they can do serious harm."

"A Family matter, *Echet*."

"As you say, a Family matter."

Marachat tilted his head to concede the point. "I understand."

"But that was a thoughtful suggestion." She sighed. "Is there any further news from Chianaise? Or Achionis? How is the teacher that was injured?"

"She seems to be recovering. And I believe that a cell connected to the instigators of the Chianaise outrage has been wiped out. Four of them, living in an apartment in a new town there."

"Good," said Linchar. "We come a little closer to peace and harmony."

Marachat purred in agreement. He drank more of the *chaola*, then nodded toward the blocks on the table between them. "Your *chera'char*, *Echet*?"

"Yes."

"It's very beautiful. May I ask you about it?"

Such effortless courtesy on his part. "Of course."

"Do you always travel with so many of your clan?"

"Oh yes," she said. "I could not be without them. My grand-fathers and grandmothers; all who came before them, and all who have come after. A reminder of everything that has made me, and everything that I wish to make. Everything that I work for. My family, a strong branch in the greater Family of Xhio. Do you not bring your *chera'char* with you when you travel, Marachat?"

"Only here." He tapped his head. "But perhaps I will, in the future." He stood up. "Good night, *Echet*. And may something good be made here tomorrow."

He left her in peace. She finished her *chaola* and put the blocks away, one by one, and with great love. *May something good be made here*. A fine sentiment, she thought, as she turned out the lights and lay down on her couch to sleep.

Lieutenant La'An Noonien-Singh stood in the transporter room on *Enterprise* waiting for the captain, bouncing up and down on the balls of her feet. She had not slept well and was, by this stage, substantially powered by coffee.

The request to change—yet again—the location for the negotiations, and the obscurity of the motive behind either of these requests, added up to Noonien-Singh's worst nightmare. All her careful preparations swept aside, and now rather than focusing on last-minute fine-tuning, her time was taken up liaising with her opposite number on Starbase 1, Lieutenant Zhovell. She could not complain about Zhovell's professionalism, or that of his team, but Noonien-Singh felt, uncomfortably, that her hands were now tied. She was no longer one hundred percent in control. Noonien-Singh was of the opinion that security should be as invisible as possible, that lives should be minimally disrupted by any measures she might enact. The downside was that people did not always realize how much preparation was involved. At various points throughout the previous evening, she had said, "This is a bad idea." Everyone agreed. Nobody could do a damn thing about it. This was her duty, and the Chionians had been very clear about their desire to move back to Starbase 1. That was what *had* to happen, and she would make sure it did.

The captain walked in, looking annoyingly bright-eyed and bushy-tailed.

"Lieutenant," he said, appraising her, "remind me to cook your favorite dinner once this is over. Whatever you want."

She nodded briskly, and they went over to the transporter platform. Soon they were walking through Starbase 1 toward the negotiating rooms. Noonien-Singh kept an appraising eye on the security arrangements as she went, and could not, as yet, see anything she would change. Holding the negotiations here had been the original plan. Station security hadn't had to start completely from scratch.

As they approached the main negotiation room, Noonien-Singh checked the time. Ambassador T'Maal and *Echet* Linchar would be here in eleven minutes. The door ahead opened. Noonien-Singh walked in and ground immediately to a halt. Pike slammed into her.

The negotiating room was in chaos. The chairs had been thrown over; at each table the carefully laid out padds were strewn around.

At the far end of the room, the screen was covered by a flag—black, with a silver device that looked like a triple-peaked mountain. The walls were covered in graffiti. The triple-peaked shape inside a circle had been painted in several places, and there was writing too. The vandal, whoever it was, had taken the time to write in several different scripts, but the message was consistent across all of them.

FREE EUXHANA.

"Lieutenant Noonien-Singh," said Pike quietly.

And Noonien-Singh—resisting the urge to point at the room, turn to the universe, and shout *I bloody told you so!*—said, "On it, sir."

2233

STARFLEET ACADEMY
LIFE ISN'T A REHEARSAL

Ensign Christopher Pike, Personal Log

Pelia roped me into a supper seminar with the plebes. She billed the whole show "Ask him anything." I felt like the prize Holstein at the country fair. Step up, step up, see the limping ensign. Nobody asked. If they had, I was going to say I fell off my horse. Metaphorically true, I suppose, but I'm glad there were no questions. I don't want anyone thinking that I would ever fall off my horse.

Can't get over how young they are. The distance between us is only a few years, but it might as well be centuries. Was I really like that as a plebe? Was I really so confident? And with so little grounds? I don't mean to be unfair, but looking at them I worry. I wonder how well they're being prepared for what's out there. How equipped they are to deal with the reality of being on a starship. Sure, their heads are full of information—those regs that Cadet Chin-Riley sets so much store by— and they do some good practical work, Pelia's course for one. Talking to them, they seem to think that they're ready for anything the universe can throw at them. And why not, when everything they've done so far has led them to believe that? These are the ones who set themselves the near-impossible goal of being good enough to get into Starfleet Academy. They worked hard. They pushed themselves, and they sacrificed the good times and the nights out that their peers were having, and they got there. They played the game and they *won*. They made it to the Academy. And that's great. More power to them.

But what about when everything falls apart?

Log paused.

So, I'm not supposed to be dwelling on what happened and running through it over and over and over again in my mind. But the thing is that I started that day thinking my superior officers would be on top of the whole situation. But they were completely out of their depth. I'm putting it mildly when I say that came as a shock. What do you do when you realize there's a void where leadership should be? That the people who should be holding things together are communicating so badly that they might as well not be there? And it would probably be a damn sight better if they weren't.

Log paused.

Anyway, I guess that is what sets me to wondering about how well these cadets are prepared for when everything just goes wrong. Obviously, I've not said this to them, and I have no intention of saying anything like this to them. My question is whether *anyone* is saying anything like this to them. Someone should. Maybe they should be completely clear what it is they're letting themselves in for.

―――

The fact was Starship Maintenance with Pelia was turning out to be a disappointment. So far, all they'd done was talk. The cadets on the *Ares IV* project had gathered around the usual seminar table and worked through the case study. They'd turned the scenario around, looked through every aspect of it, but what had they learned? Had they done anything different? As the class drew to a close, Pelia ran through the assessment. Chin-Riley listened impatiently. She could check all that herself, and when Pelia asked for questions, her hand went straight up.

"Cadet Chin-Riley," said Pelia, "you have something you'd like to add?"

"Yes," said Chin-Riley. "There's a lot to like about this class, sir—"

"Thank you," said Pelia. "However, I have the strongest sense that there is a 'but' looming on the horizon."

"Well, I wondered if it could be more immersive."

"What do you mean?"

Chin-Riley hesitated.

"Speak freely, Cadet," said Pelia.

"I was expecting that we would experience something closer to what the people on the mission did, sir."

"You mean . . ." Pelia's mouth twisted. "*Role-play*?"

"Yes *please*," chipped in a classmate. "I'm all for integrating LARP-ing into the curriculum."

Everyone laughed, including Chin-Riley.

"Not role-playing," said Chin-Riley. "That's kind of—"

"Excruciating?" said Pelia.

"Yes," said Chin-Riley. "But at the same time, there's only so much you can experience in the classroom."

Pelia looked at her thoughtfully. "What you're saying is that you want the sensation of *really* flying by the seat of your well-cut pants?"

"I wouldn't put it that way, sir. But something more immersive?" She lifted her chin. "Something that's more of a challenge?"

Some of her fellow cadets moved their seats backward.

"A challenge?" said Pelia. "You believe yourself insufficiently challenged, then, Cadet Chin-Riley?"

"So far we've been working through the background information," said Chin-Riley. "And I understand how that's essential. But—"

"No, no, no!" said Pelia. "A challenge is what you have asked for, and a challenge is what you shall get. Nevertheless, I shall need to give this a little thought. Because much as I would like to relieve myself of the burden of marking your final assignments, I cannot, alas, strand you all on Mars for weeks. But surely there would be some way to make this course more . . . what was your word?"

"Immersive, sir."

"Immersive," said Pelia with glee. "Oh yes," she said. "I think that can be done. I think that I can find a way to make sure that you are immersed." She smiled brightly. "Good discussions today, people. I'll see you in a fortnight. Expect to be . . ." Was that a cackle? "*Thoroughly* immersed."

They trooped out of the classroom. "Damn," said one of Chin-Riley's classmates as they left the room, "what have you *done* to us?"

Chin-Riley checked the time. She had a rehearsal across campus in ten minutes. She'd just about make it, if she ran.

"Cadet Chin-Riley."

Chin-Riley turned back, reluctantly.

"I won't keep you," said Pelia. "Rehearsal, is it?"

"Yes, sir."

"Good suggestion today."

Please don't punish the others on my account, thought Chin-Riley.

"I won't punish you," said Pelia, "much." Did she read minds along with everything else? "I wanted to know whether you're liking Chris Pike's lectures. Are you learning anything?"

Chin-Riley had to pause to think about that. She'd been to a couple more of his lectures, and he'd been good, but she had gotten the distinct impression that he was holding back. She learned more, she thought, from talking to him afterward. "I think so," she said. "We're going for a drink later."

"A *drink*? Don't let him give you anything—*anything*—that contains twigs."

"I . . . won't?" said Chin-Riley. Sometimes Pelia's remarks bordered on incomprehensible.

"Good. Off to your rehearsal. Did you get the part you wanted?"

"Finding out today, sir," said Chin-Riley.

"Good luck!" As Pelia turned to back into the classroom, she stopped for a moment. "You're doing good work this semester, Cadet. Sometimes I don't think we say that enough to the good students. We set them high goals and forget to compliment them on what they have already achieved."

"Thank you, Commander," said Chin-Riley.

"Off you go! Run, run, run! Do not keep *The Mikado* waiting! Rest assured I am working on your challenge."

Chin-Riley dashed off gratefully. The cast was gathering in the auditorium, and she took a seat next to Nahas, with whom she had struck up a friendship. They fell to talking about Pelia's course. Chin-Riley talked about how it was stretching them to think about engineering solutions, but expressed her frustrations about the limits of working on something like the *Ares IV* mission in a classroom. When the rehearsal was called to order, the director, a lively Andorian named Vrati Sh'zhiarreth, raised the question of setting. There was a long tradition, for good reasons, of eschewing Imperial Japan and moving the whole piece to a completely different location. On board an ocean liner. In a grand hotel. The legendary boarding school camping trip. But Vrati couldn't decide which of these settings would work, and knew only that what was wanted was something fresh.

"I know," said Nahas, when they'd gone around on this a few times. "Let's set it on Mars during an early mission." She nudged Chin-Riley. "The crew are bored out of their minds and decide to put on a production of *The Mikado*. They're pulling the set and the costumes together as they go along, and have to make do with whatever they have to hand."

It was a great idea, and everyone loved it, including Vrati. Those tasked with set and costume design started to bubble over with ideas to the extent that Vrati had to call for quiet. The parts were handed out. Chin-Riley got exactly what she wanted: Katisha, "daughter-in-law elect." Hatchet-faced, the butt of most of the jokes, but with some of the best scenes. Chin-Riley saw a flicker of disappointment pass over Nahas's face, but her friend seemed satisfied to be taking on the Mikado himself. Not a lot of singing, but a great solo and huge comic potential—and a pretty big thumbs-up for her first part with the society. They had a duet too, which meant working up a routine together.

After the rehearsal was over, Chin-Riley sent Mullins a message. *Got the part.*

Of course you did, said Mullins.

Up for a celebration? asked Chin-Riley.

Mullins didn't reply at once. *I'm with some friends. Want to join us? They'd like to meet you. They want to meet a "real" Starfleet cadet. I'm trying not to take offense.*

I'd love to.

Mullins sent directions to a café that Chin-Riley didn't know (she was seeing a lot of new places these days, she thought, what with Chris Pike's predilection for trying out somewhere different every time). The café turned out to be a family-oriented kind of place, ice creams and treats, right by a big playground. Mullins, seeing Chin-Riley, waved her over to their table. She was sitting with two others: two feline humanoids with silver fur patterned with dark rosettes and bright blue eyes. One was an older female who Chin-Riley thought looked rather tired; the other a young male whose muzzle was stuck in a padd. Mullins introduced them, respectively, as Anxha and Hax. Hax, realizing that this was the "real Starfleet cadet," put down his padd and stared unblinkingly at Chin-Riley like she was some kind of scientific specimen.

"And those two over there"—Mullins pointed toward a huge wooden climbing frame with a variety of ropes and other obstacles, where two smaller cubs were swinging around, small furry bundles of energy—"are Tilxho and Mexhano. We're here in an ongoing and largely fruitless attempt to tire them out."

It was a pleasant afternoon. When Chin-Riley explained that she'd come from a rehearsal, Hax immediately wanted full information, so she opened up her padd and explained about Gilbert and Sullivan. She ran him through some of the songs they were doing for *The Mikado*; the patter songs grabbed him right away. When she showed him "The Major-General's Song," he prized the padd from her hands and started watching intently, murmuring along with the words. The rest of the afternoon's conversation was punctuated with regular interruptions to ask for explanations about King Arthur and Sir Caradoc and *The Frogs* of Aristophanes, or the sudden arrival of the twins, demanding water and snacks or snacks and water. It was hard to get to know Anxha, but Chin-Riley did manage to work out that she was newly arrived on Earth, and that she had a daughter, Naxhana, who was not there. Mullins had been a huge help since they arrived. By the end of the afternoon, the twins were sitting on either side of their mother, wiped out, heads resting against her, and Hax (after a brain wave on Chin-Riley's part) was starting to memorize Tom Lehrer's song about the periodic table.

Eventually, the family had to leave for home. Hax, returning the padd, said decisively, "You are a very *good* Starfleet cadet."

"Thank you," said Chin-Riley.

"I'd like to visit campus one day," he said. "Please will you help?"

"Hax!" said his mother.

"I'd like you to visit," said Chin-Riley. "I'll try to set it up."

Hax nodded solemnly, and Anxha smiled. "A pleasure to meet you, Una. I hope we see you again soon."

"Me too," said Chin-Riley.

After they left, Mullins turned to her friend and smiled. "Congratulations on getting the part."

Chin-Riley waved that away. It seemed unimportant somehow compared with the family she had just met. "Are these the people you went to see that time we were out with Chris Pike?"

"Yes, same ones."

"What's their story?" asked Chin-Riley quietly. "You said they had to leave their homeworld? That they were a minority. What did you call them?"

"Euxhana," said Mullins. "That's their name for themselves."

"You said they were nomadic?"

"By choice, yes, and pretty solitary. The mother and her cubs spend the summer in the mountains—not wandering, it's more purposeful than that; they call it walking the pathways. In the winter months, they gather in these big tent camps . . ." Mullins shook her head. "At least, they used to. That whole way of life is being suppressed. Their territory is being enclosed, they're being relocated to towns, their language and culture are being discouraged. That's been going on the best part of a century. The past few years, the Euxhana have been pushing back—"

"Pushing back? What does that mean?"

"Peaceful protest, mainly," said Mullins. "It's a miracle that there hasn't been any violence on their part. The government crackdowns have been brutal. Anxha's husband was killed during a demonstration in the capital—the Euxhana came and pitched their tents in front of the government buildings, and the police rolled in . . ." Mullins shook her head. "You get the picture."

"So Anxha's left her homeworld for good?"

"Yes," said Mullins. "There's a few Euxhana refugees here on Earth, and they work on getting other Euxhana out and organizing asylum requests. The group I volunteer with is helping Anxha with her application."

"She can't go back?" said Chin-Riley, wanting to make sure. "Ever?"

"I don't see how she can," said Mullins. "Not unless something really changes back home. I don't see that happening." She sighed. "The government wants them assimilated," she explained. "They consider them primitive, hanging on to ways of life that have no place in the future of their world. I don't see the Euxhana giving up without a fight. I think it's going to get much worse there before it gets better. Anxha's made the right choice for her cubs."

Away from home for good? To never be quite oneself, ever again?

That is not a way to live, thought Chin-Riley. *That is no real way to live.*

121

Christopher Pike was sitting on a bench near the waterfront, checking the time, when Una Chin-Riley came running toward him. "Sorry I'm late," she said. "Rehearsal ran over."

He smiled up at her. "No problem," he said. "How's it going?"

"It's a riot," she said. "I think it's going to be our best yet. I'm *starving* . . ." She nodded over at the food cart across the way. It had been her turn to choose a place to eat, and she'd picked fish and chips. "Shall we give it a try?"

"Why not?" he said.

They came back to the bench clutching cartons stuffed full with battered fish, thick-cut chips that had been slathered in salt and vinegar, and a dollop of a pale green substance that the vendor had called mushy peas and wouldn't let them leave without. They sat and ate.

"Is this any good?" said Chin-Riley after a while, doubtfully.

"I don't know," he replied. "I lack context."

"I told Theresa Mullins we were coming here, and she laughed at me. *Laughed* in my face. She said you can't get good fish and chips outside of her part of the world. Even thinking about trying was a waste of our time."

"Really?" said Chris. "That sounds like one of those things that Europeans say to Americans. To which I say—your tacos are bad and your mushy peas are worse."

"You tell her that," said Chin-Riley. "This is not a hill I'm willing to die on. And you outrank her."

They fell to talking about their week. Chin-Riley described her rehearsals and her class with Pelia. ("You said *what* . . . ?") Pike recounted his dinner and seminar with the plebes and their youthful swagger. He liked talking to her, and he got the impression that she liked talking to him. Maybe it was because he understood Academy life but wasn't caught up in it. Maybe it gave her perspective. He hoped so.

"Anyway," he said, pulling a piece of batter from the cod and examining it closely, "Pelia suggested that I come up with a test of some kind for the plebes. I wanted to ask what you thought might really test them. They seem pretty . . . *confident?*"

"Isn't confidence good?" she said. "Better than thinking you're no good."

"Mm," he said, "as long as it's not overblown. I was thinking about our conversations, about gut instincts and rule following. I want something that would test that fuzzy boundary—"

"There isn't a fuzzy boundary, Chris. The regs are the regs. People make a decision about whether to follow them or not, and dress it up by saying, *Oh, I am* writing *the regs yet to come . . .*"

He laughed. "I guess we could argue about this indefinitely."

"You won't convince me," she said with a smile.

"Okay," he said. "So not that."

"Here's what I think," said Chin-Riley. "It should be something that tests ethics rather than knowledge."

"Go on," he said. "I like this."

"Something that gets cadets to reflect on the kind of officer they're going to be. What kinds of decisions are you going to make? What are your priorities?"

He looked at her with interest. "What's made you think about this, Una?"

"I met these people the other day. They're refugees from their homeworld."

"That's tough," he said.

"Yeah," she said. "Theresa volunteers with this group that helps asylum seekers. Legal advice, help with applications, but also support. Taking the kids to the park. Being someone you know you can call on for help."

"Gilbert and Sullivan not cutting it in comparison, huh?"

She shot him a surprised look; a *how did you know* look. "Not quite," she said. "But that's what I'm getting at. We only have four years at the Academy. How do we work out the kind of people we want to be? The kind of officers we want to be?" She smiled. "Maybe you don't get it. Since you've always wanted to be a captain."

He tilted his head in agreement. Having met Cadet Mullins and discussed her with Pelia, Pike thought that particular cadet needed to consider if Starfleet was really for her. He didn't say that to Chin-Riley. Not professional. None of his business. Did Cadet Mullins need a chance to reflect, now, before she graduated? Before she accepted her first posting? Did the emphasis on achievement and excellence stop some cadets from calling time-out on Starfleet? Like people who knew they should call off a wedding, but the invitations had gone out, and people were traveling from all over, and it was easier simply to go along. Maybe if that chance for reflection had been on offer, one or more of his superior officers might not have been there. Or maybe they would.

"Chris," said Chin-Riley, "do you like teaching?"

"I don't dislike it. But I'd rather be back aboard a ship."

"Still no date for the hearing?"

"No," he said. When she didn't respond, he realized she was leaving an opening for him to tell her what had happened. He didn't take it.

After a moment, she realized, and moved the conversation on.

He was grateful for how smart she was. "How were your mushy peas, or whatever the hell *they* were?"

"You know what?" he said. "I sincerely hope I never have to eat anything like that again in my life."

"Me too."

"You finished?" He nodded down at the remains of her supper. "I'll walk you back to campus."

Their conversation, as they walked along, stayed playful. But the whole way back, Pike couldn't stop thinking, *How do I keep this person in my life?*

"Theresa," said Chin-Riley suddenly. "I think I'd like to help."

It was a rare night when they were both back in their room. All evening, they had been working at the table in the sitting room, both studying, keeping each other going, stopping only to make yet another cup of tea and then get back to work. Peaceful, companionable, and productive. Still, the meeting with Anxha was preying on her mind.

"Hmm?" said Mullins, her attention still elsewhere.

"With Anxha and her family. I'd like to help."

Mullins snapped her console shut. "What do you mean, help? And why?"

"I've been looking into Euxhana history," said Chin-Riley. "There's not much out there, but an émigré group put together some fact sheets."

Mullins smiled. "I bet you could do a conference paper on it now."

"Maybe a poster," offered Chin-Riley. "But that's not the point. What I read . . . What's been happening . . . It's not right, Theresa."

"No, it's not."

"But I can't do anything about that. I can't march in and force a change of government."

"Starfleet discourages us from doing that kind of thing."

"But I can do something here and now. Something practical. Can't I?"

"You could . . ." said Mullins slowly.

"You don't sound enthusiastic. I thought you'd be more enthusiastic."

"I'm not *not* enthusiastic, Una. But getting involved with something like this is a big commitment. What do you think you could do?"

"Well, I'm not an expert in Federation asylum law," said Chin-Riley.

"Only because you haven't decided to be yet," said Mullins. "But that's okay—there are actual lawyers for that."

"It struck me that Anxha must feel pretty isolated. Her friends and family—she's left them all behind. You said there was an émigré community here on Earth, but maybe she needs a Federation friend. A local. Someone to help with everyday things."

"You think you'd be good at that?"

"I think it's something I could *do*. I got on with the kids—the older boy in particular. Hax."

"True. He's pretty shy, and he really opened up to you."

"I'd like to do something, Theresa. Nobody should feel that alone." She shrugged. "I want to help."

"Okay," said Mullins after a while. "I'll set up a meeting with Aynur Lavin. See what she has to say. It's all down to Anxha."

Aynur Lavin came over to campus to meet her, explaining to Chin-Riley in detail what their organization did (she was already well briefed), and quizzing her about her motivations. Chin-Riley gave the same answer that she'd given Mullins: how she'd like to be a kind of point person; someone on the ground who could give advice, or be there when they needed her.

"And you think you have the time?" said Lavin.

"What do you mean?"

"In between all your studies."

"I'm well organized," said Chin-Riley.

"So I've heard." Lavin sat back and contemplated her. "All right," she said, at last. "I suggest you go along with Theresa tomorrow. She's working with Anxha on her asylum application. See if you really get along. There'll be training, of course—"

"Of course."

"And I'll be your mentor on this. We'll check in a couple of times a week at first; maybe once a week as you get more confident. Come to me if you're worried about anything."

Chin-Riley went along with Mullins the next day to a neat little house across town. Anxha was delighted to see her again; so was Hax, who rattled off Lehrer's "The Elements" in no time. Chin-Riley spent the afternoon out in the garden, listening to Hax facts while teaching the two younger children the principles of baseball: *Whack the ball hard, then run.* They would need more for a full game, but for now whacking the ball and running seemed exactly what the twins wanted to do. She caught a glimpse, in passing, of Anxha's oldest, Naxhana, on her way out. Later that day, two of Anxha's friends—Euxhana émigrés—arrived, bearing food and drink.

Eight of them sat down for dinner, at a table in the garden— Anxha and her three children, their two friends, Mullins, and Chin-Riley. Food and drink flowed, and Chin-Riley had her first taste of *axho*, which to everyone's delight made her sneeze. Hax spent a large part of the evening teaching Chin-Riley a Euxhana greeting, and everyone laughed at her accent. At last she mastered it:

"Xhe'ana euxh on'axhi. Axhena mezh, alxho alxhena."

The table went suddenly quiet.

"That was beautiful, Una," said Anxha. The sun was setting. The faces of the exiles were sad. One of Anxha's friends began to sing; Chin-Riley did not understand the words, but the meaning was clear. Home. The song was about home. The next song was cheerful; a duet between a female and a male, clearly a courting song of some kind; but the one after that Anxha stopped immediately. "Not that one," she said. "Not here. Not now."

Chin-Riley glanced at Mullins, who shrugged, and clearly didn't know either why that song had been considered unsuitable. Anxha began another song instead. After it was finished, she said it was a lullaby, sung in the mountains in summer. Her little boys were sleepy on the grass. Hax was curled up in one of the garden seats, holding a padd, but not reading, watching his mother with love.

Over the next three weeks, Chin-Riley regularly visited Anxha and her family. She spent time at their home, playing with the cubs, talking to Hax and answering his questions—his many, many questions—about Earth, Starfleet, anything that came into his head. She arranged for him to visit the campus: to see the Academy buildings and watch the cadets, laughing, enjoying life. She saw his horizons broaden. While Naxhana was barely there, she met more of Anxha's émigré friends, and learned that Anxha was known to them as a painter.

"Not these days," she insisted. "Not since the cubs."

She met Aynur Lavin once a week, in between classes and rehearsals and everything else. Lavin was pleased with how well the family was settling in, she told Chin-Riley; Anxha enjoyed seeing her friendships with her children. The application for asylum was progressing well, by all accounts, and to Chin-Riley (who had taken the time to investigate the law) Anxha's seemed a clear case:

Any person fleeing persecution—or fearing for their life due to political or religious beliefs, cultural engagements, or biological truths—may seek safety within Federation space and, upon revealing themselves to authorities and making a request, may be granted asylum.

That had to apply to Anxha. The only sticking point, Lavin confided in Chin-Riley, was Anxha's activities on Xhio.

"Activities?" asked Chin-Riley. "What's that supposed to mean?"

"There's a question over the extent to which Anxha was involved in anything illegal before she left home," said Lavin. "The problem is . . ." She looked at Chin-Riley. "You tell me what the problem is."

"Well, it could mean anything, couldn't it?" said Chin-Riley. "It could mean something that shouldn't be illegal. Like talking in the street in her own language to her children. Or deciding to take a few days up in the mountains. Or her painting . . ."

Lavin was nodding. "Yes, that's right. Something that wouldn't be a crime here, but has been a mark against her back at home."

"That couldn't be counted against her."

"I'd sincerely hope not, but it's the kind of thing that can unexpectedly derail an application. I don't want Anxha to be penalized on a technicality." Lavin sighed. "It's a conversation she and I are going to have to have. But it won't be an easy one. What really matters is that Anxha is here with her cubs, and keen to make a new life. They all have so much to offer the Federation."

There was no way that Chin-Riley could ask Anxha about

these kinds of subjects, but they did come up one evening when she was at the house. The boys—including Hax—had gone to bed, but Naxhana was still there, listening to the adults talk. A couple of Anxha's émigré friends were around too, drinking *axho* and telling tales. Chin-Riley loved to hear them talk about the mountains, their home, and the old way of life. That night, the stories turned toward their younger days.

"Anxha wasn't as you see her now," said one of them. "Always covered in paint." He winked at Anxha.

"What do you mean?" said Naxhana, ears pricking up.

"Your mother was busy when she was your age. Liked to raise her voice. There was a lock-in once, wasn't there, Anxhie? At the factory?"

"Nothing like that since having the cubs," said Anxha firmly, and set her friends to taking the dishes inside to the 'cycler. Chin-Riley wondered if that could be a problem. Surely it wouldn't be? Surely protesting one's rights should not count against you?

Chin-Riley came to love the time she spent with the cubs, the two smaller ones bundles of fur and energy, stopping only to demand food and claim fierce hugs. Hax kept her on her toes, asking the kinds of questions that made her stop and think before she could give an answer. She could easily imagine him in Starfleet, a science officer, perhaps, always ready with a detailed, informed answer to his captain's question. Naxhana never came on their outings. But one afternoon, at the playground where she had first met the family, Chin-Riley thought she saw her, talking with an older Euxhana male. The girl hurried away before Chin-Riley had a chance to catch her eye and say hello. She mentioned the meeting in passing to Anxha, describing the male she had seen.

The following afternoon, Chin-Riley was going through her preparation for her next class with Sipek. She had a few more hours to do, and she had arranged to meet Chris Pike for a drink. Deep in her work, Chin-Riley got an urgent call from Anxha, asking if she could come and look after the cubs. She left Pike a message, canceling, and went over.

Naxhana had thought, many times, of going back to the café where the triple-peaked flag flew, but she had not yet summoned up the courage. Then, one morning, as she was out on one of her long walks, someone approached her in the street. It was the woman from the café, Xenanxha.

"You didn't come back," she said.

"No," said Naxhana. "I wasn't . . ."

"I understand. Mexho can be too much at times. But . . ." Xenanxha looked around; leaned in. "Come back as soon as you can, will you? There's someone you should meet."

She went the next morning. There were a few people there already sitting at one of the tables (not Mexho, blessedly), and there was a male with his back to her. Xenanxha was part of the group, and called her over to join them. She was smiling. "Look who's here," she said. "Look who's here."

The male turned. Naxhana cried out in joy. Her uncle, her father's brother, Falxho. She grabbed hold of him, covered him in kisses. "Hello, little cub," he said. "It's good to see you."

They went for a long walk together. Falxho gave a crisp and—she suspected—not completely thorough description of how things were back home. He wouldn't be drawn out either on how he got

131

away, saying only that he'd "got lucky." He wanted to hear about her, and the boys, and her mother. She was happy to talk. He reminded her so much of her father, and her memories of him were beginning to fade. She went back the next day, and the next, and on that occasion he asked, "Do you think your mother would see me?"

"I don't see why not," she said. "Why would she not?"

She went home that day, ready to tell her mother the good news, ask her to come and see Falxho, but when she went into the house, and saw her mother's furious face, she knew there was going to be a quarrel.

"Who have you been meeting, *xhixhi*?"

"What?"

"Una saw you with a Euxhana. An older male, she said—"

"Is she spying on me now?"

"What?"

"Is that what their organization is all about? I might have guessed—"

"Don't be ridiculous!"

"Ridiculous? You're the one being ridiculous." Naxhana made for the door. "I had some good news for you, but you know what? Forget it. *Forget* it!"

She left the house, knowing her mother could not follow her with the cubs to look after, and went back to the café. Falxho and Xenanxha were there, and if they noticed she was upset, they didn't press her. About an hour later, when she was feeling happy again, glad to be near her uncle again, the door to the café opened, and her mother walked in. Xenanxha, sizing up the situation immediately, left the three of them alone.

"Falxho . . ." said her mother. She looked shocked, Naxhana thought. Shouldn't she look happy?

"Anxhie," he said, rising to his feet. "It's good to see you."

"What are you *doing* here?"

"Same as you, I imagine."

Naxhana reached out to take his paw. No, her mother did not look happy. Why wasn't she happy? Falxho was here—safe and alive—he'd escaped whatever crackdown had been happening. So why wasn't she happy?

Her mother turned away. "You shouldn't have put me in this position."

"Anxha, who else was I going to turn to?"

"I have the cubs to think of!" She swung back around, blue eyes flashing. "You, here—this could put our whole case at risk! But you know that, don't you, Falxho? This is *just* like you! Irresponsible—"

"*Maxhi*," said Naxhana, but her voice had gone very small.

"It will be fine," he said. "Everything will be fine—"

"I can't take that risk! Not with the cubs' future!"

"*Maxhi*, this is our uncle," said Naxhana. "Our father's brother. Why are you talking to him like this?"

"Because he's wanted back home, *xhixhi*, and he is here illegally. No, Falxho, don't lie to me. If anyone finds out, that will be that for us. We won't be able to stay here."

"I don't want to stay here," said Naxhana. "I want to go home."

"That's a choice you can make when you're old enough," said her mother. "But it's not one you get to make for your brothers."

"I hate this world," said Naxhana. "I wish you'd never brought us here."

"But I have," said her mother. "And that's the way it is." She stood up and held out her paw. "Come with me, Naxhana," she said. "Come home."

Naxhana shook her head. "No," she said. "I won't." She looked her mother straight in the eye. "He's our uncle. *Edxhi's* brother. I'll never forgive you if you send him away."

Pike would forgive her canceling, Chin-Riley was sure of that. But for herself, she didn't like disruptions and surprises. She needed to be prepared, to know that everything was running to plan. That there was no risk of anything catching her unawares. Still, she went over to the house, where Anxha was prowling around. The kids were in the garden.

"I'm worried about Naxhana," was all that Anxha would say. "We argued, and . . ."

Chin-Riley took charge. "Go and find her," she said. "I'll be here when you get back."

Anxha left. Chin-Riley played with the cubs, made supper, talked at length to Hax, and, when the three of them were all in bed, she settled down at the kitchen table to try to finish her prep for Sipek's class. Not long after that, Anxha returned—tired, and without Naxhana.

"Everything okay?" asked Chin-Riley.

"Oh, I think so. Yes . . ."

"Naxhana not with you?"

"No . . . She's staying with friends tonight."

That was a surprise. Naxhana had always struck Chin-Riley as something of a loner. Anxha stayed standing, rocking back and forth on her heels. Chin-Riley got the distinct impression that Anxha was keen for her to leave, but didn't want to be rude.

"I should go," she said, packing up her notes. "I have an early class in the morning."

"I don't want to hurry you out the door."

"It's late. I'd like to get back."

She wasn't ready for the class. Sipek said nothing; the raised eyebrow was more than enough. Later that afternoon, grabbing her kit in their rooms before setting off to rehearsal, Chin-Riley caught up with Mullins.

"I saw Anxha last night," she said.

"Everything all right?" said Mullins.

"I'm not sure. She called me out of the blue, asked me to go round and look after the children. She didn't say where she was going."

"She's not obliged to," said Mullins.

"No, of course not, but . . ." Chin-Riley frowned. "I had to cancel plans, you know? And I didn't get a through prep. I guess I wasn't expecting . . . It put me behind in Sipek's class." She gave a wry smile. "You know how I hate that."

"Oh, I know."

"Do you think this kind of thing is likely to keep happening? I mean, I don't mind a one-off. But . . ."

"You're going to have to roll with this, Una. Anxha's life is precarious right now. There could be all kinds of reasons why she might suddenly need help. Was Naxhana there?"

"No," said Chin-Riley thoughtfully. "She wasn't."

"Naxhana's struggling with being on Earth. She's old enough to understand that they're not likely to go home. Maybe . . . I don't know. Maybe Anxha needs to be able to drop everything to look after Naxhana every so often. Maybe that's exactly what she needs from you, Una."

"You think that was it?"

"I don't know," said Mullins, "and it's not really my business. We're here to give unconditional support." She looked steadily at her friend. "You're busy, I get it. But take a moment today and be honest with yourself. Helping Anxha through this process is a huge commitment. If you don't think you can see it through, you must say. There'll be no hard feelings. None at all. This kind of work isn't for everyone. You need to be clear in your mind whether or not you can do it, and if you can't—that's fine."

"No," said Chin-Riley. "No, I want to be there. I . . . I love those kids. I think Hax, in particular, he's someone I could help. And I don't want to just *drop* them . . ."

"Okay," said Mullins, after a while. "But think about it. Really think about it."

"I will. I promise."

They went their separate ways: Mullins to class, and Chin-Riley to rehearsal, where they went through the ensemble number at the end of Act I, and everyone sang their hearts out. Chin-Riley felt a thousand times better afterward. She'd worked hard, prepared well, and singing with a group—their individual parts and voices adding up to something greater than each one of them—always made her happy. Made her feel like she really did have a place in this incredible world. It was enough—for the moment—to put aside her reservations about continuing to work with Anxha and her family. As the company brought Act I to a close and cheered their own success, Chin-Riley believed she was once again able to do anything she put her mind to. If she worked hard. If she prepared herself for every eventuality.

She went over to Anxha's as usual after Friday classes. The family was all there—including Naxhana—and there was another Euxhana, a male, one she hadn't met before.

"This is Falxho," said Anxha. "He's the children's uncle."

Not her brother? Surely she would have said that. Which,

presumably, made Falxho her late husband's brother. No wonder the two youngest cubs were clambering all over him. Naxhana too was sitting near, her paw resting on the fur of his arm, smiling, her eyes shining. Anxha seemed more subdued. She didn't often mention her late husband, and Chin-Riley was not going to press her for details. There was obviously a sad and painful story there, and that was enough to explain her reservation. Hax was sitting away from the visitor, in the corner of the room, holding but not reading a padd, his attention flicking between his mother and his uncle. Perhaps she was reading too much into this. Hax, Chin-Riley knew, took his time with people. She had been unusually favored from the outset; Anxha had remarked on this many times. Perhaps his uncle's presence brought back too many memories of his father.

The evening was convivial; fun, even. Naxhana helped Anxha with the cooking. They enjoyed as close to a Euxhana welcome feast as could be managed. Falxho was interested to hear about her life as a Starfleet cadet, and she answered his questions about her life and studies.

"And you take an interest in my little family, huh?" He looked round the table, smiling. Naxhana beamed back at him.

"Fact," said Hax. "We are *On'anxhi*. The children of Anxha."

There was a pause. Falxho looked startled; Naxhana was starting to become angry. Anxha did not say a word.

"That's the family name," said Hax. "The family takes the mother's name. Or do I have that wrong?"

Falxho smiled, and reached over to ruffle the fur on the top of his nephew's head. "No," he said. "You don't have that wrong. That's definitely a fact."

At the end of the meal, Naxhana got up from the table and lowered the lights. "There's something I wanted to do," she said.

"Something we haven't done since *Edxhi* was here. We should do it now that we have his brother back among us."

Chin-Riley sat quietly and watched as candles were brought out, six of them, and arranged in a circle. Naxhana's voice and paws were shaking as she lit the candles, saying their names, one by one.

"We should light one for Una," said Hax, when his sister was done. "She's like family."

"Not really," said Naxhana, "not like Falxho."

"Naxhana," chided Anxha gently.

"I think we should," said Hax, the fur on his brow creasing with a frown.

"It's okay, Hax," said Chin-Riley. "I think this is for immediate family. It's enough for me to be here, and see you all happy and together."

Naxhana beamed. The little boys cheered. Hax looked mollified—but Chin-Riley couldn't see Anxha's reaction. She was looking down at the table. Again, she felt that vague sense of unease. She tried to get a chance to speak to Anxha privately, when Falxho was out in the garden with the little ones, but Naxhana was there, eager to help clear away the meal, all smiles and bubbling happiness. As she was leaving, Chin-Riley pressed her hand against the soft fur of Anxha's arm and murmured, "Please call if you need anything."

As she was heading back to campus, her comm chimed. A message from Chris Pike.

Hey. Am I getting old and forgetful, or weren't we meeting this evening?

Chin-Riley blinked. Were they? Surely she wouldn't have missed that . . . She checked. He was right. She'd put it in her schedule and completely forgotten. She sent him a quick reply: *So sorry; completely forgot.*

No worries. It happens. Come now?

On my way.

Her comm chimed again; what else could he want? But it wasn't Pike this time. It was a reminder that she had an extra rehearsal tonight, for which she was surely now going to be late. Cursing quietly under her breath, she canceled Pike (again). Dashed into the rehearsal fifteen minutes late and sang badly, missing lines and cues. She left the rehearsal feeling wrong. Like she had forgotten why she was here in the first place. Like she had forgotten how to be excellent. A new experience for her, and she didn't like it. She didn't like it at all.

2260

ENTERPRISE
PASSIVE RESISTANCE

First Officer's Personal Log

"Let's hope tomorrow is a productive start," the captain said last night. Famous last words. Instead of opening negotiations on the trade agreement, we are clearing up graffiti and trying to mollify an understandably upset honored guest. Let's leave aside for the moment the fact that Linchar's repeated requests to shift the location of the negotiations have not made life easy for either Noonien-Singh or the head of Starbase 1 security, Zhovell. The fact is—someone got into that room who should not have been able to get into that room, leaving us embarrassed and with one hell of a mess to clean up.

The symbol appeared everywhere on Starbase 1—a triple-peaked mountain within a circle. I can only guess that it represents the Euxhana liberation movement. I never saw anything like that displayed at Anxha's home. Of course, Anxha was taking great pains to present herself as apolitical. Anything else would have threatened her asylum case, putting at risk the chance for her and the cubs to remain in the Federation. The friends of hers that I met were artists, writers—but I wonder now if they refrained from saying anything in my company that might have compromised Anxha. They spoke about loss and longing. They spoke about missing their home. They spoke about wishing they could go back, but knowing that they never could. There was only one person I met back then who I thought might pose a threat—even at the time, I could see why he acted the way that he did. I know what it's like to be scared of exposure. To know that one false step could mean the inside of a cell. That sick feeling, that sense of dread.

I remain conscious of our lack of information. I've reached out to my old friend Theresa Mullins, in the hope that she might have some advice. It's been a while since we've spoken—although she sent me a message after my hearing, congratulating me on the success of my case, and commending my grasp of the law pertaining to asylum seekers. I've no idea whether or not she is still working with Euxhana asylum seekers. We lost touch not long after the Academy, and I haven't kept up with exactly where her career has taken her. But perhaps she has some leads or advice that might point us in the right direction. Perhaps there are some contacts that she would be willing to share. Someone who can give us a better idea of the current situation back on Xhio. *Echet* Linchar controls what we learn about her world, and about its people—all its people. She is an erratic source, and by no means an impartial one.

Pike said there's always two sides to every story, but when it comes to the Euxhana, I am waiting to be convinced.

━━━

There had been simply no way of concealing the state of the negotiation room from Linchar, particularly when the *echet* insisted on being taken inside. She walked slowly around the table, taking in the paint on the wall, pausing at her own place name and that of Ambassador T'Maal to set them straight.

"Such disrespect," she murmured. "Terrible. *Terrible.*"

Chin-Riley was glad that Noonien-Singh wasn't in the room. She would be twitching to see that anything was being touched. "*Echet*," she said, "we should leave the room as it is until the security teams have finished completing their sweep."

Linchar showed no sign of having heard her. She carried on her circuit, stopping briefly in front of one particular piece of graffiti in Euxhana. Her teeth were bared for a moment, sharp and white and pointed. She moved on again, coming to a halt in front of the black flag that was hanging over the visual display. Reaching up, she yanked it down, hard, screwing it up into a ball. She threw the material over to Marachat, who was standing by the door. His face was expressionless.

"How?" she said, looking at Chin-Riley and Pike. "How has this been allowed to happen?"

"We all have the same questions, *Echet*," said Pike. "Lieutenant Noonien-Singh and Lieutenant Zhovell are investigating."

Chin-Riley did not know the Starbase 1 security chief, but Noonien-Singh did. She had only good things to say about him, and that was all Chin-Riley needed. The problem—the one that nobody was willing or able to raise—was that the repeated demands to move the talks had complicated security around these talks considerably. No wonder something had been missed. No wonder somebody had managed to slip past.

"I hope their investigations prove more successful than their preparations," said Linchar. Chin-Riley watched the captain struggle to think of a polite reply; he was saved by Ambassador T'Maal's arrival. T'Maal looked around the room, taking in the graffiti, and her eyes came to rest on the ball of cloth that Marachat held. "We might be wise," she said, "not to touch anything else until security have completed their investigations."

Linchar, somewhat frostily, said, "This was not the start to our formal business that I had anticipated, Ambassador."

"Nor I, *Echet*." T'Maal walked over to the symbol painted on the wall, and contemplated the image. "An interesting design. Are these three peaks meant to represent mountains?"

"That image represents the desire to violently overthrow the rule of law," said Linchar sharply. "That is the only interpretation relevant here."

T'Maal nodded. "I have come from speaking to Commander Wass," she said. "A complete review of security on Starbase 1 is already well underway. Meanwhile, *Echet*, let us face this delay with equanimity, make ourselves comfortable in our respective quarters, and wait. The commander will inform us when the room is ready."

"I wonder whether it might be better if I returned to my ship," said Linchar. Did she realize, thought Chin-Riley, how petulant she sounded? Did she realize how *childish* she sounded?

"At this juncture," said T'Maal calmly, "your comfort and happiness are my only concern. You are best placed to make decisions as to how they may be achieved. May I ask, *Echet*—is there any information that you can provide that might shed some light on this incident?"

"What do you mean?" said Linchar. "Do you think I am responsible in some way? Or someone I have brought with me?"

Touchy, though Chin-Riley, and glanced over at the captain. He was frowning.

"Indeed not," said T'Maal. "Given that you are as keen as I am for these talks to progress, that would not be a logical conclusion. We are operating with limited information, and anything that might assist us in determining who is responsible—"

"Are you intending to interview my team? The crew of my ship?"

"Of course not," Pike said firmly.

"*Echet*," said Marachat quietly from near the door. "I believe these questions are well intended, and concerned with establishing nuance—"

Linchar shot him a venomous look.

146

"Insofar as there can be nuance when it comes to these people," Marachat concluded, screwing up the flag further within his paws.

Linchar turned back to scowl at the symbol on the wall. T'Maal observed her for a moment, and then said, "I have a meeting later today with an individual representing Chionians currently living in the Federation. Perhaps he can help with our questions—"

Linchar swung around. "*Chionians* living in the Federation? You mean Euxhana! You mean that you have a meeting with someone lobbying on behalf of fringe elements—"

"I understand he is a Federation citizen," said T'Maal.

"I must ask you to cancel this meeting."

"I see no logical reason to do that, *Echet*. He has a perfect right to ask for my time, and I have a responsibility to meet him."

"These people are troublemakers! They seek to undermine the rule of law—"

"They have done nothing here on Starbase 1," said T'Maal, "except make mischief. Graffiti. Slogans. A flag. The breach of security is, of course, deeply concerning—but understandable given the fluidity of the arrangements. Considerably more damage might easily have been done. We are doubly—*triply*—on the alert now. If anyone intended serious harm—to you, *Echet*, or your team—they have missed their moment. It is logical to conclude, therefore, that no such harm was intended."

"*Harm?*" said Linchar. She seemed about to say more, but glanced at Marachat. She collected herself. "I concede your point, Ambassador. However, as a mark of respect, might I ask you to cancel your meeting with this individual?"

"A Federation citizen has approached me asking for some of my time in a matter relevant to the work of both of us," said T'Maal. "I cannot and will not cancel. I could—as a mark of respect—delay our meeting until we have more clarity on this situation. Is this an acceptable compromise?"

Marachat, who was not looking at Linchar, was nodding, ever so slightly.

"I believe so," said Linchar, after a moment's thought.

"Excellent," said T'Maal. "And let us hope, *Echet*, that we may begin our formal talks very soon." She turned and left the room.

Linchar, who looked like she was starting to realize that she had won very little and perhaps given more than she had intended, said, "Captain Pike. I shall trust to Starbase Security for a little longer. You will find me in my quarters." She swept out; Marachat, still holding the flag, followed.

Pike let out a breath and turned to Chin-Riley. "Thoughts, Number One?"

"Hard to tell where the genuine offence ended and the diplomatic maneuvering started," said Chin-Riley. "But she definitely wasn't happy to see that flag."

"No," he said. "But you're right—she's certainly willing to make capital of it."

"Let's speak to La'An and Zhovell," said Chin-Riley. "See how quickly we can get these talks started again. The sooner everyone is focused on having a constructive conversation, the better."

The talks did not start that day. Starbase 1 was plagued by constant interruptions. Songs—rebel songs, singing of when the paths to the mountains would be clear once more, promising a bright blue day on the high peaks—resounded, suddenly, throughout the public spaces of the base. More slogans appeared—not painted this time, but projections popping up onto walls. Most dramatically, a political manifesto—a charter for Euxhana rights—was projected onto the hull of the *Enterprise*, visible to anyone on Starbase 1 who took the time to look. Many did. If the intention behind the campaign was to bring about awareness of the plight of the Euxhana to a broad section of the Federation, it had achieved that aim. In Port Galley, three *Enterprise* officers were gathered, and the conversation naturally turned to the events unfolding on Starbase 1.

"I have limited sympathy with those who seek to disrupt formal and legal proceedings in this way," said Spock. "The logic extremists on Vulcan demonstrate that—despite their protestations—groups such as this seek to win through force, not reason."

"Don't they plant bombs?" said Ortegas. "Actual bombs?"

"Yes," said Spock, "they do."

"We've not seen anything like that, have we?" she said. "I kind of admire the chutzpah. Projecting your demand for civil rights over *Enterprise*? That's *punchy*. That's bold. What do you think, Nyota?"

"Mm," said Uhura uncertainly. "I don't know enough about the situation to be able to judge. Do any of us really know enough yet? But I wish I could find out more about their language."

"Of course you do," said Ortegas, with a smile.

"Did you *hear* those songs? They were so beautiful!" Uhura hummed a little portion of one of them. "That motif is so *haunting*."

"Have you commenced formal study of the language, Ensign?" said Spock.

"I wish I could," Uhura said regretfully. "There's so little I've been able to find out. From what I've been able to piece together, it has some extremely interesting features. There's no passive voice, for one thing."

"Which one is that?" said Ortegas. She looked at her colleagues.

UNA McCORMACK

"What? It's a reasonable question. Not everyone carries this information around in their head."

"'Ortegas flies the ship,'" said Spock.

Erica Ortegas leaned over and clinked the side of her glass against his. "Damn right I do, mister."

"*That* is the active voice," Spock continued. "'The ship is flown' is the passive voice."

"Now hold on a minute," said Ortegas. "Shouldn't that be: 'The ship is flown *by Ortegas*'?"

"That is still a passive construction of the verb," Spock said.

"I'm not sure I approve," she shot back.

"How about, 'The ship is flown *beautifully* by Ortegas'?" suggested Uhura.

"Better," said the *Enterprise*'s pilot. "There's no passive voice in this . . . What do they call themselves?"

"Euxhana," said both her colleagues, in unison.

"Euxhana," she repeated. "What makes that so interesting, Nyota?"

"Well, you've got to remember I don't have much to go on," Uhura replied, "but to be able to say something like 'the ship is flown by Ortegas,' you seem to have to do some pretty complicated grammatical gymnastics. And while I'm happy to do that kind of thing, I'll freely admit it doesn't float everyone's boat."

"You're not wrong," said Ortegas.

"The most common way to do it . . ." Uhura looked around at her friends. "I'm not going into too much detail, am I?"

"I for one am fascinated," said Spock.

"Hey," said Ortegas.

"Okay, well, from what I've seen, the most common way round is to borrow a construction of the verb that comes from the predominant language, the one spoken by the other group—"

150

"The Chionians," said Ortegas. "What? I do listen."

"That's right," said Uhura. "So you adopt that construction to be able to say something like 'The ship is flown beautifully by Ortegas.' But the Euxhana language *pushes* you to attribute actions to a specific actor or a proximate cause. It's almost like the language *requires* accountability." Her eyes sparkled. "Let's put it this way—it's not the language of a bureaucrat."

"Good. Ortegas *definitely* flies the ship."

"However"—Uhura took a deep breath—"I think there might be an autonomous form of the verb—"

"Whoa!" Ortegas lifted her hand. "And with that, we might be heading toward too much detail. Not yet, but on that course."

"I am willing to hear more," said Spock.

Which was fortunate, since Uhura was pressing on. "Which would translate to something like, 'The action of flying takes place.'"

"And where am *I* in all this?" muttered Ortegas. "That being the most important question here."

"What inferences can we draw from that, Ensign?" said Spock.

"Okay, so *what* that does, in a backward kind of way, is *highlight* when you really can't attribute an action to a specific person, but it also means that people can save face. I love an autonomous verb form," Uhura said happily. "They're really *very* fun." She looked at Spock, impassive, and Ortegas, baffled. "No? You don't see it?"

"I'm gonna have to take your word," said Ortegas.

"I am mildly amused," said Spock.

"Funny man," said Ortegas, patting his arm. "Anything else, Nyota?"

"This is subjective, but, you know, music is like language and language is like music, and I *really* like how the language *sounds*," said Uhura. "It's kind of breathy, like the wind in the trees, or on the mountaintops." She gave a self-deprecating laugh. "I wouldn't call myself an expert. I've had hardly anything to go on. And I'm not sure whom to ask for more."

"Nobody from the visiting team, that's for sure," said Ortegas.

"I agree that would be unwise," said Spock. "Unless you are eager to further our diplomatic troubles beyond those that we currently face."

"Definitely don't ask about the language," said Ortegas.

"Why?" said Uhura. "What's going on?"

"Didn't you hear what happened on our opening night?" said Ortegas.

"No! Nobody tells me anything!"

"Nothing is told you to, you mean," said Ortegas. "See, I was listening."

"So what happened?"

"Turns out Una knows a few words of this language," said Ortegas. "Nothing much, like, 'Hello, how's it cookin'?' The commander said that to one of the Chionian diplomats, and he stalked off like she'd told him his mother was an elderberry and his feet smelled of cheese."

Uhura burst out laughing.

"A most awkward and unfortunate situation," said Spock, frowning. "And personally embarrassing for the individual concerned. I gather that referring to his cultural heritage in public is considered far from appropriate and even borders on offensive."

"Poor Una," said Uhura thoughtfully. "She will have *hated* that . . . But why is it so offensive? What's that all about?"

"The language is not considered proper for use in public—and, particularly, formal—situations," said Spock. "In addition, I believe that it is generally considered uncouth, and that using the language in public implies that such a quality could be imputed to the person with whom one is speaking."

"He means it was rude," said Ortegas. "I think."

"But languages can't be uncouth," said Uhura. "That's not what they are. That's not what they do. It's *people* that do that to them . . ." She sighed. "I hate hearing about languages being locked up and pushed aside. They should be flying free. And this one . . . This one should be running round the mountaintops. Breathing the pure air, up in the heights."

"That's pretty, Nyota," said Ortegas, softly and appreciatively.

"Oh!" said Uhura, and she looked shy. "I borrowed that from one of those slogans."

"Well, it's nice," said Ortegas. "You're right. It's a pretty language."

"We may conclude," said Spock, "that, contrary to my initial statement, the Euxhana campaign is having precisely the effect that is desired."

"It's certainly getting a hearing," said Ortegas.

Uhura began to laugh. "You're completely right," she said. "Their language is being heard—by us."

"Uhura," amended Spock, "hears their language."

Security Chief Noonien-Singh, informed by Chin-Riley about the presence on Starbase 1 of a pro-Euxhana lobbyist, wasted no time in alerting Starbase Security. She arranged to sit in on Zhovell's interview.

"Mister On'anxho," said Lieutenant Zhovell, "thank you for your time."

On'anxho, whose silver-gray fur reflected his Euxhana heritage, smiled across the table. "My meeting with Ambassador T'Maal was unfortunately postponed," he said. "Which has left my day unexpectedly free. I'm happy to help your investigations in any way I can." His blue eyes twinkled. "I assume there are investigations underway?"

"You assume correctly," said Zhovell. "Can you tell us when you arrived on Starbase 1?"

Noonien-Singh studied the young Euxhana sitting in front of her, paws clasped in front of him on the table. Sleek, well dressed, and entirely at his ease. Did that confidence come from seeing that these disruptions were having the desired effect? Or from knowing that he was not in any way implicated? She noticed that his dewclaws were in place, and each had a bluish tinge, as if varnished. Texho, Noonien-Singh had noticed, did not have dewclaws, and neither did either of the Chionians she had seen. Was there some meaning there? Or was she dwelling on irrelevant details?

"I can do better than that," said On'anxho. "I'll make my entire itinerary available to you. I'll give you access to whatever you need to track my prior movements around the base, and permission to examine my incoming and outgoing communications to see with whom I've been in contact." He raised a paw. "I do *not*," he went on, "give you permission to examine the contents of my communications. There's such a thing as client confidentiality, and I will not breach that."

Noonien-Singh, startled by this, said, "That's extremely helpful of you—"

"It is," he replied. "Let me be frank. Much as I have enjoyed seeing the Charter for Euxhana Rights projected across the Federation flagship, and seeing political slogans plastered across Starbase 1 in both Federation Standard and my mother tongue, this is not the kind of thing with which I get involved."

"No?" said Zhovell.

"No," said On'anxho. "Fact: I am a lawyer. I specialize in asylum cases, and in particular I work with Euxhana refugees who are seeking asylum in the Federation. This is serious business. I do not play games—and interventions such as these are, in the end, games. They do not ensure the safety and security of people escaping persecution on Xhio. They do not bring about the freedom of anyone imprisoned for speaking their mother tongue in public, or trying to change curricula to include truths about Euxhana history, or simply for being in the wrong place at the wrong time. The fact is, this approach does not substantively improve the life of any Euxhana living under the current deplorable regime." He shook his head. "A waste of everybody's time."

"And yet everyone I meet is now talking about the Euxhana," said Noonien-Singh. "I've seen reports on news services back on Earth."

"At last," said On'anxho.

"This must be the most exposure that your cause has ever had," Noonien-Singh said. "Have any of your court cases managed that?"

On'anxho gave a rueful smile. "They have not. I do see your point, Lieutenant. This has without doubt raised awareness for the Euxhana and our plight. Will that materially benefit anyone back on Xhio? I'm not sure. I would go so far as to suggest that this could harm them."

"Harm them?" said Zhovell.

"The Chionian government will surely not be amused," said On'anxho. "They're a humorless bunch."

Noonien-Singh suppressed a smile.

"*I* might enjoy seeing bureaucrats like Linchar embarrassed— and believe me," said On'anxho, "I *do* enjoy it. But I also believe it will entrench people like her in their position, and reinforce the prejudice that Euxhana are unruly troublemakers." His tone became much more serious. "These disruptions are pranks, self-indulgent pranks. Already they've led to the postponement of my meeting with Ambassador T'Maal, a meeting in which I was going to draw her attention to several high-profiles cases. I don't play with Euxhana lives."

"Who do you think is behind this?" said Zhovell.

"I've no idea," said On'anxho.

"If you think these pranks are setting back your cause," said Noonien-Singh, "it will suit you if we find the culprit sooner rather than later."

"I wish I had something to tell you," said On'anxho. "My advice? Find out whether any student activists are visiting on Starbase 1. This bears all the hallmarks of that particular kind of youthful idealism as yet untouched by pragmatism and experience. Having said that . . ."

"Go on," said Noonien-Singh.

On'anxho leaned back in his chair. "How much do you know about what's happening on Xhio right now?"

Noonien-Singh and Zhovell glanced at each other. "*Is* there something happening on Xhio right now?" said Zhovell.

On'anxho gave them an exasperated look. "I see Chionian news blackouts remain as effective as ever. I'm going to suggest," he said, "that some attention by Starfleet Intelligence toward internal Chionian affairs wouldn't go amiss."

"You could just tell us what's going on," pointed out Noonien-Singh. "Particularly if you have reason to believe that people here might be in danger."

"You'll find out soon enough," said On'anxho. "No, I don't

think anyone is in immediate danger. Yes, you are going to want to review your security yet again. And when you know more about what's happening, you may find you have some leverage to use with *Echet* Linchar." He stood up. "You can thank me later."

"The upshot of all this," reported Noonien-Singh, forty minutes later, to Chin-Riley, Pike, and Ambassador T'Maal, "is that we now think that there's been a low-intensity irregular conflict between the Euxhana and the Chionian government for the best part of a decade."

"Low-intensity," said Chin-Riley from the other side of the briefing table. "What's the Euxhana death toll been?"

"I don't know," said Noonien-Singh. "Nothing we can discover."

"Probably no records," said Chin-Riley.

"Low-intensity can still have high impact," said Pike. "What kind of thing are we talking about?" He gave his security officer an encouraging smile. "I know I'm asking you to be expert in something you didn't even know was happening an hour ago."

"Thank you," said Noonien-Singh, with genuine gratitude. "We know about the two ethnic and cultural groups—"

"The Chionians are in the majority and the Euxhana are in the minority?" said Pike.

"That's right. After a century and a half of pretty systematic oppression of their culture, some of the Euxhana have turned from nonviolent actions to less subtle means of expressing their discontent. Bombings in population centers, the assassination of one admittedly quite unpleasant politician, and more than the usual number of demonstrations, some of which have turned more than usually nasty. The most recent bombing"—Noonien-Singh handed over a padd that displayed a star chart focused on the border between

Xhio and the Federation—"was on that small outpost marked in red there, not far from the Federation colony Tanial, marked in green."

"That's . . . a little too close to Federation," said Pike. "Designed to get our attention?"

"That would suggest that there are people within this part of the Free Euxhana movement who know about the subject of these talks," said Chin-Riley.

"Quite," said Noonien-Singh tightly.

T'Maal, who had been listening carefully, said, "Do we know what has *caused* this turn to violence? Acts such as this do not arise within a vacuum."

"Desperation?" suggested Chin-Riley. "Their voices are not being heard."

"Also," said Noonien-Singh, "we know there's been a fairly substantial Euxhana exodus from Xhio into the Federation for over thirty years. Many of these people are now Federation citizens. Among the second generation, there has been a move to return to Xhio and organize on behalf of their people, under the protection of their Federation citizenship. I'd say that's the proximate cause to the current instability. But the situation has been volatile for years."

"Federation citizens?" said Pike. "They've not taken General Order 1 to heart."

"They don't have to. They're not Starfleet officers, sir," said Noonien-Singh. "Many of them still have family back on Xhio, and in jail."

"What led you to look into this, Lieutenant?" said T'Maal.

"The lawyer you were supposed to meet with is a lobbyist for the Euxhana refugee community," she said. "Lieutenant Zhovell and I interviewed him. He was very helpful."

"Did he have any suggestions as to who might be responsible for these displays of pro-Euxhana sentiment?" said T'Maal.

"He did not," said Noonien-Singh. "In fact, he was rather scathing about the whole business."

"Do you believe him?" said Pike.

"I did," said Noonien-Singh. "He thought it was childish, a series of pranks and stunts, but he was happy to enjoy the benefit of the publicity it was bringing to his cause. He strongly advised that we look more closely at the situation back on Xhio. He said, Ambassador"—she turned to speak directly to T'Maal—"that it might give you leverage in your discussions with the *echet*."

T'Maal was sitting with her hands steepled in front of her, and she tapped her fingertips against the table. "More information is always helpful. Yes," she said. "I believe I can use this."

"I'll be glad if Linchar simply opens up to us," said Pike. "I'm not happy that we got no warning about any of this, particularly when you look at how close the most recent attack was to the Federation border. We could've been left open to a lot more than songs and slogans. When I think of that negotiation room . . ."

"Let's not talk about my worst nightmares," said Noonien-Singh, her voice clipped. "Ambassador, if you don't mind, I'm going to leave the diplomatic fallout to you. It goes without saying we need to think very differently about security in the light of this information—and I'd like to get back to work."

Pike, who had gone over to the comm to take an incoming message, held up his hand. "A moment, Lieutenant," he said. "*Echet* Linchar wants to speak to us, and I think your more direct approach might come in useful."

"Sir?" said Noonien-Singh.

"Because she's asking whether we might consider moving back to *Enterprise*."

"No *way*," said Chin-Riley.

"Uh-huh," said Pike.

Noonien-Singh did not say what had immediately come to mind on hearing that suggestion. "When you say 'direct,' Captain?"

"I mean direct," he said. "I do not mean rude. Use your discretion, Noonien-Singh. No swearing. But . . . I think you don't necessarily need to trouble yourself with *nuance*."

Linchar, flanked by her aides, put forward her case for a move back to the *Enterprise*. "I am no longer comfortable here on Starbase 1," she said. "These disruptions . . ."

"Stopped short of anything that could have done you harm, *Echet*," said Pike.

"Nevertheless." Linchar held up both her graceful paws.

"Lieutenant Noonien-Singh," said Pike, turning to the officer standing beside him. "You're chief of security on *Enterprise* and would be overseeing any move back there. What's your thinking?"

"You know me, Captain," said the security chief. Noonien-Singh, was that her name? *She seems to have quite a temper,* Linchar thought. Volatile. "I'm always happy to have direct oversight of security matters," said the security officer. "What I don't like is having to chop and change constantly. What I particularly don't like is not being told when there is a credible threat to a Federation ambassador."

"What do you mean, exactly?" Linchar said. She did not like the way that this young officer spoke. She sounded like she was Euxhana; angry and blunt, lacking any nuance. One wondered how someone like this was allowed to hold such a responsible position on a starship. Once again, Linchar found herself doubting if an agreement with these people was possible.

"We know that there's been a serious terrorist threat on Xhio in recent years," said Noonien-Singh. "Why you wouldn't tell us about this *confounds* me—"

"Why should we?" Linchar shot back. "It is a domestic matter. And none of what we have seen here is coming from my people. A far more likely explanation is that someone within the Federation is tacitly supporting a terrorist group." She turned to Ambassador T'Maal. "Perhaps this was the message that the Federation wanted to convey? We came to these negotiations in good faith. We did not expect to find ourselves accused of sabotage."

"Nobody is accusing anyone of anything," said Pike calmly. "We're simply pointing out that with a little more information, we might have been able to prevent these disruptions."

"Perhaps we should postpone these discussions," said Linchar.

"Nobody," said T'Maal, "wants that. You least of all. We ask, *Echet*, for some trust, in the interests of our mutual security."

"*Echet*," said Texho, "I think it would be wise."

"I agree," said Marachat.

"There have been . . . some problems in recent years," conceded Linchar. "But I would like to know who told you about this."

"Federation security is the best in the quadrant," said Noonien-Singh. "Why you didn't simply *tell* us about the severity of the situation in Xhio space is beyond me."

"None of this concerns anyone else," insisted Linchar. "It is above all a Family matter—"

"Demonstrably not," said Noonien-Singh. "Leaving aside the threat to Ambassador T'Maal—"

Linchar felt her hackles rise. Captain Pike moved to intervene.

"Thank you, Lieutenant," he said. "We're going to need a complete review of security on the ship and the station." He turned to Linchar. "What would be helpful is a clear idea of the situation between the Euxhana and your government. I'm going to guess that this is only the tip of the iceberg."

"Whatever this is," said Linchar, "it's *our* business."

"Mm, not any longer," said Pike, with a wry smile. "Someone has compromised security on Starbase 1. As well as your delegation"—he nodded toward T'Maal—"we have the safety of our ambassador to consider. If we're going to move forward with these discussions, we need a clear idea of what we're up against. Slogans and rousing music are one thing. Violence is another. I have a feeling that there *has* been violence during this struggle, and not in the distant past."

Linchar had become increasingly uncomfortable during this. "What happens on Xhio concerns us alone."

"You know that's no longer the case," said Pike.

Linchar moved to look out of the viewport. Marachat crossed over to stand beside her. Softly, he said, "*Echet*, it's time. These people have been nothing but hospitable. We owe them some answers."

Their security demanded that, and courtesy was not a negligible concern. Confess to this split within the Family? Admit to the quarrel between older and younger siblings? Linchar wondered whether the captain would be content to describe such a painful and personal breach to strangers. Keenly, she felt the failure of the Chionians to bring harmony to the Family. If only the Euxhana would *listen*, she thought, as she had many times when confronted with yet another misstep by the younger members of the Family. If only they would *understand*.

"There has been some trouble recently," she admitted.

"At last," muttered Noonien-Singh. She picked up a padd and started to tap on it.

"Recently as in . . . days?" asked Pike. "Months? Years?" When Linchar didn't reply, he said, "Or all of the above?"

Questions such as these were not quickly answered. "I'm going to ask one of my staff to give you and the ambassador a full briefing," said Linchar decisively. "I'm concerned you may be forming the wrong ideas about the younger members of the Family of Xhio. I agree that clarification of the situation will serve us all."

The angry young security officer was already halfway through the door. Linchar watched as Pike and T'Maal followed her out, and then looked at both her aides. "It appears we shall have to share our sad history after all. Texho," she said, turning to him, "would you be willing to do this?"

Marachat intervened. "I am more than happy to do this, if you would prefer, Texho."

"I believe it will be more effective coming from Texho," said Linchar.

"So do I," said Texho. He turned to Marachat. "And I have to ask myself why you think I would prefer it coming from *you*."

There was a charged silence. Linchar closed her eyes. *Disharmony*, she thought, *reaching us here*. She felt the conflict within herself; her long-standing frustration at the impulsivity of the younger branch of the Family. This was set against her desire to defend Texho, who was a credit to their world.

Marachat sensed that he had overstepped the mark. "Texho," he said, "I didn't mean that I thought you would give a partial account."

"Good," said Texho.

"I wanted to avoid putting you in a difficult situation, that's all."

"Why do you think I would find it difficult," said Texho, "to denounce acts of violence?"

Another charged silence. Linchar, deciding against intervention, leaned back in her chair. She was curious to see how Marachat would handle this.

"You're right," said Marachat. "That was crass on my part. I apologize unreservedly."

A quiet rumble, somewhere between satisfaction and irritation, came from deep inside Texho's chest. Could she ever cure him of that? No matter how long he spent with people of cultivation, something Euxhana would creep through.

"That's settled," said Linchar. "Texho, you will brief our hosts on the nature and scope of some of the recent events that have plagued our main cities. Marachat, I would like you to liaise with our people back home to ensure we reveal nothing too sensitive. I am quite sure," she finished, "that the ambassador will be sympathetic. There have been similar outrages on Vulcan. She will understand the difficulty of our situation."

Lieutenant La'An Noonien-Singh was surprised to see that Texho was sent over to *Enterprise* to give the briefing on the situation back on Xhio. As he stepped off the transporter pad, he gave her a wry smile. "Your expression suggests that you were expecting Marachat," he said.

"I . . . suppose that I was," she said. "Which was wrong of me. Why wouldn't you want to prevent terrorist acts being carried out on Xhio?"

"Why indeed," he said. "Shall we carry on? Marachat will join us later to discuss whether we can reasonably move the talks here."

"You don't sound particularly enthusiastic about that," said Noonien-Singh as they walked through the ship.

"At this point," said Texho, "I think we should get down to business."

His briefing was precise and concise, confirming a great deal that Starfleet Intelligence had already surmised, and filling in many points of detail and information, particularly about the attack on Chianaise, which was Starfleet's primary concern. Partway through Texho's talk, Marachat arrived.

"I've got a question," said Noonien-Singh when Texho finished. "Do you think that this movement is on the rise? Or do you think this is the last throw of the dice? A few high-profile attacks, done in desperation?"

Texho looked at Marachat, who shrugged.

"I believe this is a growing movement," said Texho quietly. "I believe that a younger generation, primarily living elsewhere, romanticizes the plight of the Euxhana. They do not have to live with the consequences."

He sounded surprisingly like Mister On'anxho. Noonien-Singh turned to Marachat. "What do you think?"

"I think . . ." Marachat glanced at Texho. Uncharacteristically, he was without words. He'd always had something smooth and conciliatory to say before. "I think it's a very difficult situation . . ." His voice trailed off.

Noonien-Singh nodded. "Thank you both for your frankness," she said. "This has been very helpful." She escorted them back to the transporter room. Once they had beamed off the ship, Noonien-Singh took the turbolift to the bridge. Pelia, who had sat in on the briefing, was in the cab, waiting for her.

"What did you make of all that?" said the security chief.

"I have found, over the years, that I invariably end up rooting for the underdog," said Pelia. "I should know better by now. Backing too many lost causes can give someone a decidedly catastrophic cast of mind."

"Do you think that the Euxhana cause is a lost one?" said Noonien-Singh.

"Well, what, really, do *I* know?" said Pelia. "I hadn't heard anything about them until this week. At least, I don't think I had heard of them. There are a lot of oppressed species out there. The underdog can have a pretty nasty bite if pushed too far. I think the Chionians may be learning this lesson." She gave Noonien-Singh a wide-eyed look. "What do *you* think?"

Noonien-Singh, who had some sympathy for the Euxhana, kept her own counsel. "It's not my concern. My duty is to ensure everyone's safety."

"But?" said Pelia.

"I don't like the way the Chionians talk about the Euxhana."

"Indeed not," said Pelia. "Situations like this are always more complicated than they appear on the surface, aren't they? And anyone who makes them out to be straightforward is either lying or deluding themselves." She laughed. "There. The wisdom of ages, for what it's worth." She gave Noonien-Singh a sympathetic look. "Is this causing you some headaches?"

"More than a few," admitted Noonien-Singh. "It might be a relief to move back to *Enterprise*. Have everyone where I can see them."

"Be careful what you wish for," said Pelia.

They came out onto the bridge. Ensign Nyota Uhura turned from the communication station, saying, "I've got something, Lieutenant. Something you should see."

Noonien-Singh crossed quickly over to Uhura's station. "Go on."

"It's a coded communication from Earth. It's written in the Euxhana language."

"Are you fluent yet, Nyota?"

"Absolutely not," said Uhura. "There are similarities to the Chionian language, but so far as I can make out, those are chiefly to do with vocabulary. Shared lexicon. Words in common. But structurally, grammatically—the two languages are very different." She frowned, clearly trying to think of a helpful analogy. "Imagine twisting a kaleidoscope," she said. "All the same pieces of glass, all the same colors, but the arrangement is completely different."

"I see," said Noonien-Singh, nodding.

"Commander Chin-Riley thinks that a friend might be able to help, but she hasn't been able to reach her."

Noonien-Singh thought about the Euxhana lawyer on Starbase 1. Might he be persuaded to help? She said, "I don't think we should ask Linchar."

"Not finding common ground with our guest?" said Uhura.

"Absolutely not," said Noonien-Singh. "I got the distinct impression that the *echet* thought I was rude."

"Rude?" said Uhura, a smile twitching around her lips. "You?"

"Keep working on that message, Ensign," said Noonien-Singh. "I'll speak to On'anxho again. And I'll check in with Una to see if she's reached her friend."

"The whole thing might be coded," Uhura said. "I'm picking out a word or two here, but it's hard to see any pattern. It's like having archaeological fragments, bits and pieces of broken stones, and I'm trying to guess what they add up to, what they're trying to say."

"If anyone can do it, it's going to be you," said Noonien-Singh.

"Hmm," said Uhura thoughtfully. "Let's see . . ." As she spoke, another message came through. Uhura, listening to it through her earpiece, became instantly serious. "Lieutenant, you need to hear this at once."

Noonien-Singh reached for the earpiece that Uhura offered her. A voice came through—speaking Federation Standard, but mechanized, disguised. There was no lack of clarity—no attempt at nuance—in the message that the voice conveyed.

In the name of all Euxhana, in view of the persecution that we have suffered over decades, and in pursuit of the freedom—to life, to land, to language—that is our right, we have chosen this course of action.

We have not done this to make enemies of the Federation. We hope one day to offer the hand of friendship to your diverse peoples. But your continued ignorance of our situation cannot continue. We do this to secure your continued attention to the plight of the Euxhana people. We ask you to listen.

This is notification of a clear and credible threat to the Enterprise. *An explosive device has been placed on board your ship.*

We advise you take immediate necessary precautions to prevent loss of life.

Free Euxhana!

2233

STARFLEET ACADEMY
DEADLINES

Ensign Christopher Pike, Personal Log

Last time I saw Pelia, she was talking about her class on Starship Maintenance. Correction, she was *ranting* about her class on Starship Maintenance. Sounds like Cadet Chin-Riley had a few notes for her too. I tried not to laugh in her face. Pelia can be a formidable enemy, as I think Una is about to find out.

Anyway, Pelia and I ended up talking about the *Ares IV* mission and what the hell could have happened there and whether anyone will ever know for sure. The upshot of that discussion is that I've been doing a lot of reading on the subject of When Things Go Wrong and Why and What You're Supposed to Do. In other words, I'm still brooding over my present circumstances and trying to make sense of them.

Robert April, when I mentioned this, gave me one of those looks that I've come to recognize as meaning, "Sort your shit out, Ensign," and then he asked me what I was reading about, and when I listed off the usual he suggested I cut straight to the good stuff and recommended looking up what happened to the *Kobayashi Maru*, and god damn. What a hell of a situation to find yourself in.

The other thing April said was that I should get myself back on the horse. Maybe he's right. You can't go wrong with a horse.

———

Cadet Chin-Riley woke with a sense of dread, a feeling so unfamiliar that it took a few minutes for her to work out why. Starship

Maintenance this morning. She'd been over at Anxha's the night before, and once again, the situation had been tense. She'd stayed a little later than usual, worried about Anxha, then she worked into the night on her preparation for the class. Chin-Riley wasn't sure that she had mastered the material, and she was definitely sure that she didn't like that feeling. She got dressed quickly and ran through her notes. As she read back what she had written, Chin-Riley began to doubt herself. She wasn't used to this. Always ready, the result was she was always certain. It was best that way. She looked through her notes again. Nothing to be done now. She would have to . . .

Follow her instincts? She smiled, thinking of what Chris Pike would say, and dashed off to class. When she got there, the room was empty. Chin-Riley checked her comm to see if she had missed anything, and saw a message from one of the cadets in her project group.

"Where are you? You're really late!"

Chin-Riley quickly replied, *"Where are you?"*

"We're over at the holo-engineering suites. Hurry up! Pelia's spitting feathers!"

She ran over. Twenty minutes late.

"Sorry, sir, I am *so* sorry," she said as she ran into the room. The rest of her seminar group was there already.

"I'm glad, Cadet Chin-Riley," said Pelia dryly, "that you have decided to join us. This session has been designed specifically with you in mind."

"Sir?"

"Immersive. You asked for immersive. I have created immersive." Pelia ordered, "Computer. Run program Starship Maintenance Ares." She began to walk around the room, and as she did, the empty holosuite morphed around the class, becoming Mars base circa 2032. "You've all visited holo-environments," she said. "But this one is a little more substantial than anything you will have experienced. From now on, these classes will take place entirely in this holo-environment. Half of you will experience life as it was on the *Ares IV* mission during the period of their isolation. The other half will be back at mission control, attempting to make contact." Pelia smiled. "Is this sufficiently immersive for you all?"

The other cadets were walking around the environment, their expressions a combination of amazement and trepidation. Chin-Riley took a deep breath. The *smell*. Somehow Pelia had re-created the smell of this tiny cramped environment: ozone; leaking, overheated coolant; sweat; and, lurking in the background, the distinctive reek of recycled urine. Pelia, Una thought, was literally taking the piss. She thanked Mullins for adding that expression into her lexicon.

"Thank you for the challenge, Cadet Chin-Riley," said Pelia. "I may have advanced holo-engineering technologies in several interesting ways." She started handing out period-specific padds. "I considered allowing you to organize yourselves into the subgroups," she said. "And then I thought, where's the fun in that? Your assignments. Your *roles*, as it were," she added, smiling at the cadet who had mentioned LARPing. "You'll see that three of you are nominally in the roles of the base staff: Kumagawa, Novakovich, and Commander Kelly. My advice to you is that you do not attempt to play these roles as them. Be yourselves. You know already how these individuals behaved—or you should, if you have worked through the course briefings and the psychological profiles. What you do *not* know is how you would react. That is what this class involves. It is a technical challenge, and a personal challenge."

Chin-Riley had assumed she would be assigned to mission control, so she was surprised to see she was part of the ground Mars team. Interesting. Her strengths were her attention to detail and her dogged meticulousness. These would be an asset to mission control as they worked through what had gone wrong and how to fix it. Clearly Pelia didn't want to see how she would do there. She wanted to see something else. Perhaps, see how she reacted on instinct?

"Something the matter, Cadet Chin-Riley?"

"No, sir," said Chin-Riley.

"Then shall we get to work?"

And there they were. Chin-Riley was Kumagawa and her classmates were Novakovich and Kelly, suddenly stranded on this stinking base, alone, with limited resources and no idea of what was happening. The two hours of the class flew by. As the holo-engineering suite returned to its original state, Chin-Riley breathed out. She was not sure that she had acquitted herself as well as she would like.

"Thoughts on the new setting?" said Pelia.

Disconcerting, thought Chin-Riley.

"Amazing," said one of her classmates. That was the general consensus.

"Immersive henceforth," said Pelia. "Good, good."

The class began to file out, chattering away about the session. As Chin-Riley left, Pelia called after her. "Cadet Chin-Riley, do you have five minutes?"

Chin-Riley surreptitiously checked the time.

"That wasn't a request," added Pelia. "I see the phrasing might have been confusing."

Chin-Riley fell into step beside her instructor. Her heart began to sink; an awful feeling. Usually, Chin-Riley approached meetings with her instructors with the enthusiasm and confidence of the straight-A student. However, Chin-Riley suspected she might be in trouble. No, not trouble, that wasn't quite right. She suspected that Pelia might be disappointed in her, and that was far worse than being in trouble. Chin-Riley wasn't used to disappointing people. She was used to impressing them.

"Glad you found us this morning," said Pelia as they walked along.

"I am very sorry, sir. I missed the message about the change of location."

"I was worried you might not show up. I hear from Chris Pike that you've been elusive recently."

Telling tales out of school, Chris? Was that why she'd found herself in the base group? She would have to have a word with him about that. *One time*, she thought. Well, two. Arguably three, but he hadn't replied to that last message.

"I can't apologize enough, sir."

"Hmm." Pelia stepped aside to let Chin-Riley into her office. The junk shop, as the cadets called it. Every available space was covered in components and curios, odds and ends, bits and bobs. Some of the pieces of junk looked like they still had a practical purpose. Others . . . Who knew? Parts from long-defunct machinery; perhaps some missing Byzantine icons. Pelia's office was something between a wizard's chamber and a mad inventor's lab. Chin-Riley didn't like this space; she found the disorder stressful. There was too much dust, and whatever clear surface you found was usually sticky. Efrosian cocktails? Chin-Riley wouldn't put that past Pelia.

She was starting to see the downsides of having Pelia as an instructor. Chin-Riley flourished with concrete direction and clear goals. Pelia came at you sideways, a method that Chin-Riley didn't particularly like. It seemed designed to trip you up. It wasn't fair.

"Sit down," said Pelia, clearing a space on one of the chairs as she dumped the retro padds in a wooden orange crate. "Here should be safe." Chin-Riley tested the surface with her fingertips before obeying. They sat eyeing each other. The truth was, Chin-Riley was never quite able to shake her sense that, despite Pelia's age and experience, there was something of the charlatan about her. She also sensed that Pelia knew she thought this.

"So," said Pelia, after a moment or two, "is your project stuck in some way?"

"I'm sorry, sir?"

"I haven't seen a proposal from you."

"A proposal, sir?"

"Your project proposal. It was due two days ago. Is this ringing any bells?"

"I think I must have missed—"

"Missed a message, yes, there's a lot of that about right now. Every student taking the course is required to submit a proposal documenting their final project, Cadet. Your task is to select another real-world example where engineering was done under high-stress, crisis conditions. A long report in whatever form you would like. This proposal sets out your choice of case study, your rationale for the choice, and the final form of the report, along with an annotated bibliography. Are any bells ringing yet, Cadet Chin-Riley?"

Chin-Riley dumbly shook her head. Missing an assignment deadline—missing the information that an assignment was due—was so beyond her ken that she almost pinched herself to check she wasn't having a nightmare.

"Alas for you, we are no longer in the immersive experience, and you are not having a very bad dream." Pelia leaned back in her chair. "This isn't like you, Una."

"I'm sorry, sir?"

"Late for class. Missing assignments. Usually, I'd wonder whether extracurricular activities were getting in the way of studies, but that's never happened in the past." Pelia leaned forward again, as if to take a closer look. Chin-Riley discovered that if there was something worse than Pelia's vagueness, it was her full attention. "What's going on?"

"Nothing's going on, sir—"

"No?" Pelia eyed her. "Try answering that again."

"I think . . . I think I may be overcommitted."

"*You* overcommitted? Is *The Mikado* proving too much of a challenge?"

The Mikado, thought Chin-Riley guiltily. She'd missed one rehearsal because of hurrying to Anxha's, and she hadn't practiced her part in days. "I'm doing some volunteer work, sir. It's been taking up more of my time than I expected."

"Is it something you really want to do with your limited time at the Academy, in this life?"

"Yes! I mean . . ." Chin-Riley bit her lip. "I made a commitment."

"That's not the same as wanting to do it."

Chin-Riley shifted uncomfortably in her seat.

"It's difficult, I know," said Pelia, "when you feel that you've made a promise. None of us likes to think we are the kind of person who might have to break a promise. But sometimes it happens."

Never, thought Chin-Riley fiercely. She looked at the cluttered desk and longed to go at it with a sponge and cleaning fluid. When she looked up, Pelia was still subjecting her to a frankly unnerving degree of scrutiny.

"I suppose," said Pelia, after a while, "that it will do you no harm, Cadet Chin-Riley, to discover that there are limits not only to your abilities, but to the amount of time available to you. Even those of us with many, many years of experience can only do so much on any given day."

"I understand, sir."

"Good," said Pelia. "Well. Here is what I will do. I do not usually permit the luxury of an extension on an assignment, but when the student has your track record, I will make an exception. You have forty-eight hours from *now*." She pointed up to a cuckoo clock on the wall behind her. "Forty-eight hours to decide on your case study. You will check in with me in two days, after which you will have a week to deliver to me a full proposal, *at your usual standard*. Can you do this?"

"Yes, sir, absolutely."

"Good. Off you go!"

Chin-Riley stood up. But Pelia had not quite finished.

"It is not possible for us to excel at everything, Cadet Chin-Riley. Think about what you have to do, what you need to do, and what you *can* do. For what it is worth, I do not believe you are a good fit for the part of Katisha."

In the corridor, Chin-Riley thought that was pure Pelia. Advice when you didn't want it. As for Katisha? She was going to be a *great* Katisha! Chin-Riley shook her head; breathed out her frustration. She had better reach out to Pike.

"Hey, Chris," she said. "It's Una."

"Hey!" he said. *"Good to hear from you!"*

"Sorry I've not managed before."

"What? Oh, don't worry. Everything okay?"

Everything was not okay, but Chin-Riley didn't understand how or why this had suddenly happened. "Um. Not sure."

"Okay," he replied. *"We should meet up. Now-ish suit you?"*

"I'd like that," she said. The thought of being in his company—calm, no-nonsense—made her day feel brighter.

"Only thing is—I'm not on campus right now."

"I don't mind coming to where you are."

"Great! I mean . . . I'm in the Sonoran desert—"

"The *desert?*" Of course he was. The desert. Where else would someone be?

"A small one," he said dryly, *"and not far away."*

"What are you doing in a desert, Chris?"

"What do you think?" he said. *"I got sick of being in the city."*

"Yes, but there's the beach for that."

"I'm not beach ready," he said.

"But you are desert ready?"

"Always. Look, come and join me. Get some fresh air."

"Oh Chris, I can't! I have this proposal to write for Pelia."

"I can help."

"I only have two days and I've no idea where to start!"

"Send over the details. We'll talk it through. The hardest part of any assignment is working out what you're going to do. Come on! Live a little!"

Could she really just go out into the desert at a moment's notice? "I guess I could . . ."

"Great! You send over that over and I'll send you my transporter coordinates. I'll take you riding."

"Riding? You mean, on a *horse?*"

A deep sigh came down the comm. *"Yes. I mean on a horse."*

Quickly, she said, "Now, about that—" But he was already gone. His coordinates arrived, as promised. All she had to do was go. Chin-Riley looked around the busy campus. "A horse," she muttered. As if she didn't have enough to worry about. The way things were going right now, she would surely fall off and break every bone in her body.

The joy was plain on Chin-Riley's face. Horseback riding was a sheer delight, exactly what Pike had hoped. She started out with awe mingled with dread, as if he were suggesting she climb onto the back of a plate-armored, battle-hardened unicorn and lead a cavalry charge against unspecified but mighty forces of darkness. Maybe they'd do something like that one day.

"Chris, I don't think I can do this."

Carmen, the horse that Pike had picked for her, was about as sensible and gentle a creature as existed. She had this look that seemed to say, *I'm here for the hay, and maybe—just maybe, if I'm in the mood—I might consider an offer of a carrot.*

"What's the worst that could happen?" he cajoled.

"I could fall off," she said. "Break my neck."

"Really?"

"I broke my leg once, as a kid," she said.

"Not fun." His own leg twinged in sympathy.

"No," she said. "It wasn't."

Something about her tone made him look closer.

"I had a pony that broke its leg," he said. "My first pony. Sir Neighs-a-Lot." He expected the name to earn a snort of laughter and maybe even outright derision, which was why he'd mentioned it. Not something he would do with just anyone. But he wanted to disarm her. Chin-Riley only smiled wanly. "If you're really not happy," he said, "we can give this a pass. Carmen is about as placid as they come, but she won't enjoy the ride if you're not enjoying it."

Chin-Riley seemed to give herself a mental shake. "No. I'm good. I'll give it a go."

"That's the Starfleet spirit. *Per aspera ad* saddle."

She snorted. She was relaxing. Good.

"Sir Neighs-a-Lot, huh?"

Now she was laughing. Time to get her into the saddle.

Once she was up, they walked. Eventually, Carmen decided that her rider was ready for a trot, and once Chin-Riley realized she wasn't going to fall with Carmen in charge, she was ready to try something a little more adventurous. By the end of the afternoon, she was decent. Better still, there was bright color in her cheeks and her eyes were shining. That's what he liked to see.

"Good?" said Chris.

She was laughing. "I see what you get out of this!"

"Good," he said. He had been sure she'd love it. He had been sure she was on the side of the angels. "Head clearer?"

"Clearer than in weeks."

"Better still," he said. "Come on, let's get these girls home. Then we'll find something to eat."

"In the desert?"

"You'd be amazed."

"You're not going to make me camp out, are you?"

"Not on a first date," he said. He'd meant it entirely flippantly, but he immediately sensed that it was a misstep. "Joking. No date. No camping. Not this time."

She smiled, carefully, and nodded. They went back, the horses walking at a gentle pace, cooling down, and Pike said, "The *Silver Hummingbird*."

"Excuse me?"

"The *Silver Hummingbird*. That's what you should do for Pelia's proposal. It's got everything. It's one of the first starships where they had matter synthesizers. The power dipped, and there were a whole series of system failures, including the replicators and the gravity compensators. Then the replicators were pumping out water and with low gravity . . . what do you do?"

She was giving him a look that was unnervingly like the one Robert April had given him when this had come up in conversation. "How do you know about this?"

"I've been reading up on space-flight disasters."

"Super healthy, Chris."

"But useful in these circumstances."

"I guess that would do . . ."

"Not enthusiastic?"

"It *helps* to be enthusiastic about an assignment."

"Sure," he said. "If you're not forty-eight hours away from a failing grade."

"You're right," she said. "Boy, are you right. At this stage I'll take it."

"I mean, don't *kill* yourself trying to sound grateful."

Chin-Riley laughed out loud. "I'm sorry, I didn't mean it like that. It's a great idea. Yes, I can get a proposal out of the *Silver Hummingbird.*"

"These assignments, Una," Pike said, "I know they feel like everything right now, but they don't last beyond the Academy. Two days into your first posting, you'll find your perspective. You'll be surrounded by people who were at the Academy, many who did better than you—yes, even you—and who have years of experience. Anyone who's still talking about how they did at the Academy is probably not doing as well as they'd like in Starfleet. Out there."

She was nodding; she was taking it on board. Good.

They got the horses back to the stables, brushed down, fed and watered them, and made sure they were settled.

"Hungry?" said Chris.

"Mmm."

"Good. Tacos."

"Tacos?"

"There's a place I know just down the road."

She smiled at him. "I get the feeling there's always a place you know just down the road."

"If you can find somewhere good to eat," said Chris, "that's half the battle won."

It was a hole-in-the-wall, but they were great tacos. The sky was darkening to inky blue, and the stars were coming out. Everything around them was beautiful.

"Food and horses," she said. "This is your happy place, isn't it?"

"Yep. What's your happy place, Una?"

"Campus," she said, without a second's thought.

"You know you can't stay on campus forever."

"I know that."

"So what's your plan?"

"The plan is the flagship, Chris. What else?" She gave him a very clear look. "You must be thinking the same thing."

"I'm . . . not usually so up-front about it," he said.

"Oh, sure, you might not say it out *loud*," she said, "but it's written all over you."

"And there I was thinking I was subtle."

"Not to the equally ambitious," she replied. "Can I ask you something?"

"Sure."

"All this," she said. "Riding, tacos, heart-to-heart in the middle of the desert. Stars coming out overhead. What's this all about?"

"You mean, what are my intentions?"

"Yes," she said. "Because I have to be absolutely clear with you, Chris. I'm not looking for a relationship."

"Okay."

"My life is complicated enough. It's my senior year, I've taken on extra courses and some of them aren't going well, and honestly, there just aren't enough hours in the day, and then there's *The Mikado* and the Euxhana and—"

"Una," he said gently, "it's okay. I got it."

He breathed out. He looked at the stars. They were beautiful. He'd figured out she wasn't into him. But he was glad she'd asked. Otherwise, it would always have been there. It would always have been in the back of their minds. Now they could get on with things.

"Can I tell you what happened?" he said. "The reason I'm here with a limp and a bad case of the moody blues?"

She looked at him as if he'd offered her the galaxy. He had, in a way. He had offered her access to more of himself than he did with most. Una had the wits, the decency, the generosity to see that this was access he didn't offer to just anyone. He wanted to keep her around, have her in his life.

"Chris," she said, "only if you're comfortable doing so."

"It might help me to put it out there."

"Tell me as much as you like," she said, "and stop whenever you want."

A first contact mission where he was part of the away team. His gradual realization, as conflicting orders were given, that something wasn't right between his commanding officer and the first officer. The officers directly above Ensign Pike compensating for this to protect the crew. A formula for a disaster. A hasty attempt to get to safety, and one of the officers down with him didn't make it. He made the decision not to wait for new orders, but to persuade the two senior officers that they needed to stop waiting. A shuttle flight back. Suddenly, under fire . . .

"Yeah," he said, "that's what's been on my mind."

"*Chris* . . ."

"The thing is . . ." He looked at the taco cooling in his hand. His appetite had vanished.

"People would've died if *you* hadn't acted," she said.

He shrugged. "I did what I thought needed to be done," he said. "That's what they train us to do. What we're supposed to do."

"You're an *ensign*," she said.

A weight suddenly lifted off his shoulders. She was right. It shouldn't have been down to him. Nobody had said that to him; April had implied it, but Chris only realized now how much he needed to *hear* it. From someone closer to where he was. From someone to whom it wasn't academic.

"That helped," he said, and took a bite of the taco. "Who would've thought?"

"Now," she said, "you know what you're going to say at the hearing."

He'd been turning that over and over in his mind. What to say. Now he knew. He'd be mad not to have Una Chin-Riley in his life.

"I need help," she said, in a quiet voice. "Particularly from someone that isn't caught up in campus life. But someone who understands what it's like. Not a colleague . . ."

"What you're describing," he said, "there *is* a word for it."

"Is there?"

"Friend."

Taken aback for a moment, she began to laugh. "I guess it is."

"I can do friendship," he said. "I'd be glad to."

"I'd appreciate that." She breathed in, deeply, then out. "I took on some volunteer work."

"With your friend Theresa?"

"A refugee family, Euxhana. Heard of them?"

He shook his head. "No."

"A mother and four kids. Cubs, I should say." Her expression softened. "They're so sweet! At first, it was spending a few hours with them, doing some cub-sitting, so the mother could work with her lawyer on their asylum application. The past couple of weeks, though . . ."

"Go on," he said.

"I'm trying not to break any confidences," she said.

"This is all off the record," he replied. "You know that."

"A relative has arrived. An uncle. I'm not sure about him. It's been causing family arguments. I've had to drop things, several times, to go over, look after the kids. I knew when I went into this that it was a commitment. But I'm wondering if I'm in too deep? I can't afford to fall back like this . . ."

A shadow went over her face. Pike wasn't sure why.

"It seems to be taking up a lot of your headspace," he said. "A lot more than it should."

"I guess . . . The mother has had a tough time. She's just about holding things together. They're so far from home."

"What is it about this new arrival. This uncle?"

"I think he's political. I'm not sure. The Euxhana have been suffering cultural persecution . . . There's something off about him."

"Violence?"

"I don't know. I don't think so."

"You know more about this situation than I do. But I'd say you should be careful."

"Careful?" She shot him a sharp look. "I thought I was supposed to be following my gut. That's what you said."

"I did say that, didn't I?" he agreed. "So what's your gut telling you?"

"Nothing," she said. "I guess my instincts need more of a workout."

"Not to the extent of carelessness," he said. "Look, this is straightforward. I've got the clearance level to run some background checks. I'll find out whether this uncle is someone you should be worrying about."

"I'd appreciate that," she said. "Anxha, the mother . . . I couldn't tell whether she was pleased that he was there or not. It could be something very simple. Maybe it's too painful, seeing someone from her past. That must be hard."

"Maybe," he said.

"That's my impression, my gut . . ."

"Don't worry," he said. "Send me over the information. I'll find out what's going on."

"Thanks, Chris." They sat for a while, companionably. Then she asked, "We're okay?"

"Yes!"

"Good," she said.

"Though I can tell you what happens next."

"What happens next?"

"What happens next is I introduce you to my best friend and the pair of you run off and get married . . ."

"Never," she said firmly. "Absolutely not going to happen."

"I have some really nice friends, you know—"

She thumped him on the arm. "Stop now."

"Ow! Okay."

After Chin-Riley was gone, he went back to his cabin and settled in for the evening. The aches and pains were from the riding and not from anything else, and were relieved by a sake and the warmth coming from the chiminea's fire. He sent out requests for information on a Euxhana called Falxho.

After that, he sat and thought about their day together. He liked the idea of being friends with Una. He liked that idea very much.

The files came through. They were based on accounts of the asylum seekers. Sad stories of loss of land and home. Pike felt a wave of sympathy. The notes from Starfleet Intelligence were limited. No reliable intelligence about the situation back on Xhio, but the obvious inference was that there was some kind of trouble back there. Some intelligence suggested that some refugees might be involved in the unrest. Protests or something more serious, no one was sure. The Chionians had provided a very long watch list, and the file contained vague descriptions.

Pike wondered what advice he should offer. The best thing for Una, he thought, was that she should back away. It was clearly consuming her attentions, and he wasn't sure it was good for her. He doubted she would follow his advice. She had made a commitment, given her word, and she didn't strike him as the kind to back down. But it was her decision to make. He sent the files over to her.

Here's what I've found. For what it's worth, my gut tells me: Be careful.

Chin-Riley arrived on campus late in the evening. The rooms were empty. She settled at her desk and went looking for information on the *Silver Hummingbird*. No time like the present. The day out had been a good decision, acting like a reset. Chin-Riley felt as if windows had been opened in her mind. She felt clear-headed and focused. Absorbed in what had happened on the *Hummingbird*, she laughed out loud when she read the crew's solution. (They'd got the replicators working and made some giant sponges.) She wrote up the rationale for her choice of case study, throwing in some suggested section headings for the report for good measure, and sent the file over to Pelia. Fifteen minutes later, she got a reply.

Not the most inspired choice of project. (She must remember to mention that to Chris.) *But one that will give you a sufficient engineering problem/solution to chew on. Progress to full proposal! You have a week! The cuckoo clock is ticking.*

Start tonight, she thought. First she made a cup of tea, obediently following Theresa's rituals. She sat down, head leaned against the back of the chair, thinking about the day. The ride, the food, the company. She felt like she'd won something. Not a romance. Friendship. Chris Pike felt rock-solid. Someone she could rely on. Someone she could . . . trust? Maybe. Maybe one day she would. Not yet. Her comm chimed, and she smiled to see that the message was from Chris, the promised files. Completely reliable. That was her last moment of cheerfulness. She got no more work done that night. The second face on the Chionian watch list looked like Falxho.

Be careful.

The hours that followed were incredibly difficult. Chin-Riley thought about contacting Chris Pike, but what would she say? That she recognized someone on the watch list? What did that mean, exactly? What Starfleet Intelligence knew could not be discovered, even with Chris's security rating. What did this mean for Anxha, for her cubs, for their application? Should she warn Anxha? The information Chris had sent over should not be passed along to anyone outside of Starfleet. Chris had sent it to her in good faith, and she wouldn't break that trust.

Behind all this was the old, awful, lurking fear—that somehow someone would find out about her. Find out her secret. That she was a fraud, a fake. An Illyrian. Suddenly, she was gripped by the terror—the old terror—of exposure. There was nobody to whom she could turn. Not to her friends back home, who had not forgiven her for making this choice to conceal her true self in order to come here. Not to family, whom she communicated with only rarely, for fear of being discovered. And certainly not to her new friends, here at the Academy, who could be implicated.

In her crime . . .

Day-by-day, Chin-Riley had begun to persuade herself that her genetic enhancements didn't matter. Over her time at the Academy, she had proven her talent and her mettle. She had proved that she deserved to be here. She had not given anyone any reason to suspect that she was anything other than what she showed to the world: a hard-working and talented cadet, one of the best, on her way to a glittering Starfleet career. Now she could see that she had been fooling herself. She could try to outrun her past, but it would catch up with her when she was least expecting it. She had tried to help Anxha and her family, and instead had opened herself up to exposure. Was it always going to be this way? Was she always going to have to live like this, always confronted with the grim reality of her situation?

Fact: She could not take the risk of continuing to help Anxha. Cub-sitting, running errands, reading through their applications. Putting herself in a position like this, where she could be found associating with someone on a watch list? That was a risk she couldn't take. She hated how the lies she had told to bring her here to the Academy were trapping her into further lies. She was becoming a person who—for all her formal excellence—was not one to admire.

She spent hours that night thinking through every angle, every possibility. But in the end, she felt she had no choice. She sent a message to Aynur Lavin, asking if they could meet. She tried to go back to her studies, but her peace of mind was gone. She went to bed, her mind racing. She was still awake when Theresa got back, but she didn't call out or get up to talk to her. Broken promises; half-truths and evasions. How could she live like this? How had she ever thought that this could work out?

Aynur Lavin was away at a conference, but could meet with the cadet the following afternoon. She'd offered to speak on the comm, but Chin-Riley had been insistent that the meeting had to be in person. They met at a café on the waterfront. Chin-Riley was there already, staring down into a cooling cup of coffee. She refused the offer of a fresh drink.

"Aynur, I'm sorry," she said. "I have to stop working with you. I have to back away."

"All right," said Lavin slowly. "Do you want to walk me through your reasons?"

"I made a mistake. I've taken on too much and my work's suffering. It's my senior year. I thought I could do everything. I can't. Maybe last year, when the pressure was less, it might have been different. I've taken on too much," she said, again, as if she had prepared this line. "My work's suffering."

Lavin studied the young woman in front of her. She thought the cadet looked anxious and unhappy. "Una," she said gently, "is there something else going on?"

"No. What makes you ask that?"

"You're a good match for Anxha and her family. You get on so well with them. She was saying to me only the other day how much Hax in particular loved your company."

For a moment, Lavin thought that the cadet might burst into tears. "I did. I *do*! But I've taken on . . ." She didn't finish the rehearsed line. Something more honest came out. Honest, but not the whole story. "I can't," she said. "I *can't*."

There was something else, Lavin was sure, but she couldn't press further. She didn't think Chin-Riley would tell her anything. She watched the young woman take a deep breath.

"This year is my senior year. Everything counts so much more. I made a mistake thinking that I could do so much, and I need to step back. Do you understand? I hope you understand. Please understand."

From everything that Lavin had heard, not least from Theresa Mullins, Una Chin-Riley was a first-rate cadet. Beyond that—she was, apparently, something of a star. And while it was true that sometimes the best students put themselves under too much pressure, Lavin sensed that this was not the whole story. That there was something else going on behind this decision.

"You've heard, I imagine, that there's been trouble back on Xhio," said Lavin. "It's been a worrying time for Anxha, waiting to hear news about her family."

Chin-Riley's face paled. "I know. I've heard."

"Is that part of what's troubling you?"

There was a moment's pause. Lavin listened, carefully, to what Chin-Riley would choose to say next.

"I've taken on too much," she repeated. "I'm sorry."

Lavin sighed.

"I don't know how to let them know," said Chin-Riley wretchedly. "I don't know what to say."

"I'll speak to Anxha," said Lavin. "I'll explain that you have to concentrate on your studies."

"Should I send a message? To Hax, in particular. He was coming to campus again. I'd hate to think that he thought I was cutting off contact. No goodbyes."

Unfortunately, that was exactly what Chin-Riley should do. There was no benefit, in Lavin's experience, in keeping lines of communication open. Clean break. "I'll speak to Anxha. And to Hax. I'm sure they'll understand, Una."

A lie. Lavin was quite sure the opposite was true. Hax was going to be devastated. But there was nothing to be gained from saying that to this young woman, who was clearly distressed enough. "I know this wasn't an easy decision to make," she said. "I appreciate your honesty, Una. I'll keep an eye on them—particularly Hax."

"Thank you."

"Is there something else?" Lavin said, wanting to help. "Something else that's troubling you?"

Chin-Riley shook her head. "No. Nothing else. I'm sorry. Again—I'm so sorry. I wish things could be different. I really do. Give them all my love."

Chin-Riley sat at her desk, staring at her notes.

The cuckoo clock was getting closer and closer to having cuckoo-ed, and Chin-Riley had nothing that resembled a project proposal. She hadn't been able to think straight since seeing Lavin.

The door to their rooms opened, and Mullins came in. "Hi," she said.

"Hello," said Chin-Riley. "I'm guessing from your expression that you've spoken to Aynur?"

Mullins didn't reply. She took off her jacket, made herself a cup of tea, and then sat down. "I wish you'd spoken to us sooner," she said. "I wish you'd said something."

"I'm sorry. I know you said at the start that it was a big commitment. I didn't realize how much. I was out of my depth—"

"The thing is, Una, I don't believe you're ever out of your depth."

"I'm missing deadlines. I'm messing up."

"That's what I mean. It's not like you. You're always on top of things. Is there something going on? Something at home? Family?"

"No, honestly," Chin-Riley said—and it wasn't a lie, not really, because surely Mullins was asking about illness or other troubles, but it still wasn't the *truth* . . . "I just . . . I made a mistake. I'm trying to put it right, but I know there's no real way to do that . . ." Her voice faded away.

"Those kids loved you."

"Please, Theresa, this doesn't help—"

"Hax *adored* you."

"Please, don't! I feel bad enough as it is. I'm so, so sorry!"

Chin-Riley watched the conflicting emotions pass over her friend's face. Disappointment, anger, confusion. She waited.

"I don't want us to fall out over this," said Mullins at last. "You have your own reasons for making this decision, and I have to trust that they're good. But I wish you hadn't offered to help."

"I wish that too," said Chin-Riley. She felt wretched. If anything, the offer to move past this whole situation made her feel worse. It would almost be easier if they quarreled, if Mullins ended the friendship. It was surely what she deserved.

Mullins sighed and stood up. "Well, there's nothing more to be said, really. I won't pass on news about them, if that's okay. Please don't ask me to. It's not fair to any of us, and particularly not to them. They need to move on."

"Of course," said Chin-Riley. She felt terribly sad. "I understand."

"I knew you would." Mullins ran her hands through her hair. "Oh, what a mess. Let's try to put this behind us, Una, as best we can. Anyway, I'm tired. I'm off to bed."

Chin-Riley sat for a while by herself, thinking. Was this how it was going to be, her Starfleet career? Living this lie. Living with duplicity. Always having to juggle the precarity of her own situation, and finding out that there were times when she would—quite inexplicably—disappoint people. That was the worst thing—the disappointment. Not being able to explain, to tell the truth about herself, to be completely honest. Would there ever be a time when she could be? Would her future always be full of lies?

Chin-Riley took a deep breath, stood, and cleared away the mugs. This was what she'd chosen. The child looking at Starfleet, thinking, *That's what I want. That's where I'm going to be.* The applicant, telling a lie so big that nobody would guess it, nobody would think that someone would have the audacity. The cadet, excelling at everything. This was going to be harder, Chin-Riley saw now, than she had realized. But the alternative—quitting the Academy, going back home, failing completely, abandoning all those dreams—she couldn't bear that. Somehow, she had to make this work, even if the sacrifices along the way were as painful as this one.

The mugs in the recycler, Chin-Riley tidied the shared space. It calmed her mind enough that she was able to sit at her desk and open the files for her project proposal. Take stock of where she was; of where she needed to be; of how she could get from here to there. Before she began work, there was one last thing to do, one last loose end to tie. She sent an anonymous message to Anxha, warning her that Falxho was on a Chionian watch list.

2260

ENTERPRISE
EXPOSURE

First Officer's Personal Log

An act of terror is meant to instill terror. A bomb on *Enterprise* can be quickly dealt with. We have protocols, and a supremely professional crew. Carry out sensor sweeps, look for anomalies, locate the device, transport it off the ship as quickly as possible, no trouble.

The trouble comes after. Trying to determine who was responsible. Trying to discover how the device came aboard. And, most important of all, trying not to think about what could have happened if our training, expertise, and professionalism had been insufficient for the task. Because sometimes that can happen. You have to put this out of your mind, because if you let that creep in, if you start to catastrophize, then you're doing exactly what they want. You're letting them into your head. You're letting them take control. Note to self: keep an eye on the crew for the next few weeks.

Preliminary assessment of the scans taken of the device before we beamed it off *Enterprise* indicate nothing about its components or materials that's out of the ordinary. This is going to take some good old-fashioned detective work. The kind that suits La'An. In the meantime, the negotiations are in tatters.

———

Linchar, understandably, took some time to be assured of her personal safety.

"We don't know if you were the target," offered Captain Pike.

"We think whoever planted this device seized a moment to make a statement. I'm glad that you were on Starbase 1. For the moment, Lieutenant Noonien-Singh advises that you stay here."

"There is something else that we need to discuss with you, *Echet*," said Chin-Riley. She glanced at Pike, who nodded. *Go ahead.*

"Not another threat?" said Linchar.

"We're not sure," said Chin-Riley. "Which is why we need your input. Shortly before we received the bomb warning, we intercepted this message. As far as we can tell, it's written in Euxhana."

She held out a padd, which showed the message that Uhura was still trying to translate. Linchar, taking the padd, read the words on-screen. Her jaw clenched.

"Who sent this?" she said. Her paws, holding the padd, were trembling—in anger, Chin-Riley realized. "Do you know?"

"We don't know yet," said Chin-Riley. "What we do know is that it came from Earth—"

"From *Earth*?" said Linchar.

"That's right," said Pike cautiously.

"Who was this meant for?" said Linchar. "The recipient? Who was the intended recipient of these words?" She shook her head. "So offensive. Captain, whoever was intended to receive this message is surely connected in some way to this latest outrage."

"*Echet*," said Pike, "I'm missing context. Could you explain what this text is saying that's so problematic—"

But Linchar was no longer listening. Her distress was evident, and her anger was rising. "Captain, *what* exactly is happening right now on Earth?"

"Excuse me?" said Pike.

"This was surely the signal to prime the bomb. It came from Earth?"

"We've no evidence that this was the signal to prime the bomb," said Chin-Riley. "Is that what the message says?"

"No, no, that is not what this message says," said Linchar. "It's a verse. Doggerel. But it has particular connotations. There will surely be something else included in this message, perhaps something encoded in the transmission signal. Or it may be that this is part of a cipher, a code Starfleet has not yet cracked."

"Could it simply be exactly what it seems to be?" asked Pike. "Some verse?"

Linchar glared at him. "The Archenioni dialect—"

"I'm sorry," said Pike, "what is that?" He glanced at Chin-Riley: *Any ideas?*

"I think the *echet* means the Euxhana language," said Chin-Riley. She remembered a conversation she'd had once with Uhura about language suppression. One tactic was to claim that minority languages weren't true languages. Instead they were described as dialects, implying they were derivative in some way. She should certainly check in with Uhura on this. "At least, I think it is."

"It is a *dialect*," said Linchar, her tone brooking no disagreement. "Ask any specialist in Chionian linguistics. And it is *never* simply what it appears to be. Captain, this is very serious. A message has come from Earth, using this dialect, these words. I have to ask you again—what is happening there? I know that the Federation has received a large number of—"

"Asylum seekers?" said Pike.

"Runaways, fugitives," said Linchar. "And while I applaud the Federation's generosity of spirit in this respect, I wonder if you have a full understanding of the situation, and the kinds of people involved. What processes, for example, are in place to monitor these individuals? Are you monitoring them? Are they under *any* form of observation? Subject to *any* restrictions? Have they been allowed, for example, to gather together?"

"Excuse me?" said Pike, a note of incredulity entering his voice. "You're asking whether the Federation is restricting people from congregating?"

"It's well known," said Linchar, "that individuals who believe themselves subjects of persecution reinforce their sense of grievance by seeking out like-minded others. I assume from what you've said that they've *not* been stopped from gathering?"

"No," said Pike.

"So we have disgruntled fugitives," said Linchar, "many of whom have fled because of their connections to recent outrages back on Xhio. They have learned, through some means, of our negotiations here, and have inevitably taken actions to disrupt them. You tell me that this message was sent shortly before a warning was received about a bomb on your flagship. Is it possible that Euxhana terrorists may now be operating from Earth?"

"Now hold on a minute," said Pike.

"If this is the case," said Linchar, "is Federation Security not as concerned about this as I am? I understand from Ambassador T'Maal there is a Euxhana exile on Starbase 1. Some kind of agitator, I imagine—"

"He's a lawyer," said Chin-Riley.

"A *lawyer*?" said Linchar in disbelief. "Is that what he told you?"

"A well-respected one." Chin-Riley struggled to keep her tone even. "He's also a Federation citizen." She turned to Pike. "Captain, this isn't reasonable—"

"Number One." Pike raised a hand. *Calm. Keep calm.*

"*Echet* Linchar," said T'Maal, her voice soft, but her authority undeniable. "These responses are not logical. There is no proof that this message is anything other than what it appears to be. I suggest that we allow the crews on the *Enterprise* and Starbase 1 to continue with their investigations, and provide us with hard information."

"We're exploring every avenue," said Pike. "We'll take a closer look at that message, see if there's anything else to it. We're working on tracing the source on Earth. We'll find out who sent it, where it came from, and who it was for. You have my personal assurance on that."

"And mine," said T'Maal.

"What about this Euxhana lawyer?" said Linchar.

"Federation citizen," countered Chin-Riley.

Linchar ignored her. "What will you do about him?"

"We'll speak to him," said Pike.

"And the Euxhana living within the Federation? I must be entirely clear who these people are and where their sympathies lie. Ambassador, this is not negotiable. I must be satisfied that something will be done about them!"

Chin-Riley caught the captain's eye. She could see exactly what he thought about the idea of hammering on the doors of asylum seekers to interrogate them about a communication sent to a starbase on the other side of the quadrant. Imagine coming all that way, seeking sanctuary, only to discover that they were not beyond the reach of the Chionian government. That was insupportable.

"Let's find out as much as we can about this message first," said Pike quietly. "Once we have the origin point, we can go straight to the source."

Linchar was not happy. "You already *know* that this message came from Earth. Why the delay? Am I supposed to wait until there's another attempt on my life?" She turned to go. "I must speak to my government. In the meantime, until I have your complete assurances that Euxhana terrorists have not found sanctuary within the Federation, we must consider these conversations on hold." She left.

Chin-Riley turned to the captain. "Chris, the Euxhana within the Federation have fled cultural and political persecution. And we're supposed to go knocking on their doors? Should we wait until the middle of night to drive the point home?"

"Number One."

"Federation Security is not a branch of Chionian state security."

"Yes, I know that. But there's been a threat—within *Federation* space—to a Federation diplomat and a Federation starship, and to a visiting diplomat. We have to be open to every explanation, Number One. Could militant activists have decided to export their grievances? Everyone's talking about the Euxhana now."

"They achieved that from projecting a demand for rights on the *Enterprise*," said Chin-Riley. "Why lose sympathies? Why risk that?"

"Enduring loss leads to people making bad choices," said Pike softly. "You and I both know that. I don't deny the maltreatment the Euxhana have faced, Number One. I don't deny their suffering. An influential government member from Xhio has at last come to Federation space. Within striking range. Isn't it possible that someone in pain might decide to inflict pain in return? Isn't that *possible?*"

The first officer, who had seen Euxhana in fear, had seen where that desperation could lead, had to concede that it was indeed possible.

"We need more information," said T'Maal. "Lieutenant Commander, nobody will be accused unjustly."

"I hope that's true," said Chin-Riley. "I sincerely hope that's true."

Analysis of the message did not provide any leads. Hearing from Noonien-Singh that Uhura had finally worked out whom the message was meant for, Chin-Riley went to speak with the security chief.

"It's not good news," said Noonien-Singh. "It looks like the intended recipient was Texho."

Chin-Riley's heart sank. "Oh no."

"I suppose we shouldn't be surprised," said Noonien-Singh. "He *is* the only Euxhana member of Linchar's staff. But . . ."

They looked at each other, understanding how they each felt. Was Texho being framed because he was Euxhana? Neither officer wanted to see anyone judged for a characteristic like their cultural heritage or their descent. For both of them, that cut too close to the bone.

"Could it be completely innocuous?" asked Chin-Riley uncertainly. She couldn't keep the doubt out of her voice. "We still don't know what the message says. We only have Linchar's word that it means something subversive."

"If we translate the message, it still could have been the signal to prime the bomb and send the warning," said Noonien-Singh. "We don't know, because nobody here speaks fluent Euxhana."

"Linchar knew what it was," said Chin-Riley. "But she said it was verse. Doggerel . . ."

"Texho, presumably, also knows."

Again, that pause.

"I really don't want to believe it's him," said Chin-Riley. "It's too convenient, for one thing. The only Euxhana here? *Really?*"

"Unfortunately, he *is* the obvious suspect," said Noonien-Singh. "He was on the *Enterprise* giving that briefing."

"So was Marachat," said Chin-Riley.

"Either could well have taken the opportunity to plant that explosive device."

"What about this lawyer?" said Chin-Riley. "Could he be involved in some way?"

"On'anxho?" Noonien-Singh shook her head. "He said he was working within the system. Of course, he could have been lying. Everything is possible, and I'm taking nothing for granted. Zhovell and I will be asking him a few more questions."

"Perhaps he could help with the translation," said Chin-Riley. "Whatever this thing means, Linchar was absolutely furious at the sight of it."

"Uhura's doing her very best," said Noonien-Singh. "One of the problems is—she tells me—that given the extent to which the language has been suppressed, there aren't any easily available grammars, and practically no vocabulary. We know it's not in code. If Linchar recognized the text, then it can be read at surface level. Whether or not we miss any"—she gave a wry smile—"*nuance*. Let's get it translated."

"Speak to the lawyer," said Chin-Riley. "See if he can help. In the meantime, we're going to have to ask Texho to help."

"Really, Captain," said Linchar. "To accuse my aide—"

"*Echet*," said Pike quietly, "the message could have been for him."

"Texho has been by my side for years."

"We're not saying that he's done anything wrong," said Chin-Riley. "There's no crime in being sent a message."

"On the contrary," said Linchar, "given what the message says."

Chin-Riley and Pike looked helplessly at each other.

"Would it help matters," said Texho softly, "if I simply admitted that the message was for me?"

Everyone in the room turned to look at him.

"Was it for you?" said Pike.

"Yes," he said.

"Texho . . ." Linchar looked horrified.

"Can you tell us what the message says?"

"I don't think I need to," said Texho. He nodded toward Linchar. "*Echet* Linchar knows."

"I recognize the material, yes," she said. "But I don't know what else may be encoded within the message."

"There's nothing encoded within it," said Texho. "It is exactly as it appears. A simple verse—"

"You and I both know that there is more to those words than that," said Linchar.

"Can you tell us who it's from?" said Chin-Riley.

Please, Texho, she thought. *We are trying to help you . . .*

Texho considered this. "No," he said, at last. "I don't think I can."

"That is not a logical response," said T'Maal.

"Can't tell," said Pike, "or won't?"

"Won't," said Texho. "The message was for me. It is a private matter. You have my personal assurance"—he was addressing Linchar primarily now, Chin-Riley saw—"that it contains nothing relevant to this investigation."

"Sir, we need more than your word," said Pike.

"I'm afraid I have nothing more," said Texho. "*Echet*," he said, looking directly at Linchar. She was not looking back. "I know that you find this material distasteful."

"Distasteful," she murmured.

"But I assure you that it is nothing more than it seems. Verse. And I remain everything that I have always been."

Now she looked up at him, and her expression was cold. "I am starting to fear that might be true."

Hearing those words, Texho looked stricken. Chin-Riley's heart went out to him. She recognized Linchar's look. She had seen the distaste—the revulsion, even—from some, when the truth of her enhancements became public, and from people whom she had called friend. Hearing Admiral April say that he would not have sponsored her application, if he had known, had hurt. Was this how Texho felt right now? Linchar was looking at him as if his true self had been revealed, and that she did not like what she could now see. Texho gathered himself, and his dignity. "I have done nothing wrong," he said quietly. "I have nothing to apologize for or be ashamed about, nor have I done anything that requires a defense. I have received a message. That's all."

"Very true," said Pike. "But you were aboard the *Enterprise* just before we received the warning, and it would reassure everyone if you could tell us who sent the verse, and why."

"That," said Texho, "I prefer not to do." He turned to look at Linchar. He tilted his head. "Honored *Echet*," he said. "I ask you, please, to bear in mind my long years of service to you and the Chionian government, and permit me to keep my own counsel."

Linchar was shaking her head. "I should have known better," she said. "I should have known better than to trust someone like you."

"*Echet*," said Texho, "nothing about me has changed. I am as I have always been."

Linchar turned away from him to T'Maal. "There is nowhere suitable on our ship to hold someone securely," she said. "Might I prevail upon the *Enterprise*?"

Say no, Chris, thought Chin-Riley.

But within minutes, Noonien-Singh was there, with a security team, to escort Texho to the brig.

"Captain," Noonien-Singh said quietly, "are you sure it's him?"

"I'm not sure there's anything else we can do," Pike replied.

Texho went with Noonien-Singh quite willingly, as if he had always expected this to happen.

"Captain," said Chin-Riley, "I'm sure it isn't him."

"What can we do if he isn't going to talk? Do you think we can get him to trust us?"

"Let me talk to him," said Chin-Riley. "He knows that I know something about the Euxhana. Maybe he'll open up to me—"

"No," said Linchar. "I cannot accept that—"

"*Echet*," said Pike, turning to face her. "I'm not going to prevent my first officer from carrying out her duties by speaking to a suspect in an ongoing investigation. You're overstepping your authority," he said. "I'm happy to listen to your opinions, but a bomb on a Starfleet ship is a Starfleet matter."

"We must consider our negotiations to be on hold," said Linchar, and strode out of the room.

The captain turned to T'Maal. "Ambassador, I'm sorry, but—"

"*Echet* Linchar is in error," said T'Maal. "The negotiations cannot be on hold when, in fact, they have not yet begun. Continue as you see fit, Captain Pike," she said, sweeping toward the door as grandly as her opposite number. "I shall be in my quarters, waiting to hear any news, when you are ready." She added, "Let us see what can be done for this unlucky aide. Make sure that every avenue is explored."

Once back in her quarters, Linchar sat at her table but could not bring herself to take out her beloved *chera'char*. It felt tainted in some obscure way. Texho had sat opposite her—in that seat right there—and spoken to her about it. The symbol of her history, her family, and he had the audacity to speak to her about it. But this was the Euxhana, was it not? He had knocked the blocks over, carelessly. What else should she have expected. But after so *long* . . .

A bowl of *chaola* was put down beside her. She looked up to see Marachat.

"Sit down," she said to him. "Please."

He took the seat opposite. "*Echet*, I cannot bring myself to believe this of him."

"Unfortunately, it seems to be the truth of our situation," she said. "I have been looking back," she went on. "Scrutinizing all our interactions in recent days. It was Texho who suggested we move over to Starbase 1. Who insisted that *he* should be the one to give that briefing to the *Enterprise* crew."

"Yes," said Marachat, "but I was the one pressing for the briefing to happen." He rested his head in his paws. "Oh, I don't know . . . I don't know what is to be done."

"Do you not think that Texho is responsible?" said Linchar.

"My heart says no," he replied. "I had not met him before joining your staff for this mission. He seemed completely loyal."

"Did you see the message that was sent to him?" asked Linchar.

"No, *Echet.*"

She passed over the padd, and he read the words.

"I see," he said. "I see."

Lieutenant Noonien-Singh was down at the brig when the first officer arrived.

"Has he said anything?" Chin-Riley asked. "Offered any explanations yet?"

"Not a word." Noonien-Singh shook her head in frustration. "We asked whether he wanted a lawyer. Nothing. He curled up on the cot and closed his eyes. There's barely been a twitch of an ear or a whisker since. I hope you can get him to see sense, Una. This isn't going to turn out well for him otherwise."

Noonien-Singh dropped the force field, and Chin-Riley went inside the small cell. She was uneasy, being in a place like this again, so soon after her own close call. Una hated seeing someone like Texho—dignified, self-contained—here. Texho, registering her presence, moved slowly to sit up. Chin-Riley sat down at the other end of the cot. She looked back over her shoulder. Noonien-Singh was hovering in the opening.

"Give us some privacy," Chin-Riley said. "I don't think Texho is going to harm me."

"I can be here within seconds," said Noonien-Singh. "Texho, please bear that in mind. And the lieutenant commander is a formidable opponent in her own right."

The force field was raised. Texho said, "I don't intend you any harm. I don't intend anyone any harm. I never have, and I never will."

"I believe you," said Chin-Riley. "I absolutely believe you."

"Thank you for that," he said, "and thank you, too, for taking the time to come and speak to me. From your expression, I don't think that you have any good news to report."

"I'm not sure how much I can do for you," said Chin-Riley. "You need to meet me halfway. Help yourself. This is serious, Texho. This has gone well beyond graffiti, songs, and slogans."

"I know how serious this is, Commander. Better than you do," he said. "I've told you everything that I can."

"But not everything that you are *able*," she said in frustration. "I don't think you had anything to do with any of what's been happening. But I don't need convincing."

"I know," he said again and sighed.

"Are you all right?" she said, remembering how lonely she felt. How exhausted.

"I'm tired," he said. "More tired than I've felt in my whole life. After all these years . . . they have come at a cost. I never realized, while I was living them . . ." He gathered himself; focused again on her. "Commander, I appreciate your kindness and your faith in me. I hope this investigation finds the real culprit. But I . . . I can't say anything more."

"No," said Chin-Riley firmly. "That's not good enough."

That got his attention. "Not *good* enough? What do you mean?"

"I've been where you are now," she said, "in a place exactly like this. I was under investigation, for the crime of being myself, just like you. I was caught between who I am and what everyone else thought I was. The only way out was to tell my truth."

"After which everything fell into place, and life became livable, yes?"

"Actually?" said Chin-Riley. "It did."

Texho gave her a very dry look. "I'm glad for you, Commander.

But that will not happen here. The truth?" He gave a low rumble of laughter. "Linchar knows her truth, doesn't she? The truth about what Euxhana are, even her most trusted and senior aide."

"What do you mean?" said Chin-Riley. She didn't like the sound of this. This sounded like surrender.

"The truth is," said Texho, "that no matter how they try to teach us, no matter what advantages we are given, or the confidence we are shown—Euxhana are not to be trusted. We are disruptive. Unteachable. Ungovernable. We will always be more trouble than we are worth."

"That's a lie," said Chin-Riley. "And you know it."

"It has the force of truth," he said. He leaned back against the wall. "Let me tell you a story, from when I was young. After I left boarding school, I did very well. I earned a place at the higher schools. I was the only Euxhana there, that year. I clipped my claws the week before I left to take up my place." He held up one of his large paws, from which the dewclaw had been removed. "Do you understand what that means?"

"I don't," she said. "The Euxhana I met, all those years ago, they all still had their dewclaws. I noticed yours were gone."

"I imagine they did keep theirs," he said. "But one cannot progress, as Euxhana on Xhio, with such clear evidence of one's uncultivated past in place. They had to go, if I was to progress further. I did what was needed, and I moved on and up. When I arrived at the higher schools, I was a curiosity. Everyone wanted to look at me, although nobody wanted to talk *to* me." That rumble again. "There was plenty of talk *behind* me, much of which I think I was intended to hear."

"I'm sorry," she said. She thought of her own time at the Academy; how happy she had been, even while she was hiding the truth.

Would it have been worse, she wondered, if everyone had known? But she would never have been accepted to the Academy, not without that first lie. "I really am so sorry."

"It was a long time ago," he said. "I made some friends. They fancied themselves better for making my acquaintance. They can be like that, the rest of the Family. Chionians can be very pleased with themselves, simply for knowing us. Still, they were friends, and I was lonely. We met often, to discuss our classes, even to socialize. One of them gave me my first taste of *chaola*, showed me by example how to hold the bowl and pass it around. There was a lot of watching to work out how to do things like that correctly. One evening, after supper, we were so busy with some debate or other— you know how students are—that I forgot to pass the bowl along. 'Careful,' said one of my friends to our host, 'they take whatever they find.'"

Cruel, thought Chin-Riley. It was like hearing that all Illyrians were an existential threat. La'An must have heard plenty of comments like that also.

"That's awful," she said. "Thoughtless . . ."

"I'm not entirely sure, looking back, how it was meant," said Texho. "Perhaps it was simply the gaucheness of youth, making a joke about the obvious difference in the room. That's the kindest way to think about it. Or perhaps it was a long-standing prejudice that he held, taught by his family, set free by the company and the *chaola*. Opinions like that are so widely held that it's surprising I hadn't heard them before. Or perhaps he even thought that he knew me well enough to be familiar, and that I would be amused."

"Did anyone call him out for it?" Chin-Riley asked. "Tell him he'd gone too far?"

"What? No, of course not! He laughed, the host laughed,

everyone laughed. *I* laughed, and then I passed the bowl along. But I'm not a fool. I saw everything in that moment. I saw exactly how my life would be, if I participated in their society. If I chose to walk that pathway. I saw that there would always be slights, jokes that were barbed and that stung. I knew that beneath it all, there would always be that mistrust. The belief that, in the end, we are wanderers without a sense of property or propriety. Light-fingered. Uncultivated. Nobody would ever really believe that I could be anything but Euxhana. So I told myself, I will be the one to prove them wrong."

Chin-Riley was sure similar opinions must have been said about her when her augmentations were revealed. *What do you expect? Not to be trusted.* In a way, it was true. Her whole career in Starfleet had been built on a lie. "You *will* prove them wrong," she said. "If you'll only *talk* to me."

"I don't think I can," said Texho. "Here I am"—he held up his paws to gesture around the holding cell—"proving what everyone knew. I am Euxhana, with all that implies. My mistake was believing that I could persuade anyone otherwise."

"You haven't done anything wrong," said Chin-Riley. "I'm sure of that."

Texho looked at her. He was big, powerful; his paws were huge and Chin-Riley knew the damage they could do. "How, exactly, do you know that, Commander?" he said. "What, really, do you know about me? Maybe I've finally had enough. Maybe I've decided, after all these years, to throw myself into the Euxhana cause. Maybe I have been playing a long game, sliding myself into positions of trust, biding my time until I could reveal my true loyalties, my true nature. And it's only to be expected, isn't it? We are not to be trusted." He smiled. "Leave this be, Commander. Let it fall out where it will."

"No," she said firmly. "I'm not giving up. I'm not giving up on you."

"Why?" he said curiously. "Why does this *matter* so much to you? Who are we to you? You said you've met Euxhana before. Those words that you said to me, when we met. Someone must have taught you that. Someone gave you those words."

"I have met Euxhana before," said Chin-Riley. "I was a cadet, still at the Academy, when I met a family seeking asylum. A mother and her four cubs. I tried to help. I tried to be a friend. But I made a lot of mistakes, and I didn't do enough for them. Worse than that—I let them down. There were reasons—I was in a difficult place, one that could have cost me my career and put me where you are now. But my situation these days is completely different. I regret what I did."

"And you want to make amends?"

"Something like that."

"Ah, I see . . ." Texho gave a low rumble of laughter. "A chance to revisit a mistake in your past. A chance for salvation!"

"That's not what I meant—"

"The only trouble with that, Commander," he said, "is that I refuse to be the means by which you can ease your conscience." He lay back down and closed his eyes. "You'll have to find another cause, I'm afraid. I am not willing to play that part for you. I am not willing to play any part any longer."

"That's not what it is, Texho," said Chin-Riley.

Who doesn't, she thought, *want to make amends?* But that was not why she wanted to help him. She wanted to help because she believed an injustice was being done, an injustice that had been done to her, and that was not right.

But Texho was not willing. Chin-Riley stood up and tapped on the frame to let Noonien-Singh know that they were finished. The force field was dropped, and she said the words she had learned all those years ago.

"*Xhe'ana euxh on'axhi. Axhena mezh, alxho alxhena.*"

Texho did not reply.

The frustration of the interview with Texho was mitigated when Chin-Riley received a message that she had an incoming communication from Earth. The sender was Theresa Mullins, from an organization called World of Sanctuary. Chin-Riley took the message in her quarters.

Theresa, appearing onscreen, looked much the same. Twenty-five years older—but then, weren't they all? She was relaxed, confident, and delighted to see her old friend from her Academy days.

"*Lieutenant Commander!*"

"Theresa," she said, "how are you?"

"*I'm thriving, thank you. Look at you, first officer on the* Enterprise. *How's that handsome ensign you didn't fancy in the slightest? Has he turned out to be as good a captain as everyone predicted?*"

"Meh," said Chin-Riley. "He's all right."

"*Sounds like he was rock-solid through your recent trials and tribulations.*"

"He went above and beyond," said Chin-Riley, quietly, and with great sincerity.

"*We were all blown away here by your case,*" said Theresa. "*It's huge. Landmark. You've rewritten case law, Una.*"

"My pleasure and my privilege."

"How can I help you? What do you need?"

"The Euxhana have come up on my sensors again. I quickly hit the limits of useful information. In fact, my little bit of knowledge may be hindering rather than helping."

Theresa was nodding. *"There's a Chionian delegation at Starbase 1, yes? Trade negotiations, isn't it? I didn't realize* Enterprise *was there. I would have reached out sooner. So what's going on?"*

Quickly, Chin-Riley gave her a summary of events, up to and including the bomb, and Texho's arrest. "We have one of the Chionian delegation in our brig," she said. "The only Euxhana on their team. Theresa, I don't think it's him. I think he's sitting behind a force field for no other reason than that he's Euxhana."

"Poor fellow," she said. *"Does he need a lawyer?"*

"You know, I didn't think to ask—"

"Go and ask. We've got someone there on Starbase 1 already."

"Who?"

"One of our people. We sent him out to lobby Ambassador T'Maal about Euxhana rights. Hasn't he been in touch?"

"Security spoke to him in connection with the graffiti on Starbase 1 . . ."

"Graffiti? Not his style. That's not his style at all." Mullins was smiling. *"You know, Una, you really need to speak to him. Face-to-face. If you want an expert in Euxhana rights—and a fluent speaker in their language. His name's On'anxho."* Again that smile. *"Reach out to him, Una. You won't be disappointed."*

They wrapped up the call with renewed expressions of friendship and promises to stay in touch. Chin-Riley sent a message to the station and On'anxho replied at once, inviting her to a meeting room he was using on Starbase 1.

As the doors opened, a Euxhana male stood to greet her. He

was tall, less round-faced than usual, although with those icy eyes, and he wore a very smart suit. The nails of his dewclaws were tinted blue.

"Mister On'anxho," she said, "thank you for making yourself available so quickly. I'm very glad to meet you."

His blue eyes twinkled. "Fact," he said, "we have met before."

"Oh," cried Chin-Riley, recognizing him at last. "*Hax!*"

"Hello, Lieutenant Commander Chin-Riley." He placed his paw over his heart and gave her a mock bow. "*Here's* a pretty how-de-do."

2233

STARFLEET ACADEMY
NO-WIN SITUATIONS

Ensign Christopher Pike, Personal Log

I was still out in the Sonoran desert when finally I got the message from Robert April. The date for the hearing has been set. They want me a week before Thanksgiving. He asked me where I was and if I was okay. Messaged him that I was in the desert and that I'd got back up on the horse. Heard straight back.

Good work, Chris.

Clear night tonight. The stars are looking good. Won't be long now before I can get back out there. Back where I belong.

＝＝＝

Anxha sat watching her boys play. They were thriving on Earth, Tilxho and Mexhano, free to roam and explore without the constant warnings she would have to issue at home. *Be quiet. Stay here. Don't go near them.* Every moment spent being guarded, trying to make sure they behaved in a way that brought no attention to them. Gone was the casual sneering: *Isn't that exactly like the Euxhana!* Anxha had tried to spare her children from this creeping self-censorship. It had been necessary to instill it in the older two. Hax had remained impervious, although Anxha suspected there were hidden depths to her oldest son that he had not yet revealed. The damage was clearer in Naxhana, who, no matter that she was now free, had been harmed by the life they had led on Xhio. Restless and unhappy, she lashed out and was quick to anger. But the two smaller ones? Anxha *hoped* for them, truly hoped. She believed that they could be free, here on Earth. It was not home—but then, home had not existed for a long time, and was not ever coming back.

Chin-Riley's disappearance had been a blow, and Anxha worried most about Hax. The news that they would not be seeing the Starfleet cadet again had clearly come as a shock to him. No wonder; she was his first genuine attachment here on Earth. He'd adored talking to her, learning from her. He'd loved the tour of the Academy campus that Chin-Riley had arranged. Once, in passing, Hax mentioned he might join Starfleet. Chin-Riley had told him that there were science officers, who were there to know everything about everything. Then Aynur came and told Anxha that Una was not able to see them again; she was struggling with her studies and needed to focus. Anxha wasn't entirely convinced, but it was a story that Hax could understand. (Who would want to do badly in their studies?) Still, Anxha had seen a change in him since the news. He had become, if possible, even more reflective. He looked older too, leaner, less like a cub and more full-grown. On Xhio, he would be getting ready to walk his first pathway. He would have gone out with his father, learned those walks, before taking his first solitary walk. Here, Falxho would have done this for him, which made what had to happen even more painful.

The sight of the two little ones, so happy and carefree, was giving Anxha much-needed strength today. If she could keep this in mind, then she would maintain her resolve throughout the conversation she must have with Falxho. Her responsibility, she told herself, was to these cubs. To make sure that nothing prevented them from becoming part of this world, this Federation, where, she dearly hoped, they would flourish and become their fullest selves. Still, she would be saying hard words, and the thought of that—the thought of what she must say to Tarxho's brother—brought tears to her eyes. Quickly, before any of them could see, she wiped them away.

"*Maxhi,*" said Hax. "I have a fact for you."

She glanced at her oldest boy, holding up his padd. Strange, wasn't it, how Hax somehow always intervened with a piece of information when she was feeling at her lowest. It was almost like he did it on purpose.

"Go on, *xhixhi,*" she said, stroking, tenderly, the soft white fur beneath his ear.

"There's a place in the Himalayas called the Valley of Flowers. Isn't that pretty? I think that's really pretty. What do you think, *Maxhi?*" He sounded anxious, as if he meant this as a gift, but was not sure whether it was sufficient or even appropriate.

She leaned over to nuzzle her face against him. He was warm, and she loved him so very much. "I think it sounds wonderful, *xhixhi,*" she said. "I think we're lucky to be here on Earth, and I think we should go there one day."

Naxhana wasn't around when they got back home, but Falxho was, half-asleep on the long couch. He had clearly spent the day cooking; the whole house was full of the rich warm smells that made Anxha's heart clench in her chest. Perhaps they should do less of this kind of thing: trying to re-create the tastes and scents of home, singing old songs about places they would never see again. Perhaps they should stop trying to rebuild the lost world here, and instead embrace the new life this planet offered them. Part of her thought this would be the wisest option, but the other part rebelled. So much had been stolen from her, from her four children. Why should they not comfort themselves? Why should they have to forget? Hadn't they sacrificed enough already?

"Out!" she said cheerfully to the children. "You too, Hax—the sun's still up!" When they were all safely out of earshot, she went to speak to Tarxho's little brother.

"Falx," she said softly.

"Hmm?" His head was propped against his left paw. He didn't look much like Tarxho, taking more after their father, although here and there the patterns of some of his rosettes reminded Anxha painfully of his brother. When Anxha didn't say anything more, Falxho opened his eyes and looked straight at her. There, she thought; there was the resemblance to his dead brother.

Tarxho, she thought, *I am sorry. I have to put the children first.*

Falxho was wide awake now. He sat up, his paws flat in front of him, his head hanging down. He looked like a lost boy. He looked like Hax.

"Anxha," he said. "Please don't—"

"It's the cubs, Falx," she said. "I can't risk them."

"I've nowhere else to go."

"You should have told me. The moment you arrived, you should have told me that they were looking for you."

"So you could turn me away at the door?" he said bitterly.

"Falx," she said—gentle, but remonstrating.

"Please," he whispered. "I don't have anyone else to turn to. I've got nowhere else to go." He started to cry.

It was one of the most desperate things Anxha had ever seen, made worse by the fact that she was the cause. But she must not yield.

"What would *he* want you to do?" said Falxho. "What would Tarxho—"

"Don't you dare," she whispered fiercely. "Don't you *dare* use him like that! With *me*! Of *all* people! Don't you *dare*!"

Falxho didn't say anything else. He sat for a while, head resting in his paws, shoulders shivering, but dreadfully silent. "You're right," he said after a while. "I shouldn't have put you in this position. I should have told you. I'm sorry." He stood up. "I'll go now."

"Where?" she said.

"I'll think of something." He sniffed; wiped his face. "Better, probably, that you don't know. In case anyone asks. In case they try to make it a condition for you to stay."

"Thank you," she said. "I won't forget this. I won't forget everything you have done for us. Everything that you mean to us."

"Well," he said. "I love those cubs. I wouldn't do anything to . . . to hurt them."

He padded softly to the door, turning to smile at her, sadly, before leaving. "Goodbye, Anxha. Good luck. Tell them I love them."

"They know."

He left. Anxha closed the door behind him, and leaned her face against the cool window. These cruel choices that were forced onto them, when all she wanted was to live with her family in peace; for her children to have the chance to thrive and flourish, and to know who they were and the lost world that had made them. She heard voices behind her; quick paws moving; the boys were back inside. She went into the kitchen.

"Snacks?" said Tilxho.

"Snacks," agreed Mexhano.

"Where's Uncle Falx?" said Hax, looking around—and then he caught his mother's eye. "Yes, snacks," he said quickly. "Go on," he told his younger brothers. "Find something for us to eat."

Small hunters, they raided the kitchen, bringing back a feast. Little pots and tubs full of treats that Falxho had made for them. Anxha thought perhaps the two younger ones had not noticed his absence, but then Tilxho, mouth full, said, "Where *is* Uncle Falx?"

"He's had to go," said their mother.

"He'll be back?" said Mexhano.

"No, *xhixhi*," she said. "I mean—he's had to go away."

It was like watching a ball deflate. Both of them, their shoulders slumped, their eyes suddenly wet. They had been doing so well. But then, there had been so many sudden disappearances, hadn't there?

"This is like Una," said Tilxho. "Only worse."

"Much worse," said Mexhano.

"Una is busy with her studies," said Hax. "She just doesn't have much time right now. It'll be different when the holidays come around."

Anxha glanced quickly at her oldest son. Did he really think that? His expression was bland, giving nothing away—but she could tell. He knew. He knew that Una wasn't coming back. He was trying to keep the twins cheerful. Support she hadn't realized she had. He really was growing up.

"Maybe he'll come back soon," suggested Mexhano.

"Yeah, he wouldn't go away without saying goodbye," agreed Tilxho. "Not for a long time. Not a proper goodbye."

"Not to us."

"You've got another hour," said their mother, "before you have to go to bed."

Up the pair of them jumped, food in paw and mouth, racing to be the first back outside. When they were out of earshot, Anxha said to Hax, "Thank you."

He shrugged, and stood up. "Maybe they're right," he said. "Maybe he will come back. Maybe Una will too. Maybe everyone will." He disappeared upstairs, into his room, into the quiet security of his endless studies, the blissful certainty of his facts.

There was one more conversation to be had, and Anxha did not believe that it could possibly go well. Since her uncle arrived, Naxhana had been the happiest she had been in a long time, certainly the happiest she had been on Earth. She came home after the younger two had gone to bed. Hax was still in his room. Naxhana came in, looked around, and frowned. The house was quieter than it had been for a while. Usually, when Naxhana came home these days, there was food, and lights, and company, and conversation.

"Where is everyone?" said Naxhana. "Where's Uncle Falx?"

Anxha sighed. "He's gone, *xhixhi*."

"Gone? What? Gone out for the evening? Is that a good idea?"

"No," said her mother.

"Oh," said Naxhana, "you mean he's gone."

"Yes."

"And he just decided, did he?" she said. "To get up and go tonight? On a whim?"

"*Xhixhi*—"

"There's a lot of people just deciding to go these days, aren't there?" said Naxhana. "Like that Starfleet cadet. She seems to have given up on us too."

"I'm sure she had her reasons."

"Did Uncle Falx have his reasons? Or did something else happen?"

Anxha raised her chin. She wasn't going to lie. "I think you know what happened. I asked him to go. And he agreed it was for the best."

"You *asked* him to go?"

"Naxhana, this is complicated."

"Complicated?"

"There are no easy choices here. But I have to put you, all of you, first—"

"I wouldn't ask you to do that for me," she said. "I bet the boys wouldn't either."

"The boys aren't old enough to make those decisions."

"Hax is. Do you think he'll forgive you for this? After what happened with Una?"

Stung, Anxha said, "I did or said *nothing* to make that young woman go away! I welcomed her here. She made her own decision."

"Hurts, doesn't it, to be cast aside?" said Naxhana. "At least she didn't really need us. Not like Uncle Falx does—"

"Naxhana, I can't risk us getting sent back." She lowered her voice. "He's wanted. They want him back home. He's on some kind of list . . . A watch list. I don't know what that might mean for us. He might have done something foolish."

"You mean violent, don't you? You think he's a terrorist."

"I didn't say that—"

"He tells jokes, *Maxhi*. He tells jokes that make the authorities look stupid, and that's why they hate him. What did he do, exactly, to get on this list?" When her mother didn't answer, Naxhana's eyes narrowed. "Did you even *ask* what he did?"

Anxha swallowed. She hadn't. She had no idea what he might have done. She knew only that they wanted him on Xhio, and that fact alone put her and the children at risk. She hadn't wanted to ask. There was safety in ignorance.

"You didn't even ask," said Naxhana. "You just threw him away, to save yourself."

"To protect us," Anxha said firmly. "Falxho understood. He left willingly."

"Oh, tell yourself that," said her daughter. "Tell yourself that, if it helps. Oh, my soul," she cried, "forced too far from the path, that longs for the sweet heights of the mountains! Is this what we are now? Is this what this Federation demands from us? I wish we'd never come here! If this is what it means, being here. Giving up people that we love. Giving up everything we love. If that's the price of being here—I don't want to pay it. But I don't get to choose, do I? You make all those choices. I wish I'd never come here. I wish we'd stayed in Rechzan."

"It wasn't safe there."

"It's not safe here, either, is it? At least, not for Uncle Falx. What if he's not the only price you're asked to pay, *Maxhi*? Who else will you give up? Me?"

"You're not wanted by the government."

"No," said her daughter. "Not yet, anyway."

Anxha was filled, suddenly, with terror. "Oh, *xhixhi*," she whispered. "You're not doing anything foolish, are you?"

"Do you think I'd tell you now, if I was? Do you think I'd trust you?" She moved toward the door. Anxha moved quickly, trying to block her exit, but Naxhana was faster, and stronger, and Anxha was not willing to hurt. Naxhana pushed past and opened the door.

"Please don't go out," Anxha begged. "Please don't . . . *don't!*"

"I'll come and go as I please," said Naxhana. "This is a free world, isn't it? Wasn't that the point of coming here? To be free?"

She went out into the night, the door hissing shut behind her. Anxha suppressed a sob.

"*Maxhi.*"

She turned to see Hax, standing at the top of the stairs. He had plainly been there throughout. Slowly, he came down and gathered Anxha into his arms. Was he taller than her now? She wasn't sure. They changed so quickly. They grew, so quickly.

She leaned against him, and he nuzzled the top of her head. "Fact," he said. "You are a good mother. The best. I'm glad you brought us here." He looked straight at her. "Don't worry, *Maxhi*," he said. "I'm here. I'll take care of you. I'll take care of us all."

Chris Pike got back to the city in time for his regular Wednesday drinking session with Pelia. Her choice this time. A bar without fuss or complication.

"How was the desert?" she said.

"Exactly what I needed."

"Silence and a big sky, huh?" Pelia started to laugh. "You know, you've not *really* experienced silence and big sky until you've lived through a collapse of civilization. I think it was best right after the Roman legions withdrew, because there wasn't much in the way of technological infrastructure to miss. It was much hairier after the Atomic Wars." She observed, "You don't know how much you rely on well-maintained roads until someone stops maintaining them. I think that's what sparked my interest in engineering."

"How's Una Chin-Riley?" Pike said. "I haven't heard from her in days." Not since he'd passed on that information she'd asked for. He hadn't even heard what she had decided to do.

"Hmm . . ." said Pelia.

"That good?"

"I *hope*," said Pelia, "I sincerely hope that our star student is starting to get back some of her sparkle."

"Problems?" Pike felt bad. He should have checked in sooner. He should have chased after her, found out how she was doing.

"Missed deadlines. Puzzling absences. I even had to give an extension. Unheard of from Cadet Chin-Riley! She's the kind whose work arrives early. The kind that you have to ask, 'Why do you think I want this on my desk when it can still be on yours?' But I was not expecting work to come in late. Not from her. And I was surprised at how shaken she was by our little holo-seminar."

"Surprised by the what now?"

"The students taking Starship Maintenance complained—more precisely, Cadet Chin-Riley complained—that the course wasn't immersive enough. Immersive! So I created the best damn holo-experience ever. Made them *really* feel like they were stuck on Mars with no way home. Ha!" She laughed out loud. "The place stank! *Real* seat-of-your-pants stuff. Chin-Riley didn't like that—no, she didn't like that at all. Where is your god now, Cadet Chin-Riley? Where are your *regulations?*"

Pike thought it didn't sound like Una to be thrown by a new experience. Look at how she'd got over her fear of riding a horse. "It sounds impressive," he said. "How are the other cadets handling it?"

"They love it. I should have made it more difficult. I should have made it *impossible.*"

"But not Una."

"No," said Pelia. "Disappointing, and a little surprising."

"I know she's been preoccupied with some volunteering she was doing," Pike said carefully. He didn't want to betray any confidences. "It got more time-consuming than she expected."

"Yes, I was aware of that," said Pelia. "She's no longer involved with the group. Or so I understand."

"What?" said Pike, startled.

"Yes, she's pulled out. Cadet Mullins told me." Pelia eyed him. "You look surprised."

"I am," said Pike. "From the way she was talking about it, she'd got to know the family pretty well. Was close to them. I didn't think she'd back away completely."

"When you put it like that, it is a puzzle, isn't it? Not the kind of thing you might expect from Cadet Chin-Riley." Pelia sighed. "I sense deep waters around that cadet. But the main thing now is for her to get her year back on track. The signs are positive. So *far*. The project proposal that she sent over was not the most inspired. The *Silver Hummingbird*!" She snorted. "She is going to struggle to impress me with *that* choice."

Pike decided against fessing up. He had troubles of his own, and he didn't want Chin-Riley to get a bad grade. Not this late in the semester. And he wouldn't put it past Pelia to retract his own A+ for Starship Maintenance. He'd enjoyed the course, and he liked the sound of this holo-scenario. That would focus your mind . . .

"But at least she is communicating with me now," said Pelia. "Let us hope this continues."

Pike hoped that too. That Una had decided to back away from her volunteer work—from a family to whom she had clearly become attached—had come as a real surprise. He'd thought that was what she needed to do, but he hadn't suggested it because he didn't think she would follow his advice. He had thought she would dig in, find a way to make it all work. For a moment, he wondered whether she had seen something in the information that he'd sent her. Something that had worried her. But she was conscientious, intelligent, sensible. She would surely raise any issue with her instructors. She knew the regs, and she had no reason not to trust the judgment of her superiors.

"You know," said Pelia thoughtfully, "I'd hate to have to fail her. I'm not sure how well she would handle that. She's not used to getting things wrong."

"Would you actually do that?" Pike said, shocked. He couldn't imagine something like that happening with a freshman and certainly not with a senior. The recruitment procedures were too good, the quality of cadets was too high, and the culture of working hard and doing your best too entrenched. Cadets didn't fail. Perhaps this was something that needed addressing. He remembered the look in his captain's eye when she realized the situation was spiraling out of control. *How has this gone so badly wrong?* The panic rising as the two most senior officers realized they didn't have a way out, and they didn't think that they could trust each other's judgment.

"If the paper is bad enough? You bet I'd fail it," said Pelia, eyes glittering. "I don't think it will be, though. I think it will be . . . *passable*." She gave a rather wicked laugh. "Whether passable is good enough for Cadet Chin-Riley remains to be seen."

No, Una wouldn't like that, Pike thought. In some ways, failure was an easier pill to swallow than mediocrity. You could make a real impression by failing, but never through mediocrity. There was something that cadets could learn. "Do you think the Academy makes life too easy for them?" he said.

"Hmm?"

"The cadets."

"Easy?" She peered at him. "Have you forgotten how hard we work them here, Chris?" she said. "You're not turning into one of those *appalling* people who say, 'Oh, these kids, they haven't been in space . . .'"

"Do we make them think of failure as something that's to be avoided at all costs? They are going to have to deal with failure at some point. Not missing a deadline or getting a lower grade than you wanted. Real failure."

"Go on," said Pelia.

"There's too much emphasis on excellence. On achievement. Cadets get every chance to exceed their own capabilities."

"Is that a bad thing?" pressed Pelia.

"It's not. But does the Academy ever give them a chance to fail?" He was warming to his idea. "These cadets—they self-select for the Academy at younger and younger ages. They push themselves to do everything brilliantly, to the best of their abilities. But life isn't like that. Starfleet isn't like that. Sometimes things just don't work out. Do they ever have a chance to learn that?"

"School of hard knocks, Chris? Never thought I'd hear *you* advocating that."

"I was thinking of something a little more subtle. Something that tests their ability to cope with failure. A no-win situation. Think about your current class taking Starfleet Maintenance. How would they cope with that? Because I'll bet you some of them would fall apart. And the last place you want to fall apart is on a starship, or your first post, or worse, your first command."

"Sounds like a setup—"

"The idea wouldn't be to trap them," said Pike. "That wouldn't be fair, and that isn't the point of the exercise. I want them to understand what it's like to fail. You know what cadets are like."

"Oh yes . . ." said Pelia.

"They think they're the best, the smartest, the sharpest that the Academy has ever seen. And that might be true. It's also possible that it won't be *enough*."

There was a pause as Pelia thought about what he was saying. "Do you have the date for your appearance at the hearing yet, Chris?"

"Yes," he said. "Next week. And yes—this has been preying on my mind. Of course it's been preying on my mind. I watched—in real time—as my superior officers realized far too late that they had failed. Maybe they should have known much, *much* earlier in their careers that this was possible. That all their excellence and talent and ability to extemporize might one day not be enough. Do we tell the cadets that? I'm thinking of people I knew when I was here. Cadets I've met in the past weeks, even Una. How does someone like her cope with failure? How do we get them to understand that they might not be sufficient to the moment?"

Pelia was leaning forward. He had her full attention now.

"Keep talking."

Chin-Riley surfaced from a long day of proposal writing, and was running across campus to rehearsal. It was a chance to spend time with friends, doing something profoundly unserious. It was raining, a fresh autumn rain, and all around was that deep rich scent of leaves getting ready to fall. Chin-Riley breathed in deeply. She'd earned a few hours away.

They were running through the last half of Act II of *The Mikado*, so everyone was there. Vrati had brought in some of the set designs and the cast spent the first ten minutes looking them over. Chin-Riley was reminded uncomfortably of Pelia's holo-seminar, which told her that the design was spot-on. The costume design was a riot, cobbled together from the kind of hazmat gear that would have been on the base in the twenty-first century, garlanded with ribbons of duct tape. Exactly how it would look if a bunch of bored Mars colonists decided to fill the hours with Gilbert and Sullivan. Fatima Nahas was thrilled.

"You know, it was an off-the-cuff joke," she said. "I didn't think we were going to be able to make it look so *amazing*."

The rehearsal went well; everyone was on form. Chin-Riley fell in with the collective energy, doing some of her best singing of the semester. She sat and listened to Nahas ace her solo as the Mikado. Great first part for her; she was going to make her mark on the society. As the number came to an end, one of the other performers came over and whispered in Chin-Riley's ear.

"Una," he said, "there's someone here to see you."

Chin-Riley looked back over her shoulder at the doors leading into the rehearsal room. To her complete surprise, she saw Naxhana standing there. The girl's fur was damp—it must be raining outside. She was breathless, as if she had been running. When she saw Chin-Riley, she stopped.

"Five minutes?" Chin-Riley said quietly to Vrati.

"Sure. I was about to call a break anyway."

Chin-Riley hurried through the room. "Naxhana," she said. "It's good to see you."

"So this is the rehearsal," said the girl. "It looks like it would be fun."

"It is fun," said Chin-Riley. "Stressful, sometimes, but mostly fun."

"Stressful?" said Naxhana. "Sure."

"Is everything okay?" said Chin-Riley.

"What do you think?"

"What's happened?" A sudden fear gripped Chin-Riley. "Is Hax all right?"

"Nobody's *hurt*," said Naxhana. "Not yet, anyway. It's Falxho."

"What's happened?" said Chin-Riley, cautiously, not entirely sure she wanted to know.

"*Maxhi* told him to leave. She said she can't have him near us any longer. We didn't even get to say goodbye!" Her eyes were flashing, and her voice was getting louder. Chin-Riley was painfully conscious of her friends, who were pretending to be busy, but hearing everything. "He was on some list or other—"

"Naxhana, I'm so sorry."

"I know what *Maxhi's* thinking," said Naxhana. "That he's done something really bad. But she's wrong. She's completely wrong. Do you know what he did? What he and his friends did?"

"No," said Chin-Riley. "I don't. But that's not what this is about—"

"Have you heard of *Evechet* Achar A'Rechan?"

"No, I haven't."

"Of course you haven't," she shot back. "Because you don't actually know anything about us, do you? Yet you thought you could help us. You thought you could walk in and help us, like some savior or something. Until it all became too much trouble for you. Until *we* all became too much trouble for you!"

"Naxhana, please," said Chin-Riley, reaching out for the girl's arm. She was very aware of how quiet the room was behind her. What could people be making of all this?

Naxhana pushed her away. "I don't know why I came here. Uncle Falxho said not to trust Starfleet. He said they wouldn't do anything to risk their friendship with the government. And he was right!"

She stormed out of the room. Vrati, who had been maintaining a discreet distance, came over. "Una, is everything okay?"

"Yes, yes . . . I'm so sorry, I didn't think she would come here." Chin-Riley took a deep breath. "Should we start?"

Vrati looked at her in surprise. "Don't you want to go after her?"

"I don't want to interrupt the rehearsal."

"I think you should go after her. She seemed pretty upset." Vrati nodded over at Nahas. "We're doing the duet tonight, but don't worry—Fatima can double up parts again this evening."

Gratefully, Chin-Riley left. She ran out of the auditorium into the rain. She saw Naxhana, up ahead, hurrying away. "Naxhana!" she called out.

The girl didn't slow down. Chin-Riley chased after her, catching up with her before she reached the public transporter, and reaching out to touch on the soft fur of the girl's arm. Naxhana turned, glared at her, and pushed Chin-Riley's hand away. "I've said all I have to say."

"But I haven't," said Chin-Riley. "I want to say sorry. I should have spoken to all of you directly, but I was advised not to. I took the coward's way out, and it was wrong of me. I'm sorry." She breathed out. "How are you? How's Hax?"

"How *are* we? How's Hax? How do you think he is? He doesn't make friends easily, and he thought he'd made a friend in you. He loved talking to you. He loved it that time you brought him here."

Chin-Riley, ashamed, could think of nothing to say.

"And *Maxhi* has made Uncle Falxho move out." Naxhana eyed her suspiciously. "You weren't behind that, were you?"

"I don't know what would make you think that," said Chin-Riley, unwilling to tell a direct lie, but certainly not willing to offer the truth.

"It was because of him that you gave up on us, wasn't it?" said Naxhana. "You heard what they were saying about him, and you believed it." She was getting angry again. "You've not even got any idea of what he did!"

"Then tell me," said Chin-Riley. "You said a name. Achar . . ."

"*Evechet* Achar A'Rechan," said Naxhana. "You don't even know that name. You don't know anything—"

"Please explain," said Chin-Riley. "Who is that? What does it mean?"

"He was a war hero, a great general—well, that's what they teach in the Chionian schools. But we know better. The Euxhana know what he did to us. They don't teach that. They don't talk about him rounding up mothers and cubs as they walked the pathways. They don't talk about the poisoned wells and streams and having to come to the town in the summer so that people didn't die of thirst. They put a statue of him up in the middle of Rechzan. We don't even want to live there, and there's that statue, right in the middle of the town. You have to pass him every morning on your way to their schools that tell lies and pass him again every evening on your way back home. Uncle Falxho and some of his friends—"

"Did they pull it down?"

"What?"

"The statue."

"Pull it down? What do you think they are? No, of course they didn't pull it down! They're not *vandals*! They didn't even put graffiti on it. Do you know what they did? They made some banners, and they tied them around it. Around that old bastard. The banners made jokes about him. They called him Old Big Ears. Stupid, dumb jokes that made everyone laugh. And they made a hat and covered it in mountain flowers and stuck it on his head. But do you know what the real crime was?"

"No," said Chin-Riley.

"They used our own language! Imagine that. Could anything be more outrageous? That's all they did. Nothing violent. No bombs, no threats, nothing. Jokes. That was enough for him to have to run away from Xhio, in fear for his life. They're making out like he's some kind of terrorist!" She gave a bitter laugh. "Makes you wonder, though, doesn't it? How scared they must be of us, if a few jokes in our language can make them so upset." She held out her paws, displaying the dewclaws proudly. She had painted them bright red. "But then we're savage, aren't we? Untamed. Dangerous."

"Naxhana—"

"Jokes, Cadet. But that was enough for you to drop us. Enough for *you* to run away."

Chin-Riley found her temper rising. Naxhana knew nothing about her life, not really. She saw the Starfleet cadet and nothing more. "You know, life is complicated. Sometimes people don't have the luxury of making pure choices."

"*Luxury?*" Naxhana gave that awful laugh again, filled with a kind of weariness about the world that nobody so young should have. "Have you seen this planet? You and your friends, the way you live? You're protected from everything here! You play at being soldiers and officers during the day, and then you mess around dressing up and singing songs at night. What do you know about making difficult choices?"

"That isn't fair," Chin-Riley said. "You don't know anything about me—"

"You didn't give me the chance to find out. You walked into our lives, pretended you could help, and then when things got uncomfortable you walked out. Hax *adored* you. Hax wanted to join Starfleet because of you. And you walked out on us. On him."

"I'm sorry," said Chin-Riley. "I'm so sorry."

"The least you could do is say *why*."

"I *can't* . . ." She shook her head. "It all became too much."

"Yes? Well, try living it. Every day."

I do, thought Chin-Riley wretchedly. Naxhana shook her head one last time, and then headed down the street. Shaken, Chin-Riley went back inside. The rehearsal was underway, so rather than disrupt it, she stood at the back of the auditorium, listening. Nahas was singing her part in the duet:

To the matter that you mention
I have given some attention
And I think I am sufficiently decayed . . .

She sounded good, thought Chin-Riley. It was easy to make the part of Katisha completely comedic, like a pantomime villain—but there was pathos to the character too. She was sad, and lonely, and a really good performer got that, put it out there for anyone to see who was paying attention. Nahas had it down perfectly. She didn't just sound good, thought Chin-Riley; she sounded terrific.

The deadline drew closer; the cuckoo on the clock was clearing its throat. Chin-Riley hid in her room, seeing nobody and talking to nobody. Chasing down references, reading sources, trying to put together the outline of a project that would convince Pelia. The *Silver Hummingbird* was turning out to be a mixed blessing. The parameters of the project were clearly defined, but every so often she was beset by doubts about the entire premise. Was it too narrow a case study? Was she was treading over familiar ground? She wasn't used to struggling. She wasn't used to being only good enough. She was used to excelling. Working with unpromising material with one eye on the clock did not bring out the best in her.

She was staring at words on the screen and thinking about making another cup of tea, when the door chime softly sounded.

"*Go away,*" she muttered. "*I'm busy.*"

But the chime came again. Half-irritated by the interruption and half-grateful for it, Chin-Riley padded over to the door. Standing in the corridor was Falxho.

"Falxho?" she said. "What are you doing here?" Another thought struck her. While parts of the campus were accessible to the public, the cadet dorms certainly weren't. "How did you get in here?"

"That was the easy part," he said. "As to why I'm here? That's simple enough too. I want your help."

"My help?"

"Yes." He swallowed. "I'm desperate," he said. "Anxha has thrown me out. She's asked her friends not to speak to me. I've got no one to turn to. You're the only other person on Earth that I know."

"If Anxha doesn't want her friends speaking to you," said Chin-Riley, "then I can't either."

"What do you care about Anxha?" said Falxho. "You dropped her as soon as life became difficult for you."

"That isn't fair—"

"Has Anxha ever talked to you about her past? Has she told you what she was like when she was younger? Before she met my brother?" He laughed. "Looks like she didn't. I think she's almost forgotten herself. She was the radical! Did she ever tell you about the sit-ins? The disruptions at the factory where she worked? All the machinery that used to break down, so mysteriously? Did she ever mention any of that? That's who Anxha was, when she met my brother. Anxha was the one that got him involved. Now he's dead. He'd dead, and she's turned on me, and I'm going to be next."

He was sobbing. It was awful to see, and Chin-Riley felt herself weaken. "Look, I can put you in touch with people who can help you. Help you with an asylum case."

"Asylum case?"

"Friends of mine—they're working with Anxha. They know about what's happening to you, to the Euxhana. I'm *sure* they'll be able to help you. There's all kinds of reasons that you can ask for asylum. Listen, I've learned about some of the laws: if you're fleeing persecution, if you're in fear for your life because of political beliefs, or cultural engagements, if you make yourself known to the authorities and apply for refuge. This applies to you, Falxho. They can help you. They know what they're doing."

But Falxho was shaking his head. "They can't help."

"Why not? You said you didn't do anything. Naxhana said all you did was mess around with some statue." Chin-Riley stopped to look at him. "That is all that you did, isn't it?"

"What do you care? And what does it matter, anyway? They fake evidence, you know. They don't want us out here, free, talking about what's going on. They want me back."

"Then it's even more important that you make a case for asylum," said Chin-Riley. "These friends of mine will know how to help you. They know what they're doing."

"I don't want their help," said Falxho. "I want to get away from Earth. I want you to help me get away from Earth."

"Get away? How can I help you get away?"

"You're a Starfleet cadet, aren't you?"

"Yes, emphasis on *cadet*. Do you think I have access to *starships* or something?"

"I don't know. I don't know anything about Starfleet."

"That's clear!"

"But I know that you could do something for me if you put your mind to it." He gave her a bitter smile. "After what you did to my family. Dropping them. It's the least you can do."

That strengthened Chin-Riley's resolve. "You need to leave," she said. "I'm going to give you ten minutes, and then, if for any reason I think you're still on campus, I'm contacting security."

"So they can take me away? So they can send me back? Make an example of me?"

"You need to go," said Chin-Riley, firmly. "Now."

She reached her hand out to press it against the door panel. Falxho, desperate, pushed forward against her, grabbing for her arm. Chin-Riley had watched Tilxho and Mexhano wrestle often enough, but even so, she was not prepared for the sheer strength of an adult male Euxhana. She fell back into the room, Falxho on top of her, but she kept her cool, shoving back against his weight.

"Stop this!" she hissed at him. "This is doing you no good—"

"You've got to help me!"

She grabbed one of his front limbs to push it away, but his other paw came in to grab her wrist, and, catching against her arm, his dewclaw tore at her flesh. She felt the cut, she felt the pain, and then she felt the healing begin. That warm glow, which should feel so comforting, reminding her of her strength, her individuality, her real self. Instead, it felt like betrayal: her treacherous body, always lying in wait to give her away.

Falxho stared at the golden glow. "What's happening?" he said. "What's that?"

His moment of confusion—of distraction—was enough for Chin-Riley to get away from beneath him. She went into panic mode. She had to cover this up. She had to cover this up. She scrambled to her feet. She turned—and saw Mullins standing at the door, staring into the room. They locked eyes—only for a moment, one hideous endless moment—and then Mullins ran in, pulled Falxho to his feet, and dragged him out into the corridor. Chin-Riley dived to close and lock the door. She ran over to her desk, hands shaking as she pulled out the dermal regenerator that she kept there. Soon the wound was gone; there was nothing to show who and what she was. But she had no idea what Mullins might have seen. She had no idea what Mullins might do next. She knew only what the law required. What honor demanded of a Starfleet cadet.

2260

ENTERPRISE
THE CALL FROM THE MOUNTAINTOP

First Officer's Personal Log

The past is present. I had no expectation that I would ever meet anyone from Anxha's family. And there he was. Fact.

Could he forgive me?

=======

"Hello, Lieutenant Commander Una Chin-Riley." Hax placed his paw over his heart and gave her a mock bow. "*Here's* a pretty how-de-do."

Gilbert and Sullivan. *The Mikado*. What else? Who else could this be? Looking at him, she could see the young cub that he had been, on the very edge of adulthood, gawky and intense, eager to be her friend, to learn about her and the galaxy that she represented. More than anything, she regretted the loss of contact with that boy, the damage that must have been done with her sudden withdrawal from his life. But he was looking at her with curiosity, to see who she had become, and with delight, at the sight of her. Chin-Riley did not know if she deserved this, but she was glad of it. He offered her his paw, and she reached out to take it. There was a little rosette on the back that looked exactly like a daisy. She remembered that. She remembered everything.

"On'anxho," said Chin-Riley. "I should have picked up on that straightaway, shouldn't I? Son of Anxha."

"That's right," said Hax. "I wondered if you'd learned enough

Euxhana when you knew us. When I heard nothing from you, I assumed you hadn't. Of course, it was all a very long time ago."

"Feels like yesterday to me," said Chin-Riley.

"Me too," said Hax.

They sat down, Chin-Riley pulling a seat around so that they were side-by-side. "So you went into law." Not Starfleet. Perhaps he had lost his enthusiasm for Starfleet.

"Asylum law," he said. "A specialism in Euxhana cases, but I've taken on plenty of others. I followed your career with keen interest, Commander."

"Una, please," she said.

"Una," he said, "thank you. I hope you know that your case caused something of a storm within our part of the profession. We'll be working out the ramifications of that decision for a while yet." He looked at her steadily. "I understood a lot more, when I read what happened, about why you decided to move on from us."

"That's kind of you," said Chin-Riley. "It wasn't my finest hour. I never got the chance to say sorry. I never even got the chance to say goodbye."

"Yet here we are again," he said. "Turns out it wasn't goodbye after all."

"I'm glad to see you, Hax," she said warmly. "How are they? Your family?"

"They're thriving," he said. "All of them."

"Your mother?" she said. "Is she painting again?"

"Oh yes. Has been for a while. She's got a show up." He laughed. "I didn't realize she was so good! I guess we never think that about our mothers, do we? That they might be someone in their own right. Anyway, she's great. I'll send you the details of the gallery."

"Please do! I'm so glad to hear she's painting again."

"Once the four of us were out in the world, on our paths, she was able to get back to her old work. She's part of a group—artists, writers, musicians—all Euxhana émigrés. I think you met a couple of her friends, back in the day. All trying to get the word out about what's happening on Xhio. It was such a part of her life, before my father. Before she had four cubs to worry about."

"Protest art," said Chin-Riley.

"Every painting, every song, every written piece," said Hax. "Each one works to disprove the biggest lie about us. That we are without culture. That we are crude and without nuance. That we require civilizing." He sighed. "Of course, one of the biggest injustices is that so much of our creative lives—so much of the work that we have to do in the world, so much sheer damn *energy*—is taken up denying what is said about us. Imagine what we might do if we were free of that. Imagine what my mother might have done."

"She was amazing when I knew her," said Chin-Riley. "To bring the four of you from Xhio. To set you all on your paths in the world. That's *triumphant*."

He smiled at her. "Yes, it is. I'll tell her. She'll be very pleased."

"Really?" said Chin-Riley anxiously.

"Absolutely," he said. "She wanted to know all the details of your case."

Maybe she understood now why Chin-Riley had made the decision back then. "What about your brothers?"

Hax snorted. "That pair of layabouts? They lead guided tours around some of the more remote parts of the Himalayas."

Chin-Riley laughed. "Really?"

"*Fact*," he said. "You know, I was never entirely convinced that anyone was listening when I came out with those Hax facts.

Turns out that all the stuff about the Himalayas was going right in. I envy them, sometimes. They were exactly the right age to leave home. Sometimes I think they've never quite grasped what it cost to come here. And then they surprise me. They've traveled around the Federation. Made a lot of friends, many of whom visit *Maxhi*. She loves having them there. And every single one of those already knows about the Euxhana. About our cause." Hax laughed. "Soft diplomacy. Who would have thought it could involve backpacking around the Federation and bungee-jumping off alien mountains? Wherever those two go, they are Euxhana."

"What about Naxhana?" Chin-Riley asked.

"That was a struggle for a while," Hax admitted. "She never really felt like Earth was home. She was older than the rest of us. Remembered more of what it was like back on Xhio. She's back there at the moment. She's part of an organization that works for Euxhana rights."

"Is it *safe* for her?" Chin-Riley said.

"She's a Federation citizen, Una. I don't think anyone would touch her."

"You'd hope not. Is she happy?"

"She's doing what matters most to her," Hax said. "And that, I think, is the closest thing to happiness she will ever find. Unless the paths to the mountains open once again."

"And you, Hax? What about you?"

"Well, as you can see, I decided against Starfleet."

"I can see. Why? Was it anything to do with . . . ?"

". . . with you?" His eyes twinkled at her. "Una, you think rather highly of yourself!"

Chin-Riley couldn't help but laugh. "You got me," she said. "What I meant was—I hope I didn't leave you with an unfavorable impression of Starfleet cadets and you judged the rest of them by *my* failings."

"On the contrary," he said gently, "you were a hard act to follow, Una."

She smiled at him. "Generous to a fault, Hax. And much too kind. I was young, and confused, and way out of my depth."

"I understand that now," he said. "But no—you were not the reason that I decided against Starfleet. In the end, it seemed like running away from my responsibilities. Choosing Starfleet would have meant putting the Euxhana cause second. And I couldn't do that. There aren't many of us in Federation space," he went on. "And it seemed important that at least some of us worked on behalf of those we left behind. I found I couldn't enjoy the benefits of being in the Federation without using some of the privileges it gave me. Hence the law."

"Lobbying ambassadors on behalf of the Euxhana," said Chin-Riley.

"It's a dirty job," he agreed with a laugh, "but someone has to do it. And it was a good choice for me. All those facts about case law to memorize. And sometimes, you get to help a friend."

"I do need your help," said Chin-Riley. "Or, rather, I'm trying to stop someone from making a mistake, and I hope you can help."

"The Euxhana member of the diplomatic team?" Hax sighed. "Poor fellow. I suppose he might have expected this outcome to his career. He could never be trusted."

"How much do you know about what's going on?" said Chin-Riley.

"I know about the graffiti and the projection onto *Enterprise*. And that the talks are . . ." He eyed her. "On hold?"

She blinked her *yes*.

"I also have a feeling that something far more serious happened recently," he went on. "I'm guessing that something may have happened on the *Enterprise*. A direct assault on the *echet* . . . ? No, I don't think so. A bomb threat?"

Chin-Riley's fingers twitched upward.

"I see." Hax's expression became very serious. His blue eyes narrowed. "This is not helpful. This is not helpful at all."

"From talking to La'An, I figured you might think that way."

"Fact: direct attacks reinforce prejudices against us," said Hax. He gave a short laugh. "Mind you, if Naxhana were here, she'd say something completely different. She'd say something like, 'How else are the Euxhana to get their point across? What else do you expect, after so long?' And she would tell us that 'It's a miracle that the Euxhana have not turned to violence sooner.'" Hax shrugged. "We have gone round this a thousand times, my sister and I," he said. "I doubt we'll ever agree. I doubt you could persuade her to help this Euxhana diplomat. She would say, 'He chose his path and he can walk it to the bitter end.'"

"But not you, Hax."

"I think that the choices that our people make are always fraught, Una. Always involve sacrifice. *Maxhi* made hard choices when she brought us to Earth. I know that you, of all people, understand. I've been lucky, shielded by being a Federation citizen. But if I had been a clever young Euxhana, forty years ago, wanting to do something meaningful with my life, something that might help my own, then I could see myself making the same choices as this man. Choose the boarding school, the exams. Remove my dewclaw. Shed my habits, my culture, and my language. Put on a costume that would let me play the part of loyal servant. I can certainly see myself making those very same choices. And I can see where it might end where he is now. They're putting the blame on him."

"Unfortunately," said Chin-Riley, "there's some justification."

"Oh yes?" Hax frowned. "What's happened?"

"He received a message from Earth," said Chin-Riley.

"From Earth?" Hax looked startled by this news, as if wrong-footed in some way. "But who—?"

"We don't know who it's from, and we don't even know what it says. We know that it made *Echet* Linchar furious, but she won't say why, and neither will Texho. We don't know enough of your language. Our poor linguistic expert is going mad."

Hax laughed. "I can help there. Grammars, vocabularies, whatever she needs."

"Uhura will appreciate that. As far as we know, the message contains the instruction to plant the bomb on *Enterprise*. Texho, Linchar's aide, was on *Enterprise*. He's not talking."

"I imagine not," said Hax. "I think I should see this message."

Chin-Riley handed him a padd. She watched his face closely as he read. He seemed to be taking a moment or two to decide what to say.

"Well," said Hax, "I can tell you for sure that this isn't an instruction to plant a bomb on the flagship."

"What is it?"

"It's . . . a line of poetry."

"*Echet* Linchar called it doggerel."

"Doggerel?" Hax snorted. "She would say that. I bet she said it was written in dialect too. Doggerel! This is an excerpt from a poem that is so poorly conceived, so badly written, that publishing it is illegal on Xhio. Ownership of a copy of the text is an offense that has seen people imprisoned for up to a year. Remarkable, really, the power of doggerel." His eyes sparkled dangerously. "You might start to think there was something more to it."

"What's the poem about?" said Chin-Riley.

"Love, of course, what else?" said Hax. "All Euxhana poetry is about love. And pain, and longing. It's written by a Euxhana in exile. It takes the form of a letter to their beloved on Xhio, but it's really an address to all Euxhana. Some of the lines have taken on potent symbolism. Let me think of an example. *Xha'na hezh'xha techanexh.* Translated, that means something close to . . . 'The paths will be opened in summer.' In certain circumstances, that might be construed as a call to arms. It's the use of the autonomous form of the verb, you see . . ." He smiled at her. "Let's not get into that right now."

Chin-Riley wished she had brought Uhura with her for this. "Is the line quoted in this message one of those? One that could be construed as a call to arms?"

"No," said Hax. "I would imagine the sender will have been quite careful about that."

Chin-Riley leaned back in her seat and folded her arms. "If I asked you who sent this message, Hax, would you be able to tell me?"

"You could certainly ask," he said. "I'd rather you didn't."

"Texho's future could depend on this," said Chin-Riley.

"More than one future could depend on this," said Hax. He was looking back down at the padd. His expression was very serious. Chin-Riley was sure he knew who had sent this message. This information might save Texho.

"I know I made a mess of everything all those years ago, Hax," she said. "But I want to help now. I want to do the right thing—for everyone."

"Sometimes," he said, "that's not possible."

"I can help," she said. "Let me help."

Lieutenant Una Chin-Riley went down to the *Enterprise* brig. Noonien-Singh was waiting there.

"How did it go with the lawyer?"

"It went well. He's told me some important information."

"Good news?" said Noonien-Singh.

"Yes." Chin-Riley nodded over at the cell where Texho was being held. "I need to talk to him again," she said. "And I need some privacy."

"All right," said Noonien-Singh. "Can you tell me why?"

"Can I see how this conversation plays out first?"

Noonien-Singh nodded. She dropped the force field to Texho's cell, and Chin-Riley stepped through. "Give me a wave when you need to be left alone. Keep an eye on him. I don't like the look of those paws."

Chin-Riley went inside. The force field rose behind her. Texho, who had been lying down, sat up. "Commander," he said, "are you here to take me away?"

"No," she replied. "Your chance for self-sacrifice will have to wait awhile yet. I'm here to talk some sense into you."

"Ah," he said. "No change. On either side."

"I think there is," said Chin-Riley. "Let me put it like this. Can you tell me why somebody on Earth has sent you a passage from *The Call from the Mountaintop*?"

Texho started, but quickly recovered. "Your knowledge of Euxhana has improved, Commander. A few days ago you were only able to say hello. A fairly florid hello, but hello nonetheless. Now it seems that you're able to speak knowledgeably on the subject of minor works of poetry." He gave a rumble of laughter. "I wonder who has been tutoring you?"

"It's not a minor work of poetry, is it?" Chin-Riley came back. "It's probably the most significant piece of literature written in Euxhana in the past century. I've had an excellent tutor. And as a result, I know a great deal about this poem. It's a love poem, written by a Euxhana in exile. He's addressing his love, who may be back on Xhio, but may also no longer be alive. As the poem goes on, it becomes clear that's he addressing all the Euxhana he's left behind, living and dead. He's speaking to them from his place of comparative safety, conscious of the new trials that they face, and he wants them to know that they're not forgotten. That the call has been made. That one day everyone will hear about the Euxhana and their plight."

Texho was trembling slightly, Chin-Riley saw. "You *have* learned well."

"Apparently it broke stylistic ground in your language. You'd have to speak to Lieutenant Uhura if you wanted a really good discussion."

"I know the gist of that argument already," said Texho.

"I know that it's illegal to publish this poem on Xhio," said Chin-Riley. "Ownership of a copy of the text has put people in jail for over a year."

"Fortunately for me, I do not own a copy," said Texho. "Unless we are counting this line. I would argue that possession of that was forced on me. I've never denied this message was for me. But I will say that I did not *ask* to be sent it—"

"Also," said Chin-Riley, "I know who wrote the poem, and who wrote the message."

She saw Texho's eyes widen. She raised her right hand to signal Noonien-Singh. "The security devices in this holding cell have been turned off, Texho," she said softly. "Anything you say now will be to me, and me alone, and will go no further." She leaned forward. "I don't know where your brother is, and I won't go looking. But others will—unless you talk to me, right now. You can't keep this secret forever."

He sat for a while, studying her. "Why do you care so much about us, Commander? *Nobody* cares about us."

"I told you. I met a family of Euxhana refugees, long ago on Earth."

"These are the ones you failed to help."

"Yes, I failed to help them," Chin-Riley said. "I was a cadet at Starfleet Academy. I was there under false pretenses. I'd concealed the fact that, as a child, I'd been genetically enhanced."

"Isn't that—?"

"Yes, it's illegal under Federation law. I became convinced that my involvement with this family would bring me under scrutiny. I backed away. It wasn't the right thing to do, and I'm not proud of what I did. I failed them. Don't tell me that I don't know what it's like to have to hide away a part of you to be able to lead a livable life. Don't tell me that I don't know what it's like to be feel ashamed of something that is the very essence of you. And don't tell me that I don't know what it's like to be sitting in a room like this, ready to give up on everything you've worked for. I know *exactly* what it's like. And because of that, I will do everything in my power to help you and your brother. But you need to talk to me."

Texho, who had listened to this with his eyes getting wider and wider, took a deep breath. "Not everything you seem, are you, Commander?"

"In many ways," she said, "I am the very model of a modern Starfleet officer. But Starfleet contains multitudes."

Suddenly, Texho's whole posture changed, from taut and formal and on the defensive to something more relaxed. Something more trusting.

"My brother . . ." he said, and laughed. "Half brother, to be precise. He's much younger than I am. He always was trouble. Too many questions, about everything, about why things are the way they are, about why they have to stay that way. He's a writer, Commander, and a very good one. So good that the government took against his writing. You're right—he did write this poem. This doggerel . . ."

"I think it's beautiful," said Chin-Riley.

"So do I. But the problem was, he wouldn't stop asking his questions. Why are things the way they are? Why do they have to stay that way? And there were a few questions in particular that he kept on asking: Why must we denounce Euxhana misbehavior in uncertain terms, when we do not denounce Chionian behavior in the same way? Why do our leaders expect compliance, when they have taken our lands and our language, and driven the best of us into exile?"

"I should imagine that the government leaders didn't like those questions," said Chin-Riley.

"Absolutely not. My brother was labeled a dissident, and such was his influence that the government categorized him as being as dangerous as those who commit violence. Fortunately, he had left Xhio before that ruling, otherwise he would surely be in prison now. Not least because of what he has written in exile. 'The most significant piece of literature written in Euxhana in the past century,' you said. That's only half of it, Commander."

"Where is he now, Texho?" she asked.

"I don't know exactly," he said. "Better that way. But he wanted to let me know that he was safe and well. That's what the message is. His call, to me, from the mountaintop. *Don't give up, big brother.*"

"The next thing I have to ask you will not seem fair," said Chin-Riley. "But I *urge* you to answer me. Is the message exactly what it seems on the surface? Does it contain any encrypted information that you know about?"

Texho gave a rumbling laugh. "Forgive me. The thought of Xexho sending coded messages! The only instrument he's ever wielded competently is the pen. He's the kind that lifts a bowl to lap and spills the contents over himself, or else knocks a cup of *axho* across a table. But his words, Commander, his words are like spears. When he throws them, they don't miss the target. They *pierce.*" He smiled. "He is my foolish little brother, and at the same time, one of the bravest of us all."

"Thank you," said Chin-Riley. "Thank you for trusting me."

"What else could I do? Your teacher was very well informed."

Thank you, Hax. "I have one more question," Chin-Riley said.

"Go on," said Texho. "Bear in mind that I may not be in a position to answer."

"Wherever your brother is living right now, what's his residency status? Is he a citizen?"

"No," said Texho. "He's not. My understanding is that he lives where he does with permission."

"But that permission could be rescinded," said Chin-Riley slowly. Texho was nodding, encouraging her to push the thought to its conclusion. "If, for example," she went on, "the successful outcome of a trade deal was made conditional on his return to Xhio?"

"You see now why I wouldn't talk about this?" Texho said. "I've made many sacrifices, Commander, for this career. I've endured many slights, from both sides, those who see only Euxhana, and those who consider me a traitor to my people. But there are some sacrifices I will not make. I will *not* give up my brother to clear my name, and most certainly not to ensure that a trade deal goes through."

"There's no way that would happen," said Chin-Riley. Pike, she knew, wouldn't have it. And T'Maal, she was sure, wouldn't either. "But . . ."

"But I still remain the most likely suspect, no?"

"I'm afraid so," she said. "But even if they take that message apart, they'll find nothing to pin on you. That's something, isn't it?"

He smiled. "That, I'm afraid, means nothing. I'm Euxhana, Commander. That's sufficient to condemn me, if they decide they want to."

"It's not," said Chin-Riley. "And we're going to find out who's behind all this. I promise."

On Starbase 1, *Echet* Linchar was still pressing her case to have the Euxhana in Federation space investigated. "I've tried very hard," she said, "but I struggle to see why such people are being allowed to operate within the Federation. To gather freely and exchange extreme views among themselves—"

"We do not go around knocking down people's doors," said Pike. "Particularly when there's no proof that they've done anything wrong."

"I thought," said Linchar, "the Federation—particularly the founding worlds—were civilized. Why do you shield them? I remind you of what is happening on Xhio. In Achionis and Chianaise. I felt that this was a Family matter, best kept to ourselves. You assured me that you were concerned for our safety, that you would act. I don't believe that you have."

"*Echet*," said Pike. "Federation Security *is* taking action. We will not assume that every Euxhana within the Federation is violent."

"A mistake," said Linchar. "If even Texho . . . We are going to formally request information about the Euxhana. All of them."

"I regret, *Echet*," said Pike evenly, "that's not going to happen."

Linchar turned to Ambassador T'Maal, who remained silent. "Ambassador, you *surely* understand."

"Understand?" said T'Maal. "Please explain, *Echet*."

"Your own remarkable civilization. Its culture, its restraint. Not to mention—and forgive me if I refer now to what may be indelicate or unpalatable matters—how Vulcan put aside savagery and committed to progress. To cultivation. Your struggle against elements within your society that choose to take extreme action. Surely you understand?"

"Indeed," said T'Maal.

"Then *you* will tell us what we need to know?"

"*Echet*," said T'Maal, "I agree with Captain Pike. This will not happen."

"You would rather end these negotiations than help us stop future acts of violence—acts of atrocity—against the whole Family of Xhio?"

"A logical conclusion," said T'Maal, "based upon what I have said. I see from your expression, *Echet*, our talks are now at an end. I regret that. But so it must be."

"Mister On'anxho was an old friend?" said Noonien-Singh. "Small universe." They were on their way to the bridge to speak to Uhura.

"When you think about it," said Chin-Riley, "the Euxhana refugee community in the Federation isn't that large. I met maybe a dozen when I was a cadet. Hax was someone I cared about, a great deal."

Noonien-Singh, watching her friend, said, "Something happened?"

Chin-Riley listened to the hum of the turbolift. Finally, she said, "Yes. Something happened. Not my finest hour."

"Will that cause us any problems?"

"We've worked it out." Chin-Riley shook her head. "I was a cadet, La'An. I didn't understand half of it."

"I don't begrudge anyone the confidence of youth," said Noonien-Singh. "Speaking for myself I prefer to act from knowledge and experience." She shrugged. "I wasn't great at being young, for many and obvious reasons."

"Who I was then . . ." said Chin-Riley. "I was concerned about rules and regulations." She smiled at her friend. "For many and obvious reasons. Because of who I am and what I was hiding, I wasn't able to be a good friend to Hax and his family. I made a commitment to them that I wasn't able to keep."

"He's fine with you?"

"He works in the field of asylum law," said Chin-Riley.

"Ah . . ." said Noonien-Singh.

"He was following my case."

"Professional interest," said Noonien-Singh.

"So when it came out about my genetic modifications, he understood why I did what I did back then."

"I'm glad," Noonien-Singh said quietly, "and I'm glad he's agreed to help us. I've not been able to prize Uhura away from that dictionary and grammar he gave us."

"It should help us find out who's behind this," said Chin-Riley.

"I think I might be on to something," said Noonien-Singh. "I've, er . . . taken the liberty of examining other messages received by the Chionian ship since it docked at Starbase 1."

"Diplomatic privilege?" asked Chin-Riley. This was rocky ground they were standing on.

"I've not been reading the *contents*," said Noonien-Singh. "I wanted to check whether the messages were carrying any other information—"

"And?" said Chin-Riley.

The turbolift deposited them on the bridge. They stepped over to Uhura's station.

"The ensign has identified three messages containing embedded material," said Noonien-Singh. "One arrived immediately after the Chionian ship docked. The second arrived early in the morning before the talks started. And the third—"

"The third was right before the bomb warning," Chin-Riley finished for her.

"Yes," said Noonien-Singh.

"What's in them, Ensign?" asked Chin-Riley.

"When I looked at them," said Uhura, "I saw there was a pattern." On the screen, she showed Chin-Riley. Three spikes, like a triple-peaked mountain.

"That's the symbol of Euxhana liberation," said Chin-Riley.

"The one that was plastered all over the walls of Starbase 1," said Noonien-Singh.

"Hax told me it's become a highly politicized image on Xhio," said Chin-Riley. "It's associated with the factions who have been taking direct and violent actions."

"Explaining Linchar's reaction when she saw that flag," said Noonien-Singh.

"Do we have any idea what these signals say?"

"At first I couldn't see anything," said Uhura. "Then Pelia suggested I line them up. See?" On the screen, the three spikes now overlaid each other, showing a single peak. When they aligned, text emerged.

Chin-Riley asked, "Are you able to read it? It looks like Euxhana"

"Yes, it's Euxhana," said Noonien-Singh.

"But," Uhura added, "it's coded."

"Okay," said Chin-Riley. "Are we anywhere near cracking it?"

"Not yet," admitted Noonien-Singh.

"I think we need a key phrase," said Uhura.

"Neither of us is an expert in Euxhana literature," said Noonien-Singh.

"We have the text of the most significant piece of Euxhana writing of the last century," said Chin-Riley. "We could start there."

"It's a long poem," said Noonien-Singh doubtfully.

"I know," said Uhura, clearly anxious to get down to translating it.

Noonien-Singh said, "I wish he'd chosen to specialize in haiku."

"Try this," said Chin-Riley. "*Xha'na hezh'xha techanexh.*"

"Pretty," said Uhura. "The paths being open . . . Ooh, an autonomous verb—"

"Don't get distracted," said Noonien-Singh. "What's the significance of this line, Una?"

"Saying it on Xhio could get you sent to jail," said Chin-Riley.

"Yeah, well, you've probably done that enough for one lifetime," said Noonien-Singh.

"My accent is dreadful," Chin-Riley said. "Let's hope that doesn't make a difference. I'd rather learn something more useful than where to get the best *chaola* in Ghezha."

"I think we're in luck," said Uhura. "It's instructions to get the negotiations moved to Starbase 1. And this one, the instruction to plant the bomb on *Enterprise*. The third one . . . I *think* that might be who the contact is on Starbase 1. But it's an alias . . ."

"Where did these messages originate?" said Chin-Riley. "Earth?"

"No," said Uhura. "These all came from Xhio. They were sent to one specific person."

"Go on," said Chin-Riley.

"The *echet*. These messages were sent to Linchar."

"What does this mean?" said Pike. "Do you think that Linchar is a Euxhana sympathizer? That she's involved in committing seditious acts against her government?"

"She's gone out of the way to give us the opposite impression," said Chin-Riley. "But is that sufficient grounds to suspect her?"

"I was hoping you could answer that," said Pike.

"Chris," said Chin-Riley, "could we bring in an expert on the Euxhana perspective?"

"Who, Number One?"

Hax On'anxho made himself immediately available. When Chin-Riley briefed him on the identity of the recipient of the messages, he laughed out loud.

"Forgive me," he said, "but I don't think that's very likely."

"Why?" said Pike.

"*Echet* Linchar epitomizes a certain type of Chionian," said Hax. "Her clan is one of the most . . . what would be the right word . . .

aristocratic. Yes, they're one of the most aristocratic clans on Xhio. It goes back generations. Extensive lands in the valleys of Praichinais, just outside the capital, not to mention the size of their compound in Ghezha. Commander—this kind of family is what it *means* to be Chionian. That she is a secret sympathizer to the Euxhana cause . . . Absolutely not. I'd be more convinced if you told me that's she been instrumental in pushing forward a policy to infiltrate Euxhana dissident groups and nudge them toward violent actions in an attempt to discredit them."

The Starfleet officers looked at each other.

"Is that a *reasonable* working hypothesis?" said Pike. "Is that something that the Chionian government might do?"

"I am not an expert," said Hax, "and perhaps not the most impartial person to ask. But I wouldn't put it past them."

"The bomb might have been placed to gain an advantage in the negotiations," said Chin-Riley slowly. "Or to advance some kind of repressive agenda at home . . ."

"Where is Linchar?" asked Hax. "What's she been doing?"

"She's bending Ambassador T'Maal's ear," said Pike. "She's insisting that any further discussions are conditional on the Federation making available names and details of every Euxhana living within the Federation."

"Successive Chionian governments have been very anxious about Euxhana living away from Xhio," said Hax. "I suppose this could have been an attempt to make the Federation investigate the Euxhana? Pass on information?" His paws were trembling, and he clasped them together in an attempt to quiet them. "There are clients of mine . . . it would cause many of them considerable difficulty. They might find themselves fighting extradition to Xhio." He looked at Chin-Riley. "You know."

"I know," she said.

"What would that mean, Mister On'anxho?" asked Pike quietly.

"Prison. Maybe worse, in some cases."

"The Federation *isn't* harboring terrorists, is it?"

"I don't know, Captain," said Hax. "I'm not representing any. Unless you consider writing poetry to be an act of terror?"

"Of course not," said Pike.

"Unfortunately, the Chionian government does not agree," said Hax.

The comm chimed. It was Ensign Uhura. *"Captain,"* she said, *"there's another communication to the Chionian ship. It contains the same embedded material."*

"Directed to Linchar?" said Pike.

"Yes, sir."

"It's time we spoke to the Chionian ambassador."

Lieutenants Noonien-Singh and Zhovell followed Captain Pike to Linchar's quarters. She and Zhovell took up positions on either side of the door. Pike pressed the door's comm and said, *"Echet* Linchar, it's Christopher Pike. May I speak to you, please?"

No reply. The door did not open. Pike nodded at Zhovell, who overrode the lock and the door opened. Inside, the room was dimly lit by amber lamps. Someone was inside, by the console table, Noonien-Singh blinking as her eyes adjusted to the dimmer lights. They moved carefully inside.

"Echet Linchar," said Pike, "may we come in?"

Marachat came forward. "I'm afraid the *echet* isn't here right now," he said. "May I help you?"

Noonien-Singh moved around behind him, toward the console.

"What are you doing, Lieutenant?" he said. "Everything on that console is subject to diplomatic privilege—"

"Really?" she said. Marachat lunged over toward the desk, trying to get there first. Noonien-Singh caught a glimpse of what was on the screen. She recognized it as Euxhana text. Was this another coded communication? Not to Linchar, nor Texho, but Marachat.

He came at her, lashing out. Noonien-Singh felt his claw go through her sleeve, raking the flesh beneath. The security officer remembered Chin-Riley saying how much it hurt. She hadn't been wrong. Noonien-Singh pushed through the pain, grabbing Marachat's wrist and wrenching it around. He was strong, but he wasn't combat trained, and certainly not able to handle someone like Noonien-Singh. She had him on the deck within seconds, her knee in his back, his paws behind him. Zhovell put Marachat into wrist restraints and pulled him to his feet.

"Ow," said Noonien-Singh, looking at the claw marks. Una had been absolutely right. It *really* hurt.

2233

STARFLEET ACADEMY
THANKSGIVING

Ensign Christopher Pike, Personal Log

I gave my evidence at the hearing. I talked it through first with Una. Got everything clear in my mind. I knew what I wanted to say. They let me speak, they said thank you, and then they let me go. I didn't see my former captain or first officer. Better that way.

Robert April was there, and we went for a beer afterward. We didn't pore over the details, I'm relieved to say, but he did say one thing that has stuck in my mind. He was glad I was looking more cheerful. He'd been worried that it seemed to be touch and go with me. When I asked what he meant, April said he could see the whole business had knocked the youthful optimism out of me, and some don't come back from that. He thinks I have. So that's good.

April asked me what I thought I'd learned from all this. A teachable moment? Seriously? He asked what my thoughts were on how a captain should relate to their first officer. Not like they did, was my answer. He told me to give it some serious thought. I asked him what he wanted from a Number One. Someone bold, he said, and annoying.

I know someone like that.

I sent a message to Una when I got back to San Francisco. Just to tell her it went okay, and that she'd helped, and when she'd turned in her proposal to come over. I'd make her breakfast.

Theresa Mullins did not come back that night, or the day after. Chin-Riley sat at her desk, working abjectly on her terrible proposal, waiting for the summons to appear before her superiors and explain herself. Nothing. Nobody came. Chin-Riley worked undisturbed, going through everything she could find about the *Silver Humming-bird*. The ridiculousness of the whole situation—the failed replicators, the intermittent gravity, the water bobbing around until they soaked it up—was enough to keep her from surrendering herself to abject despair. When at last the proposal was done, and submitted, Chin-Riley emerged blinking into the bright sun of what felt like her first free day in forever.

There was a message from Chris Pike. All had gone well at the hearing, and Chin-Riley was glad, but she didn't have the energy to reply. She was tired and dispirited, because she knew that she had been hiding from the world rather than confronting it. At this moment, she did not like herself very much. She walked around campus, trying to enjoy the fresh air, trying to do normal things that would make her feel like a normal person, but she couldn't manage that. She wasn't normal, was she? She was a freak, an augment, a nonperson. Illegitimate.

Chin-Riley decided she needed a hot shower. She walked back toward the dorms, and saw Mullins heading down the path. She thought about turning away and hiding, but this conversation couldn't be put off.

"Hey," said Mullins, when they met, "did you get your proposal in to Pelia?"

"I did. Where have you been? Are you okay?"

"I stayed over at Aynur's," said Mullins. "I figured you needed peace and quiet to get your project done."

So that was where she had been and what she had been doing. Thinking about her. Thinking about her late submission. And thinking about . . . what else?

"That was really kind of you," said Chin-Riley. "It made the difference."

They looked at each other awkwardly. There was no way to ask, Chin-Riley thought. No way to say: *Did you see what happened? Do you know what I am? Do you know that I'm a liar and a fraud? That I'm here under false pretenses? What do you intend to do about that?*

What are you willing to do to keep your Starfleet career on track?

"I . . . I haven't asked—" Chin-Riley began.

"Anxha's asylum hearing is tomorrow morning," Mullins interrupted, cutting off any line of questioning.

"Oh."

"At the Federation Council building on Clinton."

"I see." Chin-Riley's head, filled with unaskable and unanswered questions, boiled over with more: *Should I come? What happened with Falxho? Who let him on campus? Why hasn't anyone been in touch to ask me about it?*

So many questions, and none of them that Chin-Riley could ask, not without risk to herself. To her own status, here on Earth, here at the Academy. "Would you . . . would you let me know how it turns out?"

Chin-Riley saw the disappointment in her friend's eyes. "You don't want to come along?"

"I don't think I should. I don't think that would be right."

"Okay," said Mullins, and moved past her. "I'll let you know how it goes."

Chin-Riley watched her go. She thought about going after her, letting all her questions spill out, getting answers, whether she wanted them or not. But she was too tired. She went back to their rooms, took that hot shower, and then fell onto her bed, exhausted, and slept.

The message from Chris Pike was unanswered.

Everyone had come to hear the decision about their case. The cubs and Aynur Lavin, all of *Maxhi*'s friends, the writers and artists and musicians were at the back of the hearing room, where Naxhana saw Xenanxha. She lifted her paw in greeting, but she did not come forward. The proceedings took a while, and the twins got restless. Naxhana took them out and found a playground. They ran around for an hour or so until Naxhana decided she'd had enough. She dragged them back inside. Padds were being stacked up. *Maxhi* was crying. What had happened? Had something gone wrong? Had it all gone wrong? Suddenly, Naxhana realized how much she wanted this—for *Maxhi*, for her brothers. For herself? Perhaps more than she realized . . .

Aynur was hugging *Maxhi*. Naxhana went over to Hax. "What is it? Is it bad news?"

"No, Naxhie, of course it isn't," he said with a big grin. "Asylum granted. We have permission to stay—indefinitely."

Aynur smiled over at her. "Citizenship next," she said cheerfully. "All you have to do now is sit back and enjoy Earth."

Naxhana looked around for Xenanxha. She was still at the back of the room. She placed her paw flat over her chest, bowed her head, and then slipped out of the room. Naxhana felt a tap on her shoulder. Turning, she saw Theresa Mullins, who gave her a small smile.

"Hey," said Theresa. "We need to have a chat."

Their party was leaving the building, gathering outside to carry on their conversation, to talk about their success. Naxhana and Theresa walked on a little way.

"Naxha," called her mother, "where are you going?"

"I'm going to talk to Theresa about schools!" called Naxhana, knowing that this would get her mother off her back. "Five minutes!"

"You *can* ask me about schools, you know," said Theresa. "I've got loads of advice about how to pick the right school. Or, more importantly, how to avoid picking the wrong one. And I think you should come and see me about that. For now . . ." Theresa took a deep breath. "You're here on Earth, Naxhana, for good or ill. I know it's not what you want, not by any stretch of the imagination, and I know you're angry about it. I don't blame you. I don't blame you for wanting to tear the universe apart to make things right for the Euxhana. All power to you! Keep that anger, and keep that sense of wanting to set things right. But for pity's sake, Naxhana, play it smart! Not stupid. Smart."

"What do you mean?" said Naxhana.

"This nearly went wrong. Your uncle getting on campus. You know he attacked Una? Hurt her? It's a good job I walked in when I did. Pulled him off her." Theresa looked around. "That doesn't go past you, okay? You got that?"

"Yes," said Naxhana. "Where is he? Uncle Falxho. Where is he?"

"You don't worry about that," said Theresa. "He's safe. Aynur's got everything under control. She's had a few words in the right places, and nothing on the record. She thinks he has a case for asylum, and she's going to work with him. Why the *devil* didn't he come to us in the first place? I just don't know. And you"—Theresa's eyes were flashing—"why *you* didn't come to us, you daft cub. This whole business could have cost your family everything. It could have got all of you sent back to Xhio."

Naxhana, listening to Theresa speak, at first couldn't make sense of what she was saying. And then she realized what was going on.

She thinks I was the one that got Uncle Falxho onto campus.

Naxhana glanced back at her family, who were still sharing their joy.

It's probably better that way.

"I know what I did was foolish," she said cautiously.

"You bet," said Theresa. "You risked a great deal more than you realize."

"I'm sorry to hear that Una got hurt," said Naxhana.

"She'll be fine," said Theresa. "Thank goodness."

"I . . . won't do anything like that ever again," said Naxhana.

"Good news. Something's getting into that daft head of yours." Theresa put her hand over Naxhana's paw. "Get smart, girl," she said. "Get everything you can from being here. Take everything that's offered. Grab citizenship when it comes your way. And then you can go back home, if that's what you decide you want. You can cause a stir so big that nobody will be able to ignore the Euxhana."

Naxhana realized that she was crying. Theresa drew her in for a hug.

"You've got choices now, sweetheart," said Theresa softly. "About the person you want to be. About the difference you want to make. Get smart." She looked back over at the family group. "Come and talk to me about schools. How to pick the right one. I picked the wrong one, and you'll want to know how to dodge that. Let's get this right for you, sweetheart. You deserve it, and your family deserves it, everyone you left behind deserves it too. Here's your chance to shine. Grab it with both paws and don't let go."

Naxhana looked around at the bright fall day; this world that was both hers and not hers. Something shifted inside her. She thought that it could be possible to live here on Earth. She would not call this planet home; there was another that came to mind when she said that word, a place to which she intended to return one day.

Now the work begins, she thought. The work that would take her back one day to Xhio.

Returning to her room from an evening run, Chin-Riley saw that Mullins was sitting in her usual chair, drinking a cup of tea. They gave each other cautious smiles.

"How did the hearing go?"

"Everything went fine," said Mullins. "Asylum granted. They can apply for citizenship in four years."

Chin-Riley closed her eyes and breathed out. "I'm really glad to hear that, Theresa."

"I know. I'm glad it's all turned out okay in the end."

Everything had turned out okay. She wasn't sure how. Putting on pajamas and a robe, Chin-Riley went back to the sitting room, finding a cup of tea by her seat.

"We should talk," she said.

"Yes," sighed Mullins. "There's been a lot of that today . . ."

"What happened with Falxho?" said Chin-Riley. "Where is he now?"

"Don't worry. I got him off campus. Calmed him down. He's . . . Aynur's on top of that. It should work out okay. The main thing is—it didn't have any impact on Anxha's case."

"How did he get anywhere near our rooms?" said Chin-Riley. "I don't understand how that happened. And I don't understand why I haven't been asked—"

"I wouldn't spend any more time or energy worrying about all this," said Mullins. "Honestly."

"I can't help but worry."

"You don't have to go over what happened that day," said Mullins. "Nobody is coming asking questions. Okay? Do you understand what I'm saying, Una?"

And suddenly, with a horrible choking sensation, Chin-Riley understood completely. She had not covered her hand quickly enough. Mullins had seen everything. Seen the cut, the healing; the truth of Una Chin-Riley and her terrible secret.

"Oh," she whispered. "I see . . . I see . . ."

It felt as if the universe was contracting around her. She had pictured, many times, what might happen next. The horror on people's faces when they found out what she was. The distaste and repulsion. The public shaming. The dismissal. Prison? A distinct possibility . . . She gasped for breath. And then she felt Mullins take her hand—the one that got clawed. The one that had given her away.

"Don't worry," Mullins said. "You don't have to worry about any of this. About *any* of this. You don't have to worry at all."

After a couple of minutes of breathing evenly, Chin-Riley was able to speak. "You saw, didn't you?" she said quietly. "You saw what happened."

"Yes, I did," said Mullins. "And if you weren't sure . . . if you didn't know who I am and what I stand for—then let me say this so that we're absolutely clear. That law is wrong. Nobody should have to hide who they are. Your secret is safe with me. No one will ever hear this from me. I promise, Una. Never."

Years later, when she was sitting alone in a cell, she would remember this moment of acceptance, remember what it felt like, and she would take heart. She realized that it was the most important gift she had ever received. Now she felt relief. Nobody was coming for her. There would be no inquiry. There would be no expulsion. There would be no public shame. She could carry on, as she was. She could stay in Starfleet.

"Una," said Mullins, "Naxhana told me that she got hold of your access codes when you were at the house. She was angry with you when you said you couldn't see them. When Falxho said he needed to talk to you, she passed on your access codes." Mullins shrugged. "Teenagers."

Something didn't ring true, but Chin-Riley wasn't sure what. "Did that have an impact on their hearing?"

"Naxhana told me what she'd done, and it didn't go any further," said Mullins.

"But there must be a record of how Falxho got into the dorms," said Chin-Riley.

"Una, listen—"

"Naxhana shouldn't take the fall for this," said Chin-Riley. "It will have an impact on her future. What if she chooses to apply for citizenship? Won't she need to stay out of trouble?"

"Yes, she is—"

"I can't let her get into trouble," said Chin-Riley. "I'll go and speak to someone. I'll say I must have made a mistake, let Falxho get through somehow—"

"Una," said her friend, "you need to keep away from this. You need to keep your head down. The last thing you need is attention."

"But what about Naxhana?"

"I've taken care of that. The story . . . The *official* story, the one I told to the authorities, is that I left my padd at Anxha's house, and Falxho used it to get your access code to the dorms."

"But that's not true," said Chin-Riley.

"No, it's not," agreed Mullins. "But it keeps everyone out of trouble. Everyone who stands to lose something. Naxhana for one. You, for another."

"But what about you, Theresa?" Chin-Riley said. "Aren't you in trouble?"

Mullins didn't reply. She took a sip from her cup of tea.

"Theresa?"

"Yes, I am. Quite serious trouble, actually. They've been trying to decide what to do with me." She didn't seem particularly perturbed.

"Theresa, I can't let you take the fall!"

"Let me finish," said her friend, her voice sterner and more serious than Chin-Riley had ever heard. "All of this has helped me come to a decision. One I should probably have made ages ago. I'm leaving the Academy."

Chin-Riley gasped out loud. The idea of leaving, of putting aside a Starfleet career? She had chosen this path no matter the cost. "You can't do that," she said. "You can't!" It was unthinkable.

Startlingly, Mullins was smiling. "You mean that *you* can't. I most certainly can. My heart hasn't been in this for a while," she said. "I enjoyed my freshman year, but every semester since has felt like a chore. A distraction from my real work."

"I had no idea! You never *said*."

"It's hard to say something like that to someone who is so thoroughly, so undoubtedly Starfleet." Mullins was laughing. "Imagine me telling you that I didn't like being at the Academy, that I didn't see the point!"

Chin-Riley found she was smiling. "I guess I would have said . . . that you hadn't found your niche yet."

"I've already found my niche. It's just not here."

"Law," said Chin-Riley. "You're going into law."

"Aynur has offered me a place after law school." Mullins breathed out, as if a great weight had been taken from her. "I am so *relieved*, Una, I cannot begin to tell you. The thought of sitting through another damn lecture on warp core dynamics—"

"Mechanics," Chin-Riley corrected her instinctively.

"Who *cares*?"

"I care," said Chin-Riley.

"Exactly. *You* care. So you can take the warp core. I am *done* with it." She reached over and squeezed Chin-Riley's hand. "This is not a sacrifice for me, do you understand? This is me making the decision that's right for me. And besides, the thought of you leaving Starfleet isn't right. You're the image that comes to mind when I think Starfleet officer." She gave it a moment's thought. "Maybe Chris Pike." She gave her friend a curious look. "Where *do* things stand with you two?"

"I've told you, Theresa, I'm not looking for a relationship. I'm looking for a friend."

"A *friend*? Did you say that to him?"

"Yes," she said.

"Poor fella," muttered Mullins.

"But that's not quite right either." Chin-Riley drew a deep breath. "I think . . . I think I'm looking for a *captain*."

"And she got there at last," Mullins said with a smile. "Legends," she went on. "I bet you're going to be legends." She placed a kiss on her friend's cheek. "Remember the little people when you're out among the stars."

"I'll never forget what you've done for me," said Chin-Riley.

Mullins squeezed her hand. "I'll bear that in mind. The next time I need a Starfleet officer."

They sat and talked late into the night: about their future

plans, the people they intended to become. Later, as she was falling asleep, Chin-Riley realized the source of this lightness. Having someone who knew her secret, it felt . . . *good*. Safe, and far less lonely. One day, she thought, maybe everyone could know the truth. But not yet. Not for a long time yet. There was work, and there was play—and proving to everyone that Starfleet was where she belonged.

She sent a message to Chris Pike. *Glad you're okay. Yes, to breakfast.*

"You recalled, didn't you," said Pelia, "when you sat down to write this proposal, what percent of the overall course mark it counted toward?"

"Um, yes, sir . . ." said Chin-Riley, although she wasn't sure. If Pelia asked her right now, she could not tell her. Not *exactly*. Not in so many words.

"Don't worry," said Pelia dryly, "I'm not planning an impromptu oral exam." She began to recite, banging her desk as she spoke. "Performance in group work, twenty percent! Report on group work, thirty percent. Project proposal, twenty percent. Final project, thirty percent. I will not believe for one moment, Cadet Chin-Riley, that you did not familiarize yourself with that when you signed up for this course."

"Of course I did, sir," said Chin-Riley.

"Bear that in mind," said Pelia, handing back her assignment, "when you read your grade."

Chin-Riley read her grade.

"A C?" she cried. "You're giving me a C?"

"Yes, I am giving you a C because the proposal that you wrote and sent me is fully deserving of that grade. I know a C when I see one, Cadet, and that proposal"—she tapped the padd—"bore those unmistakable signs."

The damn *Silver Hummingbird.* All that literature she'd trawled through. All those hours . . .

Chin-Riley looked down at the padd and fumed.

"What is the first rule of engineering, Cadet Chin-Riley?" said her very annoying instructor.

"It's 'Write everything down,'" said Chin-Riley. Pelia said that every session.

"I meant the *other* first rule of engineering." Pelia leaned in and said, in a confidential tone of voice, "You will be *amazed* to discover how many first rules there are."

"If it's not 'Write everything down,'" said Chin-Riley, trying hard to suppress her frustration, "then I don't know *what* it is, sir." Sometimes she thought Pelia played with them for her own amusement.

"Oh," said Pelia, "that's a good sign. Admitting one's ignorance is the first step along the path to wisdom."

"Is *that* the first rule of engineering?" said Chin-Riley, bewildered.

"Of course it isn't," said Pelia. "The first rule of engineering is 'If you don't want a C grade, don't hand Pelia a C-grade paper.' Go away, Cadet Chin-Riley, reflect on this experience. Remember that eighty percent of your overall mark is still on the table. And with that happy knowledge, enjoy your Thanksgiving break. When you return, I expect much better from you. Otherwise, I will be asking questions. *Real* questions."

That was the last thing that Chin-Riley wanted: questions. Not from Pelia, not from anyone. Time to put the disasters of the past weeks behind her. Time to take herself seriously again. Prove that she belonged at the Academy. That she deserved to be in Starfleet. Leaving Pelia's office, she headed across campus to the auditorium. Chin-Riley didn't go in right away. Fatima Nahas was onstage, singing Katisha's aria, pitching it perfectly between the grotesquerie of the character and her humanizing sadness.

Hearts do not break!
They sting and ache
For old love's sake
But do not die . . .

Chin-Riley studied the company; her friends, many of them in costume, some in sweats. They looked so young. Inexperienced. She thought of Naxhana's accusations: privileged people, leading privileged lives, knowing nothing about the real world. She felt a sharp stab of something that she knew was envy. None of her friends had to conceal anything; none of them had to constantly second-guess themselves. They were all so untroubled. It wasn't *fair . . .*

But why shouldn't they be carefree? Why shouldn't they be happy? Why shouldn't they lead lives that would fulfill them, that would give them joy and pleasure? The problem was not that they were carefree. The problem was that not everyone had that option. None of them had to leave the world where they were born and twist themselves into a new shape to be able to fit in.

I have worked hard, she told herself. *I have given up so much. I deserve to be here.*

Come, tell me why
When hope is gone
Dost thou stay on?
May not a cheated maiden die?
May not a cheated maiden die?

Nahas finished singing. There was a pause, and then everyone applauded. Chin-Riley made her way quietly into the auditorium. "Vrati," she said quietly, "can we have a word?"

"Of course, Una."

She sat down next to him. "I'm not going to be able to play Katisha."

Vrati's face fell. "Una, it's one of the main parts. We've been rehearsing for weeks."

"I'm not dropping out. But I've not done the work, and I don't think I'm in the right part." Chin-Riley pointed to Nahas. "There's your Katisha."

"But she's already playing—"

"I'll play the Mikado," said Chin-Riley. "I know the songs. And I'll rock that hazmat suit."

"Are you sure?"

"Absolutely," said Chin-Riley. "Fatima will be brilliant—she's already brilliant. And I'll have fun too. Isn't that the whole point?"

"I guess so . . ." Vrati stood up and called out, "Fatima. Can you come over here for a minute?"

I do not always have to be the star, Chin-Riley thought as Vrati broke the good news to Nahas and she whooped for joy. *Sometimes, I can be the supporting act.*

Christopher Pike was standing on the bridge of a starship staring at an unnervingly realistic *Kobayashi Maru*. "You're planning to inflict this on your cadets?"

"Yes," said Pelia. "A completely immersive test. A truly no-win scenario. One that will make the students actively consider what it means to fail." She grinned at him like a lunatic. "What do you think?"

"I think they're going to hate you," said Pike.

"Hate me?" said Pelia. "This was *your* idea—"

"Oh no," said Pike. "You're not pinning this on me."

"'Test their ability to cope with failure,' you said. 'Put them in a no-win situation,' you said. Make them realize that being in Starfleet is not about missing deadlines or getting a low grade. And here we are." She rubbed her hands together, the very image of a mad scientist revealing a scheme for world domination. "At last!" she cried. "With this test I shall outstrip that dullard Sepik and be known as the most *formidable* instructor ever to have walked the halls of this Academy!"

"You already have that reputation," said Chris. "Some of those cadets are convinced you met Jesus."

Pelia snorted. "What nonsense! Of course I did not meet Jesus. Although given the chance, I would definitely have dated Mary Magdalene. Chris, she was *gorgeous*."

Making breakfast under the watchful eye of Una Chin-Riley was unnerving.

"Have you heard anything about this test that Pelia is cooking up for us?" Chin-Riley asked.

"What?" said Chris. "No, I don't think I've heard anything."

Technically, that wasn't a lie. He'd *seen* it, in all its terrifying glory. This poor cohort of cadets would be the first to experience the *Kobayashi Maru*, and he was partly responsible. If they found out, they'd burn him in effigy.

"Oh well, how bad can it be?" said Chin-Riley. "That *Ares IV* thing was as bad as it could get."

"Yeah," said Chris, noncommittally. "That sounded like the pits."

"The smell, Chris. I'll never get over the *smell* . . ."

"Hush," he said. "I'm trying to make the perfect omelet."

He cracked eggs into a bowl. Whisked them together. She was watching his every move. "How's this semester been?" he asked. "Now that you've got a moment to step back and take stock?"

"You know, I thought that the worst thing that could happen would be to fail at my work."

"You mean that grade from Pelia?"

"I didn't like that. I didn't like that at all. But it's not the worst thing that could happen to me. The worst thing was knowing that I'd failed as a person. Made a commitment that I couldn't see through."

A failure of honor, he thought; not a failure of knowledge. He was concentrating on seasoning the eggs and didn't reply immediately. Would she explain, if he gave her an opening? "I was wondering why you gave up."

"Things got too complicated," she said.

Nope, she wasn't going to explain.

"I've tried to take your advice, Chris."

"Uh-huh? Which advice in particular?"

"Did you give me more than one piece of advice?"

"I've got all kinds of really good advice. You want to hear the secret to making a perfect omelet—?"

"The one about following my gut," said Chin-Riley.

"How did it work out for you? What did you learn?"

"I will never, ever break the regs," said Chin-Riley.

Not what he'd been hoping she would learn. There was something else going on here, he thought; something he didn't know about. Something he doubted that she would tell him. Not until there was a lot more trust, and he wanted to build that trust. He wanted this person—this friend, this colleague—in his life. Where he intended to go, he would need someone he could rely on, who would be straight with him, who would call him on his BS. Someone who would be bold, annoying, and absolutely on his side. He would need the best. Una was going to be the best.

"Don't hold yourself to that," he said.

She shrugged. "Are you going to tell me the secret to a perfect omelet?" She smiled at him. "It's trust your gut, isn't it?"

"Nope."

"Write everything down?"

"Nope."

She looked tired. "I give up. You're going to have to tell me."

He tipped the omelet out of the pan. He passed the plate over. He handed her a fork. She took a mouthful.

"How's that?"

"It's perfect, Chris."

"Wanna know the secret?"

She nodded.

"The secret to a perfect omelet is: be gentle."

Be gentle.

2260

ENTERPRISE
THE SECRET TO A PERFECT OMELET

Marachat, the scion of an aristocratic Chionian family, as privileged as anyone could be in their culture. A few years back, he spent two months at the family compound near Rechzan and saw a peaceful demonstration put down. Violently. And that was it, he was converted to the Euxhana cause, ready to do whatever it took to help them.

He's not sorry for anything. He said he knew we'd find the bomb, and that the Chionians do worse every day to the Euxhana. He'd do it all again. Zhovell is holding him in the brig on Starbase 1. The crime was committed within Federation space on a Starfleet station. Let the lawyers talk about extradition. Hax has gone to talk to Marachat, to see if there's anything he can do.

Texho is free and his brother is safe.

―――――――

Before returning to her ship, *Echet* Linchar met Captain Pike and Ambassador T'Maal one last time.

"May I ask, *Echet*," said T'Maal, "what you will take away from this encounter?"

"It was shocking, to say the least," said Linchar cautiously, "to learn that Marachat would choose violence. That is not the Chionian way." She seemed to draw the line at describing his behavior as Euxhana. "Or so one would hope."

"Yes," said Pike, "one would hope."

The Vulcan leaned forward. "You asked me to reflect on the similarities between us, *Echet*. Between your civilization and my own. I have been. I reflect often on our history. You directed me to recall how violent Vulcans were, how brutal, and how hard-won our peace and stability have been. If you come to Vulcan—and I hope, one day, you will—then I shall welcome you as an honored guest at my home. You would see the scars of violence everywhere. A land that is still traumatized. Breathtaking buildings now razed. Brutalized seas, no longer home to the creatures that were once abundant. I often reflect on this, the dead end that Vulcan walked into."

"I hoped that you would understand," said Linchar. "Your people, your civilization are greatly admired on my world, Ambassador. Your cultivation, your culture . . ."

"May I tell you what it makes me think, when I reflect upon who we once were?" said T'Maal. "Who we still are, in many ways. Vulcans must work every day to suppress these violent tendencies. I am grateful that we survived. I live in a time of peace. Vulcan shares this time with our partners in the Federation." A glance at Pike; she gave him the ghost of a Vulcan smile. "All of Vulcan has learned from them. They are so infinitely different . . ."

She turned back to Linchar.

"I hope, *Echet*, that you will return to Xhio committed to preserve the differences that exist on your homeworld. I hope you will reflect upon the Euxhana: their refusal to be destroyed, their patience, their endurance. I would ask you to consider if you could learn from them."

Linchar rose from her seat. Stiffly, she nodded, then left without a further word.

"Negotiations over," said Pike. "Not the outcome the Federation wanted."

"Let us not assume that door is completely shut," said T'Maal. "While we are plainly disappointed in Linchar, that is nothing to the disappointment she must feel about her performance here. While I return home wiser and more knowledgeable about the Chionians, she only has failure. Yet one can learn from failure."

"Thank you for all your efforts, Ambassador T'Maal," said Pike. "It's been a pleasure working alongside you."

"My thanks to you, Captain Pike," she replied, "and to the *Enterprise* crew. I regret that I have not had a chance to speak with your science officer. Another time, perhaps."

"Mister Spock has been busy," said Pike evasively. "Do you know his father?"

"It has been my honor to serve alongside Ambassador Sarek on several occasions. I have learned a great deal from him about the art and practice of diplomacy."

"I'm . . . better acquainted with his wife," said Pike diplomatically.

"Indeed," said T'Maal. "The redoubtable Amanda Grayson. Would you ask Spock to convey my regards and respect to his mother? I admire everything that she shares with us. If only all Vulcans did."

"I want you to know," said Hax to Texho, "that I'll assist you in any asylum request you make to the Federation. I've a great deal of experience in the field. We would have no trouble making your case. The pressure put on you because of your brother—"

Texho held up his paw. "I'm grateful, but I have no intention of leaving either my home or my post."

"It won't be easy," said Hax.

"It's never been easy," said Texho. "But Xhio is my home. It's not possible to wish the Chionians away. I am a part of that world." He smiled at Hax. "Perhaps I can make them understand what they have done wrong. Perhaps I can make them understand that there must be reconciliation."

"And restitution," said Hax. "In a different time, I might have made the same choice. You know how to contact me. If there's anything at all I can do."

"If you are able," said Texho, "I'd like to speak to Xexho. It's been years . . ."

"*Enterprise* can facilitate that," said Chin-Riley.

"Can we keep my brother's location private?"

"I have a friend who knows how to do that," said Chin-Riley.

"Do you think he's made the right decision?" asked Chin-Riley.

"I hope so," said Hax. "His name is clear for what happened during the negotiations. But he is known as the brother of Xexho On'Mezha." Hax shook his head. "Life will not be easy for Texho. Everything will depend on Linchar, on her patronage. Whether she chooses to give her support, or decides that Texho is a liability."

"Would she do that?"

"I don't know. She isn't leaving Federation space garlanded in success. She's shown a lapse of judgment in trusting Marachat. I imagine the chattering Ghezha classes are busy telling each other how they never trusted Marachat, what a terrible choice Linchar made. They're not a nice bunch."

"Texho must know that," said Chin-Riley. "He must believe that he can still make a difference."

"He's certainly very brave," said Hax. "Others would leave. I wish him good luck. May the mountain breeze lift him to great heights." He looked at Chin-Riley. "I didn't know, you know, back then, what would happen."

"Excuse me?"

"When I let Uncle Falxho have your access codes."

Chin-Riley nodded. She had always known who had been the culprit. She remembered her first thought when Theresa said that she was covering for Naxhana. She'd believed it was Hax. He was the one she had loved best; and he was the one who had loved her best.

"I'm sorry," he said.

"You couldn't know what was at stake."

"Did he hurt you badly?"

"Not on purpose," she said.

"Naxhie came to talk to me after our hearing," said Hax. "She told me that Theresa had come to her, thought it was her who had given Uncle Falxho your access codes. She told me that she'd let Theresa believe that. We made a promise then that we'd do every-thing we could with this second chance we'd been given, knowing that Theresa had sacrificed her Starfleet career."

"I don't think she's ever regretted that," said Chin-Riley.

"But we were the cause. So we made a pact. We would be ex-cellent."

She folded her hand around his paw. "I think you've both made good on that promise. More than good."

He snorted. "Well, I think Naxhana likes causing trouble. But then she thinks that I'm timid, and should get my head out of my books. We each have our own work to do. Our own pathway."

"Anxha must be proud of you both."

"I think she is," said Hax. "But I'm sorry, Una. I didn't know what was at stake for you. I would do everything differently now."

Gently, she kissed the fur on the top of his head. She said, "*Xhe'ana euxh on'axhi. Axhena mezh, alxho alxhena.*"

"From my high peak to yours, I salute you in turn," he said. "May the paths be opened in summer." He laughed. "Your accent! It's *terrible*."

Echet Linchar had never visited Texho's quarters. Why would she come here? He always came to her. Acted on her orders; anticipated them. When he opened the door, he was surprised to see her.

"*Echet*," he said, "is something the matter?"

"May I come in?" she said.

"I'd be honored." He stepped aside to let her enter. She looked around, expecting—what? Something different? Something unfamiliar? The light was less golden, perhaps, less mellow, and on the far wall, behind his desk, she saw a picture of three silver peaks upon a blue-and-white field, with white clouds passing in front of them. It was like the symbol on the flag she had removed.

"Please," he said, "do sit down."

The chair she took gave her a clear view of the painting. He made *chaola* for her in a wide bowl; in his own bowl was *axho*.

"Do you know," she said, "I have never visited the mountains."

Why would she, when the valleys were so beautiful? Why would she ever think of going there?

"I can tell you a little about them, if you like," he said. "Although I was very young when I left them, and I never *walked* them, not the way that I should have. You should speak to someone better informed, if you would like to know about the mountains." He was studying her unblinkingly. "I don't think the mountains are the reason that you have come here."

"No," she said. "I thought . . . I thought perhaps we should talk. Properly."

"*Xhi'xha axhenaxheh a rechanexh*," he said, "as my mother used to say."

"I don't understand, I'm afraid," she said. "I don't speak . . ."

"Dialect?" he said.

"Your mother tongue," she said. "I don't speak your mother tongue."

"Nor have I," he said, "for a very long time. But some things never leave us. It's a proverb. Let me see, how should I say it . . . something along the lines of . . . 'The first step on the path forward is to feel the first wind of winter.' It means that knowing your own ignorance is the first step to wisdom."

She laughed. "Yes," she said, "my mother had a saying like that too."

"We are both part of the Family of Xhio," he said. "It should come as no surprise that we share some ideas."

"I suppose not," she replied.

"Do you know the story of the two young cubs?" said Texho.

"No," she said, "I don't."

"It's our story," he said. "By which I mean—not just the story of the Euxhana. The story of us both—Euxhana and Chionian. Let me tell you this story, *Echet*, as my mother told it to me. One night, high in the mountains, when a pure wind swept about us, and we were free. The tale begins, as many of our tales do, at the end of winter, when the tents are coming down, and the snows are melting, and the mountain paths call out to us."

The *echet* listened—yes, she listened—and maybe she heard the call from the mountaintop. For a moment, perhaps, she glimpsed the precious rarity of Euxhana art and words, the singular beauty of the paths they trod.

Captain Pike and Number One convened in his cabin. The heart and the hearth of the *Enterprise.*

"Hey," said Pike as Chin-Riley took the pan from his hand, "I was going to cook for *you.*"

"My turn," she said. "I'm gonna make you a perfect omelet."

He watched, doubtfully, as she assembled everything she would require. Ingredients. Equipment. He saw her running through the checklist in her mind. She was going to do this by the book, wasn't she? Gently, he directed her toward his second-best pan.

"You showed me once. When I was a cadet. You told me the secret to a perfect omelet."

"I remember," he said.

She cracked the eggs. He resisted the urge to check whether any of the shell had made it into the bowl.

"I came back after Thanksgiving break, and Pelia unleashed the *Kobayashi Maru* on us. So nice."

"Hadn't you specifically asked her to make her classes more immersive?"

"I know whose fault it was, Chris."

"Mm?" he said, committing himself to nothing.

"Pelia told me about your hand in the *Maru.*"

"I am not responsible for the *Kobayashi Maru,*" swore Pike. "I admit that I did suggest that she might want to make her cadets think about failure. But that's all."

Chin-Riley picked up a fork and beat the living hell out of the eggs. What had they ever done to her? "Imagine if I went out now," she said, "and told everyone on the *Enterprise* who went to the Academy after me that the other architect of the *Kobayashi Maru* is you. I'd be acting captain within the hour."

Check the pan, thought Pike.

Chin-Riley checked the pan.

"Pelia's a great engineer," he said. "You'd struggle to replace her."

She said, "And that's the only thing stopping me."

She poured in the eggs. Tilted the pan as the eggs slid from side to side. *That's it,* he thought. *Distribute evenly.*

"What happened," he said, "with the Euxhana? I knew something was going on, but I didn't know how to ask. We were just breaking in our friendship."

"Oh, Chris . . . that family. Hax's family. An uncle turned up. He was on a watch list."

He put the spatula in her hand. "That's why you backed away, wasn't it? You didn't want any scrutiny, in case someone found out you were Illyrian."

"Not my finest moment."

"That's why you said the Academy should be testing ethics," he said, "rather than knowledge. In many ways, Number One, the *Kobayashi Maru* is your fault."

"Watch it, mister," she said. She was nudging the eggs around in the pan.

Good, good, keep that up . . .

"The uncle came knocking at my door. Somehow, he'd got through campus security. There was a struggle and he clawed my hand, with predictable consequences."

"Damn," he said softly. He put his hand on her shoulder. Mostly for support. But it also made her lift the pan from the heat.

"Yeah," she agreed. "My friend Theresa took the fall. She said he'd got onto campus because of a mistake she'd made, leaving her access codes lying around. She left the Academy, resigned. She covered for me, Chris, despite knowing what I was."

"That's a good friend," he said.

"She wasn't the last one to do so." She smiled at him. "But Theresa was the first, and it planted a seed in the back of my mind that not everyone would react with revulsion."

Serve it up now, Number One.

She put on salt and pepper. She folded over a third of the omelet, turned it on the plate, and folded it over again. She passed it over and handed him a fork. He dug in. Tried a mouthful. She was watching like a damn hawk.

"So," she said, "how is it, Chris?"

He looked up at her.

"Be gentle," she said. "I've never claimed to be a good cook."

He took another bite.

It was okay. Not too crunchy. Sometimes a little white lie was exactly the seasoning a friendship needed.

"It's delicious, Number One," he said. "In fact, it's perfect."

ACKNOWLEDGMENTS

My grateful thanks to the folks who steered this book through various trials and tribulations, and made it happen: Margaret Clark, Kimberly Laws, Scott Pearson, and Kirsten Beyer.

Salutes and gratitude to Dave Mack and Dayton Ward for their thoughts on the *Kobayashi Maru* test. Particular thanks to Dayton for the deepest of deep cuts—the *Ares IV* mission. O captain our captain! We stand in awe.

Huge thanks to my brilliant agent, Max Edwards, who cheers me up and cheers me on.

All of my love to Verity, who helped more than usual with this one. I hope you like it. And of course all my love to Matthew, who keeps everything going whenever I'm off in space.

ABOUT THE AUTHOR

UNA McCORMACK is the author of eleven previous *Star Trek* novels: *Cardassia: The Lotus Flower* (part of the *Worlds of Star Trek: Deep Space Nine* trilogy), *Hollow Men*, *The Never-Ending Sacrifice*, *Brinkmanship*, *The Missing*, the *New York Times* bestseller *The Fall: The Crimson Shadow*, *Enigma Tales*, *Discovery: The Way to the Stars*, the acclaimed *USA Today* bestseller *Picard: The Last Best Hope*, *Discovery: Wonderlands*, and *Picard: Second Self*. She is also the author of six *Doctor Who* novels from BBC Books: *The King's Dragon*, *The Way Through the Woods*, *Royal Blood*, *Molten Heart*, *All Flesh Is Grass*, and *Caged*. She has written numerous short stories and audio dramas. She lives with her partner of many years, Matthew, and their daughter, Verity, in Cambridge, England.